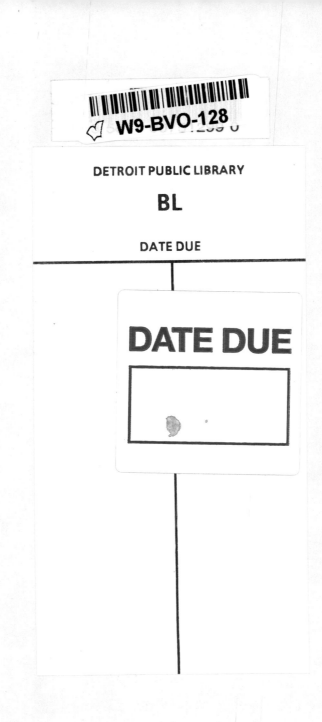

ALL MY ENEMIES

A Simon and Schuster
Novel of Suspense by

ROSEMARY HARRIS

SIMON AND SCHUSTER
New York

First U.S. printing

SBN 671-21383-0
Library of Congress Catalog Card Number: 72-82204
Manufactured in the United States of America

*...myself and a sister, both born
in an hour. If the heavens had been
pleas'd, would we had so ended!*

TWELFTH NIGHT

Prologue

'Introibo ad altare Dei, ad Deum qui laetificat juventutem
meum. . . .'

That I may go unto the altar of God, to God who gives joy to
my youth.

It has been a long time before I could say those words again.
The gap has been wide, stretching from that last day of enclosed
innocence at the little convent school in Kensington, to that
other day last summer when I knelt once more beneath the
lights of the grass-green, rose-red windows in the chapel where
Nicola and Anne, and all the other children whose names I now
forget, along with of course Elizabeth and myself, used to kneel
each morning before school.

Elizabeth, I remember, was always at the end of the pew
where only prefects were supposed to sit; just as she had the
most coveted desk before the classroom window, and the nearest
seat in the refectory to the fire. Such things fell automatically to
her without apparent effort on her part. She seemed to attract
privilege, almost to soak it up. Without effort, as I have said.

How well I can see her now, as I saw her so often during those
years of pious education; her serene and self-contained look,
her pale profile outlined against the darkness of the chapel aisle.
In many early Italian Renaissance paintings you can see the
likeness. Sometimes on a pageboy in a crowd—a child with long
legs, folded tunic, flowerpot hat and curled-under hair—or a
young servitor in a Mantegna procession; or in a portrait of a
Botticelli youth. For all its sudden flowering of the human
spirit the Renaissance must have been a disconcerting time, I've
often thought, when the two faces of life never showed themselves more clearly: purity and corruption side by side, jostling
each other for pride of place; more often than not in the same
person, too.

I remember there were generally three or four girls sitting
between me and Elizabeth. *I* never sat at the end of any pew.

She was five minutes older than me, four places up on me in class. She was in the first hockey team, I in the second. She won her silver for skating while I still worked painstakingly for my bronze. She was lovely, so everyone said, while I—as Sister John would say tartly when she found me peering into the long glass in the hall—would have passed in a crowd. By rights I should have hated my twin, but I was too busy struggling to copy the pattern set before me. I don't think hatred ever occurred to me—except, perhaps, deep down inside; just as it never occurred to me that I might have a pattern all my own.

If the nuns felt sorry for me, they never showed it; since it's no part of a convent education to encourage self-pity. We weren't there to flourish our emotions, but to learn worship and behaviour, and to pick up—I now realize!—a smattering of knowledge. Above all we learned restraint in our daily lives. Last summer, on that memorable day when I returned to see her, the most that Reverend Mother allowed herself was a soft pat on my arm, and a "We're very glad to have you with us again, child, after so long and so eventful a time." 'Child!'—I am twenty-eight. With more white hairs than most people have at forty. But in 'eventful' she had the right word.

It was always her way to gloss over those transitory and unpleasant aspects of life which seem huge as tidal waves to those suffering them at the time. Anything which might be blown up to crude and gigantic proportions she just dismissed or ignored. It was unusual for children whose parents were divorced to remain at the convent; but when Reverend Mother was a young novice our mother had been educated there, and when she separated from Father no mention was made of our being taken away. The sisters looked at us with compassion—the same look they accorded me last summer. Reverend Mother said: "You'll be with your dear mother for the holidays, Elizabeth?"

"Yes, Reverend Mother."

"And Jenny too, I suppose?"

"Oh, yes." (And Jenny, too.)

"And shall you see your father, child?"

"But he's abroad, Reverend Mother. In France, I think."

"So Jenny won't be seeing him either?"

"Oh no. Jenny won't see him."

"Ah well—enjoy your holidays." With a wave of the hand she dismissed us; and Father back to France. She had done her best for our spiritual welfare; his was certainly out of her reach, except by prayer.

'Introibo ad altare Dei. . . .'

It was Elizabeth who took away my joy; and curiously enough, in view of all that followed, it was Elizabeth who gave it back to me, although not till the false joys I had moulded for myself had been totally destroyed during those weeks of terror and wreckage and sudden death which eventually put my name into sensational headlines—no longer where it should have been: in ordinary print on one of the most famous syndicated columns in the world. I was unlucky, perhaps, for being a journalist; when horror takes the sudden incredible twist and strikes close home, and the belief which comforts most of us (it can't happen to me) is nullified, then you are where they can find you quickest, with all your vulnerability exposed: the fox in the home covert, the corn-fed, hand-reared pheasant waiting to be flushed into the air.

When I returned last summer to the convent chapel it was simply to give thanks: thanks that I was still alive, and that others, who might have died for my stupidity or ignorance, whichever you like to call it, were still alive. It was to pray for the dead, and not only the innocent but the guilty who brought them there; for because I've come the hard way to reality it is only compassion that could keep me sane.

I have come to safety while others died; now before forgiveness is complete there is something to be done, and I must do it before forgetting starts, and details blur, and the thread of memory is lost. I must do it for Ilona, because so much has been distorted in the world's press, although differently from the way it was distorted in my mind at the time.

There is a story to be told. It began on a day when I was at the peak of success, smug in my false security, happy as anyone can be. It involves not only the recent past but childhood as well, along with a promise of the future. I couldn't claim it as my

7

story alone; but I no longer feel that former driving need to be the centre of the picture. I suppose that in the centre itself, as might have been predicted right from the very start, was my sister Elizabeth.

1

Why, then the world's mine oyster . . .
THE MERRY WIVES OF WINDSOR

It was my birthday, the 15th of October, and there wasn't a cloud in my sky. Not even the kind that can be seen drifting along very thin and filmy at sunset, like a transparent scarf, and is no more than a presage of fine weather. Whichever way you looked at it I was high on a pinnacle of good fortune, well-being and fame, which seemed certain to keep me above the clouds indefinitely.

I remember that I picked up the daily paper, and all the headlines were of minor catastrophes and grimnesses for other people, which only served to underline my smugness; my enviable isolation from the cat-like jumps and tearings of reality. I can still remember the list, which began with a policeman being shot at and wounded in a gun battle, and ended with a shabby couple called Jim and Dorothea Arkroyd who had been jailed for spying.

There was a photograph of the Arkroyds, taken at their bungalow on their wedding anniversary two or three days before their arrest. She was a faded little woman with a crumpled face, like a blonde cream bun. He was a sharp type—shoe chin, slitty dark eyes behind glasses, hairline retreated from a narrow bony brow. Their spying had been of a pathetically small variety, and the length of sentence too was proof of their futility: he got two years, she, six months. Their whole lives were pitiful, like discreditable grey dust. They made me more than ever aware of the gratifyingly high-coloured success of my own.

I remember, too, my glorious certainty on waking that things were getting better and better, and would go on that way till I was gradually turned by the course of time into a brilliant old darling, loved and loving; and George developed into stateliness, a bit fat—yes, probably portly, dreadful word—but with a steady and profitable eye and attraction for the richer sort of client.

We had Ilona in for the present-giving, and then George left for his office, and I breakfasted late in bed, for once, and admired the expensive clutter. Furs, scent, gloves, books, records—and a small exciting jeweller's box. All over the floor there was tissue-paper, and the new bulldog puppy was having itself a ball. Sometimes she made a dab at my new white fox jacket, but Ilona pulled her off and distracted her, then set herself down on my feet to admire her own present to me. Pearls and diamonds from Woolworth's in the shape of a prancing horse. It was plain she thought a lot of it.

Meanwhile I sat and admired her; and in my fatal arrogance made up my mind then and there that George and I would provide her with a brother next year. After all, it was my *Annus mirabilis*, and a son and heir was the only lack in our lives. Not a noticeable one, since Ilona's birth. She was seven now, and not very like either of us, nor any member of the family I could remember. She was leggy, quick-moving and graceful, with a slow, wide, happy smile, and a shaggy head of chrysanthemum-cut hair, chestnut in colour, like mine. She was a darling and a complete satisfaction to us both, but I knew George had reached the age when he was due to get wistful about a son to follow in his footsteps—some serious little boy to enthrall with Test Match scores, or stories of a Yorkshire childhood.

Since Ilona at her merriest could be a bit of a wildcat, not to say a menace, I decided to opt for a quiet studious boy who could share the library with George. A bent for science, that was the thing these days; yes, a serious scientist son for clever, lucky, happy, thoroughly successful Jenny. Please God. It was hardly a prayer, more of a thinly-veiled demand which I expected gratified in due course. At that precise moment, I remember, the telephone by my bed began to ring.

As I stretched out a hand I wondered which of our many friends was ringing up to congratulate me now. If someone had told me that telephone call was to usher in the most terrible year of all my life, I would have laughed. Ilona and the puppy sprawled together over my ankles, and squeaks and yaps intermingled.

"Darling, please hush—*no*. Stop it—menaces, both of you. Who? Oh . . . oh, it's you, Christopher. . . ."

That was the first flat moment of the day. I tried not to sound irritated but wasn't successful, for Christopher's reply held an undertone of amusement. I counted five and then cooed back like an enamoured dove; and had to listen, fuming, while he sang 'Happy birthday to you' in a throaty and sentimental parody of Sinatra.

I wouldn't be drawn. All honey I thanked him and sent him an outsize kiss down the telephone.

" 'Say I'm weary, say I'm sad, Say that health and wealth have missed me, Say I'm growing old, but add, Jenny kissed me . . .' " said the voice approvingly in a way which showed he understood my arrogant euphoria and was out to collapse it. I felt it go, too—sliding away like a lovely dream. It had been a nice state, both above and below real happiness. Now I was on the defensive and a bit disappointed with myself, which was the effect dear Christopher always had on me. It was no rewarding relationship. I often wished that when John sent him out on some tough foreign assignment he wouldn't return; but he was usually back and typing out his stuff before most people would have got away.

"Did you ring just to say happy birthday?"

"No, Jenny love. I only remembered your ripe old age after dialling. They told me you wouldn't be in today, so I kindly sifted through your mail, and as I found something of a grand surprise I've sent it round. By hand. All same Beaverbrook."

"You've done *what*? Oh Christopher, this is too much, entirely. I just won't deal with letters here."

He only laughed. "Courage, ma belle Geneviève. Lucy Starr is on her way." Then he rang off. That's what I liked about Christopher. His manners.

I sat bleakly there, and fumed. The room looked just the same, but the euphoric world of lucky Jenny had blown clean away. Quite soon Miss Starr would appear in the doorway and give me her loving look of admiration, which always made me conscious of being a fraud. She worked nine times as hard as I did, for a fraction of the money; she had a sick mother; was on the verge of fifty-five, never took a day off, and had a variety of minor ills to bedevil and exhaust her. For all that she was uncomplaining, efficient, kind, and an inveterate admirer of myself. Whenever I compared our lots I was conscious of guilt, which drove me to write out a cheque for the sick mother.

"Was that darling Christopher?" Ilona bounced on the end of my bed. "Is he coming to your party? Did he send me his kind, *kindest* regards?"

"No, darling."

"No to what?"

"No to the party—he's got a conference. No to bouncing on my bed, too, you'll wreck the springs."

"And no to the regards? He *is* a piggy." Gloom overlaid her candid features.

"He's very busy." She heard the sarcasm in my voice, and I saw the quick look she gave me. Christopher was always the most idle man I knew, and yet he got more done in less time than anyone else; a trick, of course, like Find the Lady. And speaking of ladies, much of his spare time was taken up with burnt-honey blondes, real or false. My daughter already felt his special form of attraction. Looking at her I reflected that he would just be an age to mar her life with his mature fascination when she was eighteen, and resolved to cross his name out of our address book well before that time.

"You're *thinking*," said Ilona accusingly.

"Of you." A half truth. I leaned back and lit a cigarette. With the first slow inhalation euphoria seeped over me again. Lucky Jenny. Oh lucky, lucky Jenny to have married George, not Christopher. . . .

There was once a film called *The Seventh Veil*. The school-girls of my generation were mad about it. James Mason played the hero, you may remember—a dark, bitter type called Nicholas who was dependable, crippled, despotic, and given to striking the heroine across the knuckles with his stick while she played the piano. She ended in his arms, of course, happily doomed to a masochistic future. All over the world women thrilled to Nicholas, and I was no exception. It was, perhaps, why I fell in love with Christopher.

True, he was no cripple, and was most unlikely to strike

12

anyone. His looks were remarkably like the film Nicholas's, yet were in fact the mask to a gentle, ironically detached nature. But there was a side to him I couldn't deal with, which kept me as nervous and uneasy as Nicholas's poor heroine, while in some obscure way I was aware of being a bitter disappointment. So what began as an idyll ended as a torment; one I could well have done without, after my childhood with Elizabeth.

To go further back still, Christopher was the dark aloof little boy who lived next door to us in Kensington. We first met him at a children's party when we were eight, and as in a magazine story he grew up and got engaged, prettily enough, to the girl next door: me, Geneviève Lemprière. This proposal spelt sheer bliss. I had worked so hard to bring myself up to the high standard set earlier by Elizabeth, and to find that Christopher loved me set a seal of approval on it all; for there had always been this nagging fear that I was not quite right, somehow: not quite good enough. Years of monotonously being the lesser twin were almost certainly to blame. But if there was no longer an image of the Elder Twin in my mind to copy, there were other models available. The only hours I walked the world with confidence were those when I issued from film performance or theatre, temporarily identified with the star.

In those days a great many people found me 'sweet', which I still look on as a deplorable, damping judgment, implying milk and water lack of character: a Victorian void. I must admit that I couldn't think why Christopher got engaged to me, but I'm sure the mythical sweetness of my character had no part in it and I was convinced that this was love—undying, changeless love; but whatever Christopher thought he had in *me* just wasn't there. I spent a good deal of time in tears, and he spent his wearing a puzzled thoughtful look. In the end I was forced to realize that love either waxes or wanes; it *was* changing, after all, and in no palatable way. Christopher himself had changed, I thought. More experienced, I might have suspected another woman. There was about him an air of restlessness, of suppressed excitement, and a tension and crossness which didn't belong to our happier days. At last pride made me suggest we might be better off without each other.

Of course I longed to be hotly contradicted, but he only put his hands in his pockets, leaned back against the wall, and was ominously silent. I still remember that silence, it seemed to weigh. Since then I've known exactly what people mean when they say their hearts sank. Mine went down, down like a miniature lift. It was an awful sensation, as if every scrap of energy had been sucked out of me at once. Like Christopher I leaned back against the wall. We stayed there a long while. A Latin-American band was playing in the ballroom behind us, the tune they played was 'Caramba, Carumba, Carooo'. It gave me a fixed dislike for everything Latin-American.

At last Christopher moved, and because someone had turned off the lights near us I couldn't see his face. All he said was: "That's what you want, Jenny?"

"I think so." I felt sick.

"You don't want to discuss this any more?"

He took his lighter from his pocket and lit a cigarette. I could see his face for a moment, and wished I hadn't. It was the Nicholas twist all right, but neither despotically tender nor even sadistic; just indifferent.

"No, I don't." Then naturally, in that idiotic way all women have except the born courtesans, I began to discuss it. My voice rose to a high note of aggrievement, and although it was a bore I couldn't stop. I ended up on a wailing note of dire accusation that he didn't love me any more—if he ever had.

He said nothing. Just stood there and shook his head, like an animal with a fly in its ear.

I began clumsily to pull off his ring, but he put out a hand and stopped me. "Do keep it, Jenny. What am I supposed to do with it—pop it, or wear it on a chain? Anyway, I had it specially made for you."

The lightness of his tone made me churn inside with rage and misery and hurt. "Thanks, I'm not a golddigger by nature."

He laughed, which seemed unforgivable then.

"I never thought you were, whatever else you may or may not be. Do please keep it and wear it as a sentimental memento. It's a pretty ring."

"I've got one already," I said like an idiot; like me.

14

"Well, have two!" and he roared. "I've never heard a woman turn down jewellery with that excuse before."

"So other people have turned you down too," I said nastily, and whipped that ring off my hand as if it was stinging me.

"Not a great deal, so far." His voice was amused. It was impossible to imagine he had ever loved me. 'Whatever else you may be', and the way he'd said it sounded a thorough disparagement.

" 'Whatever else I may or may not be,' " I said slowly, now; "I'd be glad to hear exactly what you mean by that."

He hesitated, and I knew he regretted the remark.

"Why, I don't quite know, Jenny. Do you have to hold a post-mortem on something I never meant to say?"

All at once it assumed enormous importance. "But you *did* say it, Christopher."

He made a nervous movement of his hand, the red tip of the cigarette made a leap like a firefly in the dark.

"The thing is, Jenny, a lot of people may be complex, but—" The firefly moved again, with a sudden jerk.

"*I'm* not," I said bitterly. "I'm just simple naïve Jenny." Had I ever known what made other people tick?

"But that's just it," he said quite gently, "you're not simple Jenny. You're sometimes what Elizabeth might have been, or you're Jean Simmons if you've been to the flicks, or perhaps you're not really grown up at all just yet. But *is* there a Jenny? I don't believe I know."

It was the cruellest thing he could have said. I stood there in my new enchanting dress and felt that heartsunk sensation all over again. I had to be violent in order not to break down and cry, so I made the classic unanswerable gesture and literally threw back the ring. A mistake, because in the dark he couldn't see it, and it whizzed on over the balustrade and landed in the well-lit road below. I saw it fly upwards once, and the diamonds sparkled in the light like tears. Then it rolled right across the tarmac towards an enormous man in evening dress who had just paid off a taxi on the opposite side of the road.

I didn't stay to take in what he looked like. I turned and left Christopher alone. The firefly made a sudden move in my direction as I went, but then hesitated and failed to follow. I felt indecently naked without my ring, and something had to be done about it, so I went straight to the buffet and downed several glasses of champagne. If there was no original Jenny when I started, there were at least three of her before I finished, and all of them ready to confide in the first comer about the rupture of their lives.

"Jenny," said my hostess, laying a slightly nervous hand, I thought, on my arm, "may I introduce. . . ."

He looked quite as enormous in the bright lights as he had standing in the road outside. I was drunk and he knew I was drunk, but it didn't seem to bother him. At least, he held me up successfully during several dances, and some time later on I heard him, through the buzzing in my ears, tell me about the shower of diamonds from the sky.

"Most extraordinary thing, wouldn't you say—Geneviève?"

"S'Jenny. No, s'wasn't exstraord— s'was mine. He wassha *beast*." I pointed with an unsteady finger. "Over there, thassa one."

I saw a glint of appraisal in his eye: "He looks quite valuable to me."

"Schweepings off the floor," I said. "Give me almost anyone else. Plenty more about—jus' look at this room. S'like a blo-shoe. I mean *zoo*."

'Nothing succeeds like success.' Through the fog caused by champagne I noticed my partner peering at me with something approaching awe. My self-confidence and Christopher's re-dundance had impressed him. I felt thoroughly like a fraud, but incapable of explaining just *why* I had broken my engagement. That was the first and last lie, implied or straight, I ever told to George.

2

There is no doubt in my mind today that both lucky Jenny,
and Geneviève of the *Subscriber*, were the dual creation of
George. Dear, kind George. Sweet-natured, elephant-faced
George. George who, sixteen years older than I was, built me
up again out of nothing when I was in as many pieces as Humpty-
Dumpty after his fall. In the first place he entirely accepted me
as so utterly desirable in myself that I could relax and not try
so hard any more. The affectations I had put on to captivate
Christopher—the Ann Todd smile, the Elizabeth façade, all
disappeared when there was no longer need for them, and I felt
free again inside, and happy with myself, like a child. Yes,
I certainly loved what George did for me. And I certainly came
to love him greatly later on. If there was any cruelty in him at all,
and I suppose there must have been, since most men seem to
secrete a beetle-crushing urge somewhere, it was hidden deep,
and I must honestly say that I never caught a glimpse of it.

So much for Jenny. Geneviève's birth was accidental but if it
hadn't been for George she would have been stillborn.

It was about a year after Ilona's arrival, and we had friends in
to dinner; among them the *Subscriber's* editor, John Anderson,
and his wife Miranda. John had only just been given the editor-
ship, and he was full of enthusiasm, and his plans for the *Subscriber's* future. We'd finished eating, and were sitting in comfort
round the fire, when someone idly asked him how he was going
to replace that *fabulous* Gemma.

"Gemma!" I said. "What a ghastly name. Who's she?"

There was a general hush while everyone, except George who
looked mildly amused, gazed at me with shocked reproachful
eyes. It was the measure of George's success that I felt no heat of
shame, merely a genuine desire to know.

"Fame!" said someone on a sorrowful low note.

"My *dear* child, Gemma was our most famous woman columnist, that's all."

"The only female version of Oliver Shannaway," said somebody else. "Though a bit more snazzy and slightly less twee."

"Wide-eyed visits abroad with mention of duchesses thrown in, but all in a cosy way as if they did nothing but drink tea and be kind to dogs and old folks too," explained Miranda. "Mention they wash up, but don't say it was only a Spode saucer by accident."

"All animals are equal, but the rich are more equal than others."

"Revolting," was George's verdict. "*I* should just give them *Animal Farm* over and over again until they got the message." He shook his head. "John, your predecessor pandered to a disgusting lie."

"You're dead right." John closed his eyes and yawned. "But one must admit that it takes stamina and courage to go on churning out that stuff year after year and *still* make it sound as if the jet set went to Venice to say their prayers. Gemma has fully earned her retirement to the Bahamas, revolting woman, but the *Subscriber's* circulation may feel it. I wish we had an adequate replacement. I've promised Macpherson to give that sport-mad protégé of his a trial, but I don't think he's good enough."

Miranda shook her head gloomily. "He'll never make it."

"Anyone could," I put in with all the bouncing confidence that two years of George had given me. "Even I could."

They all laughed, a bit sourly, I thought.

"Sport or duchesses?" John gave me a flick-knife look from his little blue eyes. "Gemma knew those appalling people; dogs and children trusted her, etc., duchesses too. And for all her sickliness Gemma was a truly great journalist. She knew her stuff."

"She did, if she had them praying in Venice," snorted George. "You certainly won't find another Gemma."

"But it's not another Gemma *you* want, is it?" I appealed to John. "I should have a sort of ordinary intelligent woman doing rustic and seaside stuff instead—'the day I stopped at an inn and had real Cumberland apple pie with cream' sort of stuff."

"You mean an anglicized Little Madeleine?"

"I *may*. I don't know who she was, either."

18

"Oh come, Jenny. You can't *not* know about the farm in Normandy."

"Well, I don't. But find me a farm anywhere else you please, John, and I'll write it up for you. *And* I've got a French name too, so much for Madeleine." Here even George thought me a bit above myself, and he took away my glass, kissed the top of my head reprovingly, and switched the conversation on to politics.

In the middle of the night, however, after George and I had satisfactorily made love, the thought of Gemma's vacant newspaper column kept coming back into my mind, like an obsession. "George," I said softly, "how many words is a female columnist's column?" But all I got was a groan, and the suggestion that if this was all his love-making could do for me one of us had better see an analyst.

That vacant column haunted me like a challenge, so as soon as George left the house next day I went surreptitiously to his study and got down to work. We'd lately visited Provence and the Camargue, so I wrote about my prosaic shopping difficulties in Carcassonne, and my horse difficulties in the Camargue—me on Rosinante silhouetted, like Daumier's tragic Don, against a giant sky where the rosy wings of flamingos were a constant source of annoyance by their absence. I finished with a fascinating conversation between me and the Mayor of Perpignan, and drew a sketch of us at cross-purposes. When it was done, and the fever of creation subsided, I read through my work. My confidence collapsed.

'Dull as ditchwater,' I thought. 'No sparkle. God save Gemma, she knew her job.'

I left the pages scattered over George's desk and forgot about them. Ilona was teething just then, and having a painful time of it. She squeaked, and came out in rashes, and sucked frantically at my fingers with her sore gums. She was only soothed when I picked her up and rocked her and sang little lullabies. Her sufferings—and mine—put all lesser matters from my mind. So I was mystified when John's secretary telephoned and asked me to come down and see him at his city office. Three hours later I sat before him, staring like a startled rabbit at the pages of my article which lay upon his desk.

"Wicked of George not to tell me that he sent it, John!"

"Perhaps he expected opposition. But he liked it, and so do I. Care to have a crack at the column for me, Jenny? When you piped up about the simplicity of journalism I nearly slapped you down. Yet it's true that some good journalists are born, not made, and I've a hunch your cockiness might be justified. You've done a bit of writing—that's evident."

"Essays and short stories at school!" I panicked. "But *this* was just a joke. How could I keep it up? We're not very smart, you know—we're not always shooting off abroad; George doesn't have the time. You're forgetting he's a busy barrister."

"Smartness is out. Leave the rest to me," said John smoothly —a little too smoothly, I thought. "We'll supply you with copy, and we'll pay you a fifth of what Gemma earned for each article we accept. Rising by a fifth every six months until you reach her salary, if you turn out well. Agreed?"

"Lord, no. I couldn't—I know I couldn't." I was dazed. For the first time since my marriage the shadow of Elizabeth seemed to hover in the room.

"We think you could. But from now on, Jenny, it's going to be work, work, work—if you accept. Will you try?"

I took a deep breath, crossed my fingers, and thought momentarily of—not Elizabeth, but Christopher; at this very moment somewhere in this gigantic building at work on his typewriter. I longed to wipe Christopher's eye.

"If George agrees," I said.

It was work, all right. They wouldn't take much of what I wrote at first, and there was a terrible time when everything I sent came back without any comment at all, looking as clean and unread as when I typed it out. I would have given up, but by this time my pride was engaged, and I hammered on.

A week after this bad patch the telephone rang.

"Hello."

"What's the matter, Jenny," said John's voice, "aren't you trying?"

"Trying!"

20

"Listen, that first one was the goods—the Camargue and all that. I've got a hunch——"

I groaned. "Another! If it's like the first, John, forget it. I'm just no good. It's shaming, but there it is. Born for obscure domesticity, that's me."

"Oh come, don't give up so easily. Macpherson has bought himself a farm in Provence, and I was wondering——"

"If I could farm it for you. You've just a hunch that I'm a born farmer, and you'd like me to go down and live it up among the pigs. . . ."

"Do women ever listen? Macpherson and his wife are flying down there this week-end, and I've bought you a ticket and you can go along and help them settle in. Then come back here and write about it."

"Thanks one hell of an awful lot. What happens to George? And Ilona? And——"

"Leave George, it won't kill him. Take Ilona, the sun will do her good."

"Don't be ridiculous," I said, "of course I can't."

Of course I went.

That conversation with John was the true moment of Geneviève's birth, and the invention of Geneviève's farm. Naturally the *Subscriber's* readers were never told it was the Macpherson's farm, and the Macpherson's lemon trees and mimosa, and their striped curtains, and organic manure, and couscous, egg-plants and melons, and sunflowers which were probably direct descendants of the ones at Arles. I don't know why Geneviève caught on immediately—perhaps, in a world growing ever more welded into one, when the travel agencies offered exotic holidays in Rangoon and the South Pacific as a change from Blackpool, she provided an almost pre-war flavour of near-yet-far difference. A kind of French provincial Cranford touch.

John's readers lapped it up, and it was John who decided to use my full Christian name at the column's foot. He said that I sounded like a Frenchwoman when I wrote, thanks to French papa. In a short time Geneviève's Provençal adventures were being syndicated all over the world, and I was earning as much as George.

Once a month I and Ilona boarded a plane for the south, to return four or five days later with our copy for the coming weeks. I say 'our' because Ilona became an integral part of the adventure and a star of the series. Poor George never came into it at all, but survived exclusion placidly. I never knew if the readers thought that Ilona was a sort of virgin birth, or that a sad French widowhood, all crêpe veils, brooded over the whole thing.

Anyway, she was a nice baby and a charming star. She cooed and chuckled at the geese. She was an equal success with the Communist mayor and the right-wing Curé, who carried on a ferocious Don Camillo-type war with zeal and wit. She exchanged what she felt was sparkling small talk with Mère Rabat and Père Gagagne who almost ran the farm between them. As for the poor Macphersons, they must have had the impression they didn't own the place at all. I even wrote up the *vendange* as if I'd trodden every grape myself, and Ilona had done the bottling from her pram. But in spite of her star quality there were times when the column went stale, and then John would raise a gimmick for us.

Once it was a pair of Siamese cats, collected from a haughty woman who bred them up in Leicestershire. I wrote a heart-rending page about those cats and the way they joined the farm, although it was nearly my jugular that was rent when I let them out of the basket at journey's end. The Macphersons had wisely gone out, and when they got back the curtains were in strips as well as stripes, and the local doctor was applying plaster to my throat. The cats were on top of the pelmet, discussing what they thought of aeroplanes and me. It took two days and a lot of blood—mine, no one else would try—to get them down. And then John ordered a mule called Fanfarouche, in a straw hat. Ilona rode the animal, and I moved them about in the heat. Ilona loved it. Fanfarouche too enjoyed himself in the quietly ironic way mules have. He went backwards most of the time, and the more the sweat poured down my face, and the more I swore, the more Ilona chuckled and Fanfarouche showed his enormous yellow teeth in a wide derisive grin.

Ilona . .

At the age of seven she still possessed the same ridiculous throaty chuckle she had when she was two; it never failed to disarm me, even when I was on the verge of upturning her for a hearty smack. Like all natural charmers she instinctively knew her own powers, and I had often to be strict with myself in order to be strict with her. Those people who rely on charm to get them what they want, who never need to work for love or admiration, what monsters they turn out to be! Sometimes, looking at Ilona, I feared for the future of her character; but I think, and hope, that Reverend Mother at the convent will see to that for me. No dazzling innocent smile ever got past her guard, although she may have retained a soft spot for that other possessor of charm, my sister Elizabeth.

It must seem strange, but although I lost my faith a long while back; although the incense and solemn shadows, the black lace, the candles, the familiar muttered mechanical words of devotion, were for a long time no more to me than part of an inescapable milieu which emanated a comforting sadness surrounding the myths of childhood, I still intended to give Ilona a convent education. . . .

"*Mummy* . . ."

I was brought back to the present by a heavy poke in the chest.

"Do put my brooch on now." Ilona held out the pearl and diamond extravaganza. "It's very beautiful, isn't it? Much more beautiful I should *think* than the one Daddy gave you?"

"It's the most super thing I ever saw."

"The most super, super, *super* thing?"

"The most."

"So shall I pin it for you?" She advanced its heavy pin towards my nightdress, which was so sheer that even George sometimes wondered if I had it on.

I stayed her hand.

"Too good to wear in bed, sweetie. We'll put it on my suit when I get up."

"Yes, but when *are* you getting up? You lazy, lazy, lazy Mum . . ." She trod on the bulldog and it bit her.

23

"Her jaws haven't locked in my leg, have they?" She remarked with fearful interest.

"She's only a very little puppy. When she's bigger they will, so better not tread on her then."

This sent her into paroxysms of laughter, and the puppy bit her again. Blood oozed from the thin brown leg. I was climbing out of bed to deal with the situation when there was a robust knock upon the door.

"Mrs. Emerson, may I come in?"

"Please do—all this noise is only Ilona and a bulldog."

"A bulldog—why, it sounds a formidable birthday!"

Miss Starr's brisk and upright form came round the door.

"A puppy!" Ilona whisked it joyfully above her head.

"A Winston, I see." Miss Starr examined it critically from underneath.

"I thought George said it was a she," and "But we've called it Clemmie," Ilona and I said simultaneously. Ilona pushed the puppy into the secretary's arms, and with one competent hand she cuddled him, while with the other she delved into her office bag and brought out a letter.

"Here you are, Mrs. Emerson—and I forgot to say many happy returns. You *have* had a lot of lovely presents."

"But you haven't seen *this*, yet." Ilona poked the *pièce de résistance* at her.

"Isn't that beautiful?" Miss Starr's plain face gave such a beam that for a moment the hideous brooch seemed to shine with splendour in the room.

They were both happily occupied so I turned my attention to the letter. A large square envelope, with a Paris postmark, and a typewritten address. Letters sent to the *Subscriber* for me were usually addressed to Geneviève. This one was marked 'Mrs. George Emerson'.

"I'm afraid we're all very inquisitive in the office—we simply can't see what's so urgent about that letter."

"Mr. Leyton evidently thinks it is." I drew the sheet of paper from its envelope. The handwriting—large, even and assured—was unfamiliar and yet, in a way. . . .

My vision began to blur. The room, with Miss Starr, Ilona

and the bulldog, grew all at once sharply unreal—when I had last seen something like that script? A child's writing, surely, in a child's diary. . . .

"You look a little pale," Miss Starr's voice hardly penetrated my concentration. "Are you all right, Mrs. Emerson?"

"Perfectly——"

> *Hotel Mirliton,*
> *Paris, VIième.*
> (*undated*)

Darling Jenny,

I went to the opera tonight. It was *Zauberflöte* they were playing—all wisdom and beauty and charm. It really is true magic, isn't it?

I remember so well how it thrilled me that time we saw it. And I don't suppose *you'll* ever forget . . . poor Jenny! This time I saw it to the end; it cast a spell, or I might not be writing to you now, Geneviève. Or should I. . . . ?

I'll be in London on Thursday next, the 15th—could we meet? At the Hilton? At twelve? If I don't hear from you I'll take it you'll be there. Although it may merely mean that you're away, or got this too late to put me off. Anyway. . . .

Do you remember that we always signed our letters to each other

> With love, love, love,

I stared in disbelief at the signature. At one time I had dreamed of this happening, willed it, cried for it. At last decided that it could never happen, since the writer must surely be dead, or wouldn't there have been one word or sign. . . . ?

And now here was the reality; here, in this casual bridging of the immense, inexplicable gulf.

"Dear Mrs. Emerson, I know I shouldn't be so inquisitive, but please won't you satisfy my curiosity?"

I ran my hands distractedly through my hair. Ilona was very still, gazing at me with serious blue eyes. The puppy bounced unheeded at her feet.

"It's from my sister," I said slowly. "My twin sister, Elizabeth."

"Your sister? But we—I—never knew you had a sister!"

"I haven't had one," I said, "since I was thirteen."

3

The baby figure of the giant mass
Of things to come at large.
TROILUS AND CRESSIDA

I can remember every moment of that birthday—our thirteenth.
Or I suppose that's an exaggeration. Some pictures of it, anyway,
stand out in my memory with an astounding stereoscopic effect.
When I was small I had a toy which beguiled me for hours;
you placed two similar photographs side by side in a black
stand-up frame and stared through glass peepholes at them. The
pictures fused into one, and what had been flat-looking villages
in Africa or herds of Indian elephants stood out suddenly in
depth, so that it was like looking at the real thing. Parts of my
thirteenth birthday, in my memory, are like that.

I can remember how it began, with a thundercharged atmosphere. Since the divorce and the withdrawal of colourful Father
to some obscure corner of France, my sister and mother and I
had lived quietly, snugly, in our quiet, snug little house in
Kensington, close to the convent. So far as our lives were concerned our austerities were less of the post-war period than of
the Victorian. We weren't dressed like Alice but looking back it
seems surprising that we weren't. Mother was sad and sweet and
withdrawn. I suppose most people would say she had a guilt-
complex; I would have said it myself till quite lately. Her family
had persuaded her to divorce Father because everyone said it
was the only legal way to detach us from his influence. Of course
our Church didn't recognize the dissolution of her marriage, and
so she still looked on herself as joined to him. Even as a child I
realized the difficulty of being joined to someone who wasn't
there.

People said how marvellously she had taken the whole thing,
meaning, I suppose, Father. Everyone said—and particularly
the nuns said—Elizabeth and I were a credit to her. Especially
Elizabeth. We were good, and we were dull. We must have
seemed extraordinarily dull to the Leyton household next door.

I didn't mind the dullness, though. There was something

27

about Father which often gave me a sick sensation of insecurity. Literal sickness. In the early days when he was still with us— I never thought of *us* being with *Father*—my stomach often knotted itself together and heaved, for no other reason than Father's presence. He wan't exactly rude or unkind, he hovered on the verge and made me uneasy. People would say it was Freudian, but I don't think it was. He made a lot of other people uneasy before Mother divorced him. He was better with Elizabeth than with anyone else, it may be because she was better with him. She was his favourite, and I didn't mind at all, since it took his attention off me.

About every three months or so Father would reappear and take us all out for the day. This was what the Judge meant by 'reasonable access'. Things might have been less strained if Mother hadn't come too, but I was always glad of her presence even though, tight-lipped and withdrawn, she almost ignored Father, which cast a blight upon the outings. Before them Elizabeth was monotonously sick, and after them she usually ran a temperature. I used to think her reactions odd, since she never minded him as much as I did.

She was sick the morning of our thirteenth birthday. I heard her retch over the loo in the green bathroom, and then she padded back into the room she shared with me. She looked flushed and dishevelled, and as if she had a temperature already.

"Don't tell Mother," she said, "but I feel rather awful."

I felt awful, too. It was the first time that Father's day of 'reasonable access' had fallen on our birthday. The words 'reasonable access' can still give me a hollow sensation in the stomach, as the word 'thermidor' must have affected the French nobility.

"You ought to wear your slippers." Her feet looked cold. She had been in the loo some time.

She got into my bed and lay down flat beside me, pressing her icy feet hard up against my warm ones.

"Ow."

"Don't let on, Jenny."

"About what?"

"Me feeling awful."

28

"It's an awful sort of birthday," I said gloomily. She didn't reply, just lay there on her back and stared upward at the ceiling. Presently she said: "We've always opened our parcels like this, together, haven't we? Me in your bed, or you in mine. It must be odd to be a twin, don't you think so, Jenny?" She turned on her side, and her blue eyes looked straight into mine. I stared back and wondered why she looked so furious. "Just one person instead of two."

"It would be funny, but I don't suppose we could stop feeling like twins."

"That's identical twins, not us. We've never felt alike."

I felt hurt, and moved my feet away. Hers followed, and I said 'ow' again, but she took no notice, just rubbed some of the chill off against me. It occurred to me that I wouldn't object, for just one day, to knowing what it was like to be twin-less.

"I suppose we must get up," she said suddenly, "and face the fact that we're thirteen. Thirteen long exhausting years. Lord. And more ahead. I don't feel up to it."

"Exhausting?"

"Flat. Flat and dull. We must be the dullest people we know."

"But I always think the nuns feel you're rather special. Most people do."

"Oh yes, the nuns." She sat briskly up in bed.

"You look better, now."

"Gosh, I feel it. Let's get up. Thanks, Jenny." I didn't know what she was thanking me for.

Mother was tightlipped throughout the morning. Father was taking us all to an opera matinée, and was to fetch us about two o'clock; so I was surprised the tightlippedness had come on so early.

About eleven, when we were having milk and biscuits, she stood up and laid a hand on Elizabeth's forehead.

"I believe you've a temperature already. What a nuisance."

Elizabeth was writing up her diary. She did it every day in her large, neat script. No one was ever allowed to see what she put in it, not even me. She kept it locked, and the key hung round her neck on a thin metal chain. Now she snapped the square green book shut, and pushed her chair back from the table.

"I haven't got a temperature!"

Mother looked surprised. "Goodness, Elizabeth, don't shout! Jenny, fetch the thermometer. Don't tell me one of you children has picked something up *today*." She leaned against the table, and I saw she looked far from well herself. A bit drawn and grey but with flushes on either cheek. I heard her mutter beneath her breath: "These *horrible* days. . . ." I began to worry in case I had to go alone with Father, and my stomach gave a sympathetic heave.

"I'll get it—" Elizabeth rushed from the room. She came back a minute or two later with the thermometer stuck sideways in her mouth.

"*Under* your tongue, Elizabeth. What's got into you, today?"

"It's below normal—look!" Elizabeth yanked it out and shoved it triumphantly under Mother's nose.

"Well, I wouldn't have thought so."

Nor would I. My twin looked suspiciously flushed to me. Yet I supposed no thermometer could lie. Mother sort of faded away upstairs, and I sat and stared at my sister. It seemed that the combination of a birthday and Father had unsettled even her self-possession. "You can't *want* to go out with Father, surely?"

"I want to *badly*. I want to see the opera. We never go to things like that."

"It'll be hell," I said glumly. Anything would be hell with colourful Father. He always talked and gesticulated till I longed to disown him. People would look at him and smile, and then at Elizabeth, and last of all at Mother and me. He was handsome and outgoing and noticeable, and I felt that even stage performers—even opera singers—would be unnoticeable in comparison.

"You shouldn't say hell, Jenny," said Elizabeth, rather primly, I thought.

"Good grief, this is nineteen forty-eight, didn't you know?" I seldom rounded on my twin, and she looked startled.

"Oh, don't let's fall out *today*, Jenny."

"I should say it was just the right day for it." And when I heard Mother being sick upstairs I knew that I was right. It was a black thirteenth birthday, and if it had fallen on Friday the thirteenth I shouldn't have been surprised.

By the time Father arrived Mother had been sick five times, and Ellys—the Welsh girl who helped her in the house—was ringing up the doctor. Elizabeth looked worse than before breakfast, and was in the loo a suspiciously long while. I went and listened outside, but if she retched she must have done it with decorum, so that it wasn't advertised. I hadn't known she looked forward to the opera so much. It struck me that I knew very little of my twin—less than I thought. It made me feel lonely. I began to hope, selfishly, that if Mother was unable to come with us, Ellys might go instead. But when Father came he vetoed the idea.

"It's just one of those boring things, Jerôme," said Mother. She had hoisted herself on to the sofa and lay there feeble and palpitating, like a hare I had once seen hiding from pursuit. "You'd better take Ellys with the girls instead of me."

"*Mais tu es folle, ma chère Yvonne*" began Father, and then lapsed into English. "The girls, they come with me, and Ellys await naturally the doctor. It is perhaps an *appendicite*."

"*I'll* stay with Mother," I said gladly and selfishly.

"*Mon enfant*, you do no such thing. This is an expensive treat I give you all." Father began to sulk. His beady black glance raked me with a sullen look of—what? Dislike? I began to tremble. I knew Mother wished to stop the outing, but didn't dare. 'Reasonable access' hung over me, like a cloud.

The taxi, ticking up shillings on its meter, was also giving Father fidgets. So it wasn't long before Elizabeth and I were sitting one on each side of him *en route* for the theatre. I wishing that my stomach wouldn't heave, and Elizabeth calm and self-possessed as usual, but still with that bright-eyed air of fever.

Curiously enough, Father almost ignored her and gave me all his attention. When he wished, he could charm the proverbial birds off trees, and by the time we reached the theatre I was actually prepared to enjoy myself; 'theatre' of almost any kind was one of the things I liked best in life. It was the exact antithesis of the convent, and titivated my already over-developed sense of drama. I don't think this was inconsistent

31

with my dullness and love of routine. I just didn't like 'theatre in daily life.

Father left one ticket at the box office. He then led us into the auditorium, to Row D of the stalls. Our seats were by the gangway. We filed in, leaving Mother's seat empty on our left. Father bought a box of chocolates and handed them to Elizabeth; but she made no attempt to open them, just folded her hands on the lid, and he told her sharply either to hand the chocolates round or pass them over to me.

The lights had turned low, and the orchestra had begun the overture, when a large coarse-looking woman barged her way past us without apology, and sat down beside me in Mother's empty place.

"Good," said Father resonantly, "so they got rid of the ticket."

His voice was loud above the music, and I blushed for him. Also, I was unhappy with my neighbour. She was fat enough to overflow on to the arm of my seat, and her scent was like a blast of poor-quality soap. But I soon forgot my irritation. Even now I think *The Magic Flute* is the ideal first opera for a child, if the more obvious choice of *Hänsel and Gretel* is discarded. It was clever of Father to have chosen it, and my heart warmed to him. I was enthralled. And it wasn't till half-way through the performance that I realized all was not well with my twin. Elizabeth's head drooped, while she breathed almost as loudly as the over-scented woman on my left. She was twisting her hands together in her lap—always a sign that things weren't physically well with her. I saw Father glance at her sideways, and then she got up in one quick movement and stumbled out past him, up the gangway. I saw her speak to the programme seller by the entrance, who took her sympathetically by the arm and steered her away—towards the 'ladies', I supposed.

Father gave an exasperated sigh. "Stay here, Geneviève. I return." He followed Elizabeth out, looking ominously tall. I wanted to go too, but people round us had begun to turn in their seats, and frown, and I didn't dare cause more disturbance. So I began to hope fervently that I wouldn't fail him too, and my treacherous stomach heaved at the mere idea.

The interval came, the lights went up, and neither Father nor Elizabeth returned. People began to pour out of the stalls towards the foyer, and others settled down to trays of tea. Father had fixed tea for us in advance, and a tray was brought me. I sat there, balancing it on my knee, not knowing whether I dare put it on the floor and go to look for Father, or if someone would tread on it.

I was just lowering it to the ground when sure enough that beastly fat woman next to me stood up and started to barge her way out. So there I stayed, unable to think of eating, nervous of other people wanting to move, of upsetting the teapot, of bringing down Father's displeasure on my head. Then, just as the bell rang and the lights dimmed, Father reappeared. Behind him was the fat woman. 'The Bargee' I called her to myself.

"Jenny" (he never called me Jenny, and this in itself was grave) "Elizabeth is most unwell, like your mother. She cannot sit the opera out; she is all the time sick. I take her quick to the flat of friends nearby, and this lady—" here he prodded the Bargee in what I thought a familiar way, "has so kindly made a promise to see you join us there by taxi afterward."

"Oh no," I said, upset. "Please, please, let me come too, papa."

I felt quite wretched, because I knew at once that Father was furious with me. Even with the lights lowered his face gleamed red and swollen close to mine.

"This is stupid," he said. "*Someone* might as well enjoy the afternoon."

"I'm *not* enjoying it." I was reckless with dismay. Mother sick at home, and Elizabeth sick in someone else's flat! I tried to drag myself up, but that wretched teatray weighed me down. Of course at that moment the curtains parted on the next act; the music began, everyone round us said 'hush', and the Bargee sat down, firm and enormous, in Father's gangway seat, blocking my exit as effectively as a lorry would have done.

"Please, Father—" I said, very loud above the music, but he merely gave me a glance of bitter disapproval, and loped off up the gangway to wherever he had left Elizabeth. "No more fossing, will we," said the Bargee, or it sounded like that; anyway, it made me heartily dislike her.

I don't think I've ever spent a more miserable hour. I was trapped—on my right, on my left, and by that tray of tea which weighed a ton. Eventually someone took it away from me, and at last the opera came to an end. We applauded, stood for 'The King', and put our things together. I felt a great rush of relief. I even managed to down a chocolate before cramming the lid back on to the box. The Bargee, like a blockhouse, stood waiting for me.

"So, little girl, kom along now." Her words had a foreign intonation, though not a French one. I don't think she was even European, she had too dark a skin. Along with that powerful wave of dislike for her I felt, curiously enough, a distinct feeling of fear. I followed her from the theatre, thankful that I should soon be with Elizabeth and Father. We found a taxi quite easily, and the Bargee beckoned me to get inside. She put a foot on the step, and I thought she was coming too.

"Now. And so what is the address?"

"The address?" I stammered. "But *I* don't know it!"

She muttered something under her breath which sounded like 'stupid one'. "Your mother's house. You do not know the address of your own house?"

"B-but, P-Papa—Father—he said you would see me to the *flat*."

"The flat? What flat?"

"*The* flat—the one where he and Eliz—my sister, are!"

"He give me no such address." She tapped her enormous foot on the step with the air of a bored and impatient horse.

"But he did," I said weakly. "He said so."

She gave me a sharp glance, full of spite. "It is a misapprehension. I have no address. You had better go home, little girl."

The taxi man gave me a kind fatherly smile. "Sure, I'll take her."

"Oh *please*. Couldn't we—couldn't we ask the cloakroom attendant, or—or someone—" I knew it was useless.

"Come, dear, do not be silly, will we? Give the driver the address."

I gave in.

A look of triumph lit her face. She leaned forward, shoved

34

a ten-shilling note into my hand, and banged shut the door. I gazed out in despair, and saw her hurry off; her shoes went clackety-clack on the pavement with the precision of hammer blows. The taxi started with a jerk.

The rest of that day was confusion, from my arrival home to the moment when, limp from tears and exhaustion, I went to sleep at last in the room I had always shared with my twin. Her empty bed was a bitter reproach to me. Did Mother ever blame me for my dim-wittedness? If she did, she never said so. Everything had played into Father's hands: my stupidity, Elizabeth's sickness—I don't suppose she cared much what happened to her that day. It was Father's luck, always his best ally.

When, incoherent and shaking, I reached home, I found Mother almost recovered. "Friends—what friends?" she said sharply, when I reached the point in my tale where Father spoke of the flat.

"He didn't say."

Her hand went to the telephone, but withdrew again. "We shall have to give him time . . . A chance . . ." she murmured. But her features were blurred with doubt; there was something altogether too glib and neatly dovetailed about the separation of me from my sister at the theatre. As I left the room I heard her pick up the receiver, this time with decision, and call the police.

At first they didn't take it seriously. Why should they? They hadn't my distrust of Father, nor Mother's bitter knowledge of him. But as afternoon gave place to evening, as lights pricked out everywhere and glittered on rainy pavements, and still there came no news, no taxi stopping at the door, no sudden strident shrilling of the telephone, our inner doubts were shared. Then I found myself required to re-tell my story until Mother put an end to the repetitive probing, and sent me, tear-stained and exhausted, to my bed.

"Try not to worry, Madam," said the sympathetic police-sergeant, as I closed the living-room door, "he won't get her out of the country, we'll find them first." (When the divorce went through, Elizabeth and I had been made Wards of Court;

35

Father could go to jail for contempt, if he tried to take my twin abroad.)

'We shall find them first.'

They never did. Nor did they locate the Bargee. What's known as 'a nation-wide hunt' took place; it extended to the Continent, and Elizabeth attained notoriety in the Press as 'the Missing Twin', until she became one of those unsolved cases relegated to the dusty files in newspaper offices, and left open in the annals of the police.

Except for one incident which drew the hunt temporarily to France, she vanished from our lives as completely as if she had died; and she took nothing with her, not even a brush or comb. That was one thing the police asked Mother and me. But the idea of complicity was quite ruled out. We knew that Elizabeth, with her simple calm, her love of home and school, was the last person to rush off with our alarming, unpredictable parent; she had never shown marked signs of preference for him, although she could manage him better than anyone else. (Mother never told me till years later that the sole reason Father tried to fight the divorce had been his reluctance to lose Elizabeth; perhaps she thought it would hurt my feelings.)

I mentioned a trail to France.

Two days after the disappearance Mother made me return to school. I was just leaving, after breakfast, when the telephone rang. I picked up the receiver.

"*Allô—allô. Ici Paris. Madame Lemprière? Quelqu'un vous demande—*"

I stood there bewildered, my mouth open to call Mother.

"Jenny!" It was a light gasp, almost a breath, into the telephone. It sounded very far away.

"*Elizabeth!*"

"Jenny—is Mother—is she—"

"Wait, I'll call her, I—"

"No—*no*, don't go, Jenny, oh don't—" again the gasp, "is Mother all right now?"

"Yes—oh yes . . . *Mother!*"

"*No*, Jenny," the whisper sounded frantic. "I *can't* . . . he's coming . . . Good-bye, Jenny—good-bye."

36

As Mother reached my side the line went dead.

That was the last we heard of my twin. The call was traced to a small hotel in Paris where she and Father had breakfasted. After that the trail faded out. They were sought all over France, and for months afterwards we were bedevilled with rumours—they had been seen here, seen there; but in the end it all dribbled away to nothing. The rest was silence, and a question-mark. To what bolthole he smuggled her, and where and how he had managed to spirit them both away as easily as a conjurer whisks his accomplice off the stage, remained a mystery.

Poor Elizabeth! For years she haunted me. I saw her round every corner; in every crowded bus I craned to get a glimpse of her, although I knew in my heart it was hopeless, Father could never bring her back to England. How would he dare? The thought of her life with him made me shudder—to what sort of existence had she gone? Impossible to imagine it, far from the placid, rational lives of Mother and myself. Particularly I shuddered when I thought of the quirks of destiny, and how Elizabeth, on the morning of our thirteenth birthday, had complained of the certain, incurable dullness of our future. . . .

4

. . . there's something in't
That is deceivable. But here the lady comes.
TWELFTH NIGHT

"What a fantastic story!" said Lucy Starr.

I looked round at my audience, like the traditional story-teller watching his effects. At the foot of the bed Ilona stared back at me with round enthralled eyes.

"And you really never heard of them again? They disappeared—"

"Like a puff of smoke in a high wind."

"I don't suppose Daddy would take *me* away like that." There was a touch of disappointment in Ilona's voice. I hid a smile.

"Darling, I'm afraid he won't. Do you really want to go?"

"No, *but*—" She stroked the puppy with her foot. He gnawed it.

I grinned to myself. "The adventure would be smashing?"

She rushed at me then, and flung her arms round my neck. "Of course I wouldn't *truly* want to go, Mum, you see, *but*—"

I rocked her lightly in my arms, and over her head saw Miss Starr watch me rather curiously.

"What's on your mind, chum?"

She shrugged. With that movement of hers I noticed the shabbiness of her one good office suit, and made a mental note to offer her another. "Mrs. Emerson, you've been a 'name' for years, and yet she never got in touch with you before."

"Why should she have put me and Geneviève together?"

Miss Starr gave an elegant version of a snort. "Why put you together now?"

It was my turn to shrug. "I suppose I'll find out—at the Hilton. My present guess would be—the office biography."

"Yes, of course. Well, everyone in the office was against it—except Mr Leyton. And look how right he was—as usual!" Her voice was a little dry, and I sympathized, for I, too, had suffered from Christopher's appalling rightness at times.

The office biographies had been one of John's inspirations

38

for pepping up the flagging moments in his columnists' careers. In Geneviève's case it had introduced her public to the shadowy form of Jenny, along with Jenny's home life and—unemphasized—George. It hadn't, of course, revealed that Geneviève's ownership of the farm was purely mythical; nor touched on Elizabeth and her disappearance, that early heartbreak which I had never dragged out in public again.

"Put in a bit about your parentage, and your maiden name, didn't he?" went on Miss Starr, pursuing her own thoughts. "I remember. And cut out about your grandfather's invention. Lucky he did too, otherwise you'd never know—" She stopped.

"If you mean," I was on the defensive for my twin, "that we wouldn't have known if Elizabeth's reappearance had something to do with *that*. . . ."

"Well, would you?"

"You don't understand, how could you? You never met her. She was a complete Puritan—odd thing for a Catholic to say, but she was. She got it from Mother, I suppose, who could be rigid. Elizabeth just wasn't interested in money."

"We were most of us pretty lofty at thirteen. And people change. And I've yet to meet the person who's not interested in money." Miss Starr smoothed down her worn shirt. "I'm interested in it myself."

"It wouldn't be that," I persisted in the face of her scepticism. "Anyway, she's welcome to her share. I'm sure if Grandfather had known she was still alive, *and* what would happen to his funny little patent after his death, he would have wanted us to halve the proceeds."

That was certainly true; Grandfather—Mother's father—had adored Elizabeth. I think her disappearance had literally broken his heart. He died soon afterwards, leaving Mother to struggle on alone to bring me up. And it was a struggle all right, without the small allowance he had given her from the annuity he lived on. He was so generous always, with a creative streak somewhere which came out in an inventive turn of mind. "Your Grandfather's hobbies," my mother used to say, with her amused smile. She would have been startled if she could have guessed what the 'hobbies' would produce—an ingenious device for locking the parts of aeroplanes together which was to be used eventually all over the world, wherever aeroplanes are made.

The patent had come to me. How were we to know that something which brought me in a few pounds a year was to snowball until it made a fortune? It was just another of those fabulous things which had happened for lucky Jenny when she no longer needed it. I still speak of it reluctantly now, for in a way I'm ashamed of the fortune on good fortune which came my undeserving way during those years of high-coloured plenty; too much good fortune in a world pitiless to other people.

While I was thinking of this, Miss Starr glanced at her watch, exclaimed, and rose hurriedly to her feet. "Good heavens, look at the time! I must get back to work and our Mr. Leyton. It's been a fascinating tale—I wouldn't have missed it for anything."

"I'm amazed it didn't leak out before," I said, and was surprised to see her colour up an unbecoming pink; perhaps she thought I was hinting that she gossipped. I hastened to add: "You can tell Mr. Leyton that if he was less of a clam you'd have known all this long ago."

Ilona, cuddled up on the bed, gave an enchanting giggle.

"I don't suppose you wanted it talked about, Mrs. Emerson, it must have been very hurting for you and your mother." She still lingered, and then blurted out: "Odd, isn't it—when you meet your sister you won't know anything of the way she's lived. Was your father—" a delicate hesitation, "not well off?"

"Less money than Mother, and she hadn't much. He had his pay, of course, and a small pension after the war. His parents were poor too; Mother hardly knew them, only met them two or three times when she got engaged to Father on holiday in France. Attempts were made to trace him through them, but they didn't know where he was living. They were ripely disapproving. There was generally a woman somewhere, I believe."

" I see." A tone of spinsterly withdrawal that amused me. Unlike her, I thought it. "I suppose your father's dead?"

"Goodness—he might be, or he might not." I reflected on the thought of seeing Father again, and it left me cold. No; not cold—angry. If he turned up at the Hilton there was a thing or two to say, when I remembered the return home of the scared thirteen-year-old that had been me.

"And you hope he is." Miss Starr's office shrewdness went straight to the target. "And I hope for your sake that it's so, Mrs. Emerson. You couldn't look forward to seeing him." Her hand was already on the door when suddenly she turned back to me. "I say, here's another thought—what if she's *not* her?"

"Dear Miss Starr, what *do* you mean?"

"She might be an imposter."

"Oh, but why should she be? There's nothing for her to impost about," I thought the secretary's sense of the dramatic had run away with her.

"What's a 'postor?" put in Ilona.

"A person who pretends to be someone they're not, darling."

"The Tichbourne Claimant! There's something for you to think about, Mrs. Emerson. Now I'll run—good-bye. And have a happy birthday."

While I dressed, I considered her words. The initial shock and delight of Elizabeth's reappearance had faded, and I found myself thinking coolly of my twin—if it *were* my twin who had turned up in this improbable way. For surely she could have got in touch before? When I thought of the misery her disappearance and presumed death had caused us all, her silence seemed the acme of heartlessness. Perhaps it was harsh of me to prejudge her actions until I heard her story. As if I were back at school I could hear Reverend Mother's voice, mild but reproving, say: 'Judge yourself harshly, Jenny, if you will, but never other people. Leave that to their conscience, and to God.'

Well, I wouldn't judge Elizabeth; at least, not yet. So I thought as I crossed to the cupboard where my clothes were hung. My new chestnut-brown suit had just been delivered and I decided to wear it for the meeting. It wasn't a bad match for my hair. I looked in the glass over the chimneypiece and wondered if I had changed so much that Elizabeth wouldn't recognize me. And would I recognize her? I grimaced at myself— somewhere far back in our family tree a Hungarian ancestress had contributed those high cheekbones, my wide brow and rather

41

prominently modelled lips. Features which helped to make up what George lovingly referred to as my touchingly peculiar face. In no way did I resemble the fair-haired blue-eyed English beauty that Elizabeth must have blossomed into when she grew up. In the Adam glass my eyes looked both wary and—could it be?—resentful. Was it possible, I asked myself ruefully, that I didn't *want* my twin back? Was there, somewhere deep inside, shut away from all the happiness and success, a fear that invidious comparisons were to start all over again? Did one *never* become properly grown up?

The clock striking interrupted these rather morbid thoughts. Eleven-thirty. So much to be done—or rather, so much to supervise, that must now be left, since in a few minutes I must start for my rendezvous. I wondered why Elizabeth had posted her letter so late that she couldn't possibly expect a reply in time. Perhaps she had hesitated to send it? If Elizabeth had become a ditherer, then her character had radically changed.

Some time ago Mrs. Jason had take Ilona to the little nursery school she attended nearby. She must have been shockingly late—I grinned to myself—but no doubt she would wriggle out of the consequences. It was fortunate that Reverend Mother would have the handling of her within a year. Even George, who so adored his daughter, sometimes complained. . . .

George! I put a hand to my mouth. How *could* I have forgotten him? Would he welcome Elizabeth's arrival? Too late now to get hold of him and explain. I dare not risk being delayed for the appointment. How tantalizing if Elizabeth, real or impostor, should take off and vanish once again!

I rang for Clayton. He came, wearing that smug pudgy smile of his. How I detested him, but George found him invaluable. He was the prop and stay of our household, and knew it. I would have preferred the house to fall elegantly to bits, sooner than meet Clayton's smile round every corner. But in household matters preoccupation with Geneviève had made me mildly deficient, and it seemed unfair to inflict chaos on George, so I must just put up with Clayton's smile and Clayton's feet— those particularly large feet which skimmed over the floor so softly that we seldom heard the sound of his approach.

42

"You rang, Madam?"

"Yes. I'm going out." I avoided looking at his eyes. They always gave me a sensation of discomfort. "There are all sorts of bits and pieces for the party left undone, and I haven't made a list of them."

"Madam has no need—" He spread his soft hands sideways, and inclined gently forward like a bird bowing on its perch. A giant canary—his too-canary coloured hair shone very sleek like an advertisement. "The flowers—then we are out of Campari, then the confirmation of Madam's hair appointment—"

"There's no pink, either," I said, picking up my gloves, "and my little watch has been mended—it needs collecting—"

"I collected it just now, Madam."

How had Clayton known . . ? I gazed at him in some resentment. So he had noticed its absence, had guessed it would be due back for the party—had found, no doubt, the jeweller's receipt on my dressing-table. It was extremely useful, and like being under police surveillance. There was no expression on the large fat face watching me, but I felt his amusement.

"Is that all for Madam?"

"No. Tell Mrs. Jason that I may lunch out, or I may be back, in which case I shall have a guest—" I thought briefly of Father, and added reluctantly, "perhaps two."

"Certainly, Madam."

"And your hair needs cutting, Clayton," I said. "And it's getting altogether a bit too blonde." Going downstairs I hoped that some of the amusement had been wiped away.

My taxi arrived at the hotel sharp on time, but I lingered just inside the door. I felt nervous—nervous of Elizabeth! Suppose she *was* an impostor? Suppose I couldn't be quite sure. . . .

It was then I saw her coming towards me, and all suspicion died. She hadn't seen me yet, or hadn't recognized me. For she stopped by a glass and gravely examined herself. It wasn't the sort of stocktaking a woman does for reassurance, or to correct something wrong with her appearance. There were several men waiting for people, or reading newspapers, and they were assessing her too. Even the pageboys did it, out of the corners of their eyes. She had stepped straight into the limelight, as she always had, and as always she was unconscious of it. She was, quite unmistakably, Elizabeth.

There was the well-recalled, beautifully cut profile; the same silky hair now pulled into a heavy twist at the back of her head. She wore a dress which fitted her figure almost too well, and finished in a little fur collar. On her head was a ridiculous hat—a sort of tiny fur plate endearingly like the hats worn by small Victorian girls, which took away from the insinuating appearance of the dress. Then she turned again towards me, and I saw her eyes: very wide and blue and serene, with incredible long black lashes. She looked at me for a full half-minute, during which something—shyness?—held me back from making a sign of recognition. Then her lips broke into a questioning but warm smile of pure delight.

"*Jenny*? It is, isn't it? Marvellous to see you, darling!"

We kissed each other warmly, muttering incoherent words. "Well—" Elizabeth at last drew back, and looked me up and down with a cool little stare which was somehow disconcerting. "I might have said same old Jenny, but it's not, is it? It's Geneviève. Now I've something to live up to. . . ."

I felt stupidly rebuffed and hurt, and somehow lessened. She had at once put me into the successful career-woman bracket; while there she was just being herself, which was plainly enough for anyone, to judge by the looks she received. Perhaps I was over-sensitive—she couldn't have *meant* to make me feel like that.

"Live up to *me*? Oh, Liz! Not looking the way you do."

She gave me an almost grateful smile, and her reaction jarred. For why should Elizabeth, so well-groomed, so obviously cared for, be grateful for that very ordinary remark? I said hastily: "Don't you think we might drink to our reunion?"

"Do let's." She put her arm through mine, and at once I felt more as if we were twins again.

"Poor Jenny. What a boring time you must have had when Papa abducted me."

"Boring! Understatement. . . ."

We walked to a table, and sat down. A waiter came and took our order. Elizabeth glanced at me sideways.

"You've sprung no questions on me yet."

I looked down at my hands, and then sideways at hers. She had removed her gloves, and her left hand was ringless. The question I *had* been about to ask died on my lips.

"What is it, Jenny?"

"Nothing. No questions till later." I was visited with sudden reluctance to know about her life. It was too late; with Mother and Grandfather dead, and myself ensconced in a totally new life, what interest could the other side of the picture hold for anyone? The picture that remained in my mind, of a small girl disappearing up the gangway of a theatre.

"To our happy reunion," I said, and drank. Her lips just touched her glass, and then she set it down. In that instant I had a sensation of something urgently wrong. It was one often connected with Father. So strong was the feeling that I hurriedly looked about me, but there were only five people near us; and none of them resembled Papa.

He certainly wasn't the middle-aged man sitting opposite, who might have been of vaguely Eastern origin—say Armenian, or Turkish. He kept eyeing first me and then Elizabeth as if we were objects laid out on a goldsmith's counter. There was a paper on his knee, but he made no pretence of reading it, just sat and stared at us. There was a very faint line of moustache along his upper lip, at this distance it looked almost like a line of sweat. . . . Suddenly a look of amusement crossed his face, and I grew conscious of having stared too hard. Hastily I turned back to my twin.

Elizabeth sat staring into space. Her hands were laid flat on the table before her, her lips were drawn into a thin almost colourless line. She appeared utterly withdrawn; there was something about her expression which reminded me of a little sphinx-face once seen in a museum. I felt scared—not of her, but of something I fancied almost visible around her, a miasma of melancholy, of desolation;—could it be?—of evil. No, these were neurotic fancies, and not things that lucky Jenny meant to indulge in. I heard my own voice say—and it was reassuring to hear it sound so placid: "What of Papa, Liz? Is he—well?"

Her face relaxed, and colour came back into her lips. It was like watching Galatea come alive.

"He died a few months back." Her voice was composed. There was no tinge of regret in it. Surely it had not always been so absolutely controlled, and colourless in tone?

"So he never suggested we should meet again?"

"No. He thought it was—*I* thought it was better not, while he was still alive."

I felt a surge of relief. In spite of myself Lucy Starr's words had bitten deep. Now here at least was one good reason to hang an explanation on: Elizabeth free at last to exchange one set of loyalties for another. How like her, that she should ever have seen the situation in those terms. There had always been, I thought, this natural uprightness in her character which would have made it difficult for her to lead a dual existence.

"There's such a lot to say—" I glanced at my watch. "Hotels aren't the place for family histories. . . Let's go home."

Elizabeth gave me an almost grateful smile. "That sounds wonderful. But I thought you'd lunch here with me."

"Darling Liz—you're staying with me—with us. For as long as you like."

"Jenny, you angel. But what about—George, isn't it? Won't he mind having the prodigal sister-in-law foisted on him?"

"George is the angel, not me. He never minds anything. I'm most dreadfully spoilt."

She let out a long breath like a sigh. "Oh, Jenny, I'm tremendously glad everything's turned out so well for you. If you *knew* what people could be. . . ."

It was the exact reversal of our schooldays. Here was Elizabeth envying *me*. Fantastic, with those looks of hers, that she could have cause to envy anyone. Strange, that fatality which so often haunts very beautiful women. With the one-track-minded reaction of the happily married I resolved that George and I would act as marriage brokers in the fastest possible time.

Elizabeth's things were easily put together. Her room was small, on an upper floor, and what she had with her went into two moderate-sized cases. Everything was plainly expensive, and she had some charming clothes, although not many for someone staying in a luxury hotel. Anyway, I couldn't ask what her finances were, as if I must know before she came to stay with us; and she didn't volunteer information, which reminded me of her habitual childhood reserve. We had her cases taken downstairs, paid her bill, and the doorman called a taxi.

"It's fun, Jenny, to be back again in London—and with you."

"Strange, I should think."

"Jenny."

"Yes?"

She was staring out at the street. A few autumn leaves drifted past the window. Her hair was almost the same colour as the palest of them. There was again that shadow of sadness on her face.

"Would it be extravagant of us to go right round by Kensington and the little house?"

"Let's. I'm in an extravagant mood. It's not every day I'm reunited with a twin I thought dead."

"Poor Jenny. Is that really what you thought?"

"Wouldn't you have thought so?"

She didn't answer, but a tinge of colour came into her face. She hadn't mentioned Mother, I noticed. The biography had shown that she died some years back; silence was understandable.

For years I had been a stranger to that little street. The houses, once so shabby, were now mostly done up with fashionable paint and window-boxes. There were only two houses which were peeling and dirty of façade, and one of them had been ours.

"It's for sale, Jenny—" Outside our old home was a board.

I had the conventional sensation of being a ghost—a twin ghost. It seemed the oddest thing in the world that Elizabeth and I should return here now together. I almost expected to see Christopher as a little boy waving to us from the house next door, as the taxi drove slowly past. I was relieved when the driver turned the corner. Elizabeth leaned back in her seat, sighed, and voiced my thoughts: "Didn't you expect to see Christopher, Jenny? But I suppose you *do* see him, fairly often." I didn't reply, and she went on: "That was a pretty foolish impulse. Everything looks so sad. I feel the little girls we were have been dead a long while, don't you?"

"No—in some ways I'm pretty much the same inside, al-

47

though not so unsure of myself. And outwardly at least *you've* not altered much."

"Lost innocence," she said, with gaiety, "that's me." Then: "Did you ever find my diary?"

The apparent irrelevance took me by surprise. I thought carefully for a moment, but I couldn't remember what had become of that frivolous pale green volume, with its foolish, portentous lock and key. "Come to think of it, I don't remember ever seeing it again after—when you went."

"Stupid of me, but I don't much like the idea of strangers peering at the idiotic thoughts I had when we were twelve."

"It's crumbled to dust long ago. Or if it hasn't, it probably won't be found for fifty years or so—and then you'll just be an oddity: a child of the good old just-post-atomic period."

"That's true."

"Forget it, Liz. Think of the future. I'm dying to show you my home—mine and George's and Ilona's. I simply can't wait for you to meet my family."

"Nor can I. Oh, Jenny—" there was the ring of truth in her voice, "you can't think *what* it means to me, to be here at last. Home."

5

And what's her history?
A blank, my lord.
TWELFTH NIGHT

"A fortnight." said George. He said it indistinctly because he was washing his face at the time, but his meaning was clear.

"Darling, you're a little unfair." Since a small doubt nagged away deep in my own mind, I was almost too vehement in denial.

"I'm not, and you know it. We've been very gracefully put off. A whole fortnight since your sweet sister came creeping back to us like a strayed cat and, like a cat, she's just not telling. What *do* we know about her? That your father took her abroad. That there was eventually some sort of stepmother, who died, and that Elizabeth seems to have some money now."

"She hasn't asked me for a sou," I said, on the defensive for my twin. "*Must* we be so suspicious?—Elizabeth was always very reserved."

"Another word for it is cagey."

I was silenced. Here we were, for the first time in our married life, on the verge of a quarrel. It was incredible. More incredible still that it was Elizabeth, who fitted so unobtrusively into our household, who had caused it. If she'd been unhappy with Father, she had a right not to talk of it, surely? A right to forget. It was uncharitable to poke around in Elizabeth's past, to demand that she drag out and rattle whatever skeletons haunted it. I said so.

"All right, then, I'm uncharitable." George clumped into our bedroom from the bathroom. He was a heavy man, and he moved heavily. There was an expression of hurt upon his face, but I ignored it. I was too busy trying to justify Elizabeth and my defence of her, in defiance of my growing unease about the old story that relations cause trouble in a marriage.

"Sweet, kind George. Don't be cross. You do *like* her, don't you?"

He rubbed his nose with the back of one forefinger.

49

"I've not seen anything to *dislike* yet," he admitted. "I'm just reserving judgment."

I smiled, a mean bit pleased that George hadn't succumbed to her fascination. All our friends raved about Elizabeth, and she sweetly, if aloofly, responded. Ilona followed her round the house like a child-slave, while Clayton, who certainly loathed me, spent his time anticipating her wants. Our telephone rang constantly. If I hadn't been so fond of her myself. . . .

The telephone rang.

"Damn it," said George. "Not *again*."

"Let Clayton answer. Do him good to run up and down the stairs a bit—run off some of that fat."

"You do hate him, don't you, Jenny?"

"Understatement."

"We could always do without him, if you'd really prefer it."

"Darling, no. You wouldn't be nearly so comfortable."

"That doesn't matter, Jenny, if you'd rather he went. It only matters what you want."

"Darling," I said.

"My sweet—"

There was a satisfactory interlude broken by a knock on the door: Clayton's obsequious tap-tap, like a refined woodpecker not much at home with a hardwood tree.

"Come in."

"Oh, excuse me, Madam—" Clayton's expression managed to imply that I was a lecherous, free-living woman—and with my own husband, too. "It's Mr. Leyton, Madam; on the telephone for Miss Lemprière. I thought she might be up here with you."

"Miss Lemprière went out some time ago. She's at Mass."

"I am sorry to have disturbed you, Madam. But would you wish to speak with Mr. Leyton yourself?"

"Just give him the message." Though there was now constant antagonism between us, it did strike me that he might have the common politeness to ask for me or George if Elizabeth wasn't in.

"Very good, Madam." Clayton closed the door. I relaxed again, threw my arms round George, and pressed my face into the warmth of his neck.

50

"I love you," I murmured. "I do love you so much."

He held me closer. I shut my eyes. It was the nicest thing I knew—me and George together, and everyone else shut out. Everyone else, I thought, mattered less than my little fingernail beside him. Except Ilona. I and George and Ilona snug against the universe, with even Elizabeth way, way out on its perimeter.

Presently George said in a ruminative tone. "Christopher."

"Ummm?"

"Wake up, my love. Christopher would be an excellent solution."

"This is only the second time he's rung since my party," I pointed out. "It doesn't seem a very enthusiastic solution."

"Christopher's a busy man."

"Never too busy to take out a blonde."

"Well, it was only a suggestion."

"I'm not opposing it, only saying that for Christopher the running is slow."

"Perhaps he hasn't picked himself up since the initial shock. I thought she knocked him cold at the party."

"Didn't notice," I said, and then realized it wasn't strictly true. The fact is that Christopher's behaviour on my birthday was a sore spot with me. First of all, the conference which made it impossible for him to come had suddenly faded away to a mere unimportant chat with a sub-editor which could be postponed. Or so he murmured in my ear when he arrived.

"These are for you, Jenny. Happy birthday, again." A bunch of chrysanthemums of a particularly hideous rust-colour; a box of milk chocolates, which I loathe. Decidedly not Christopher at his most tactful.

"You've brought nothing for Elizabeth?" I asked somewhat snarkily. "I suppose the only reason you've turned up after all is your insatiable journalist's curiosity."

"What a girl you are for flickknives." He stared absently round the room. "Not at all the dear polite little Jenny I used to love. Even rich successful women say thank you for presents."

"I hate milk chocolate, and I loathe rust, which you haven't taken the trouble to remember. It's no compliment to turn up with things I hate just because you want to look over Elizabeth."

"You'll be a scold, if you go on like this, I must warn George. Never let a wife fix herself in an ugly mould young, they're the devil to get out of it later." He grinned in my furious face. "Cheer up, Jenny: Elizabeth *shall* have a birthday present." He whipped the chrysanthemums out of my grasp. "Where is she?"

"Oh, *Christopher.*"

It was Ilona, bobbing up and down in front of him, and barring his path. Her face was alight with adulation. Bright face, bright hair. She looked a darling, and I could have slapped her.

"Christopher, Mummy said you couldn't come; oh, *Christopher.*"

He put her absently aside, and her face flamed with sudden hurt. My anger with them both simmered up to boiling point.

"Christopher, you selfish pig, you might just say hello to Ilona—Ilona, try not to pester people," I said unreasonably. He put his arm round her shoulders and patted her neck. "Come along, honey. Come and find me Aunt Elizabeth."

"Oh I *will.*" She gave me a triumphant and very grown-up look. "Mummy's cross tonight. I don't think birthdays suit her," I overheard the audacious whisper.

"No? Birthdays don't suit women. Never have them, Ilona."

They crossed the room together, and their laughter drifted back to me. I saw Ilona prod Elizabeth unceremoniously in the back, saw my sister turn, give a delighted cry of recognition, and hold out her hands in welcome. Someone came up to greet me then, and when I next had time to look Elizabeth was cradling the chrysanthemums, while Christopher had one arm around her and with his free hand was tickling Ilona beneath the chin. All three were having a gorgeous time.

"Yes, I *did* notice," I corrected myself now, "but it might have been just Christopher. I've seen him act knocked cold by women who might be stick insects. My sex does something to him."

"Well, couldn't Elizabeth?"

"You're very keen to get her out of the house!"

"I'm always keen to get you alone."

When I came up from under again, I said: "Christopher

would be a scourge as a brother-in-law. We see more than enough of him as it is."

George smiled at me tenderly, and looked pleased. He had no cause to be jealous, but perhaps most men like to hear their wives speak slightingly of former boy friends. "I should think you've almost had one already," was all he said.

"One what?"

"Brother-in-law." He grinned at my surprised face. "So much for women's powers of observation and intuition and all that. Haven't you noticed that your twin has worn rings on both hands? The marks are still there—you can just see them against the remains of her summer tan."

I gazed at him in astonishment. "George, darling, talk of Maigret!"

He looked a bit smug. "Noticed it when she drove my car the other day. The fact is, Jenny, you aren't all that observant in small things."

"I know." Indeed I did. That was why we had Clayton. "Poor Elizabeth; a broken engagement—it explains why she's reticent."

"Perhaps. To some extent. She could at least tell us where she lived."

"In Paris."

"She told you so?"

Had she? No—come to think of it, she hadn't. I had *assumed* Paris, because her letter came from there.

"You see?" said George. "It's all done with mirrors; we haven't the faintest idea what the conjurer's up to."

"She'll come clean in time, you'll see." But I spoke without conviction, and the time was to come when I would bitterly, tragically regret that I assumed any confidence at all.

And my twin remained clam-like. Soon I ceased to expect revelations, and George said no more about it. He seemed to accept her as part of the household, and to forget his qualms. True, we were both so busy in November that we allowed Elizabeth to slip more and more into the background of our lives. Now and then we saw Christopher—socially, I mean; in Fleet Street I saw him often. Sometimes he called for Elizabeth

53

and took her out, but I saw no signs of anything serious between them.

So things went on for several weeks, broken only by the alarms and excursions of journalism, the usual bouts of 'flu, and that terrible party hurdle, Christmas. We weathered it gaily, which meant that we went on till we dropped on drink and pep pills and too much food. Elizabeth spent a lot of time at the convent and eyed me, I felt, with reproach whenever I failed to acccompany her to Mass. But you can't force yourself to faith, I told myself fiercely. At least, when George and I were together, I felt thankful for the happiness I had.

It was January, with an icy, whining east wind which came tearing out of a blind blank sky. Not even furs were protection from its brutish fury. I felt tired right through—through and through as though Christmas had never got out of my bones. I lay down exhausted at night, and ached when I got up in the morning. Eventually I was so tired I couldn't sleep, and little pills of all sorts crept into the drawer of my dressing table: iron and calcium and vitamins and sodium amytal. One evening I came home at half past five wondering if the exhaustion I felt could possibly be another baby—that little boy so arrogantly decided on in October.

Elizabeth was in the drawing room. As I stood on the threshold it struck me that she might have been the mistress of the house. It was a charming sight: the curtains were not yet drawn against the grim January night, and by contrast the pretty room was a glowing, welcoming place. There was an overriding smell of woodsmoke, of flowers, and of Elizabeth's scent.

She sat on the sofa, one arm along its back, her blonde hair spread untidily behind her. She wore tight black silk jeans, and small jewelled slippers with Turkish toes to them. Her high-collared shirt was sea-green, and turned her eyes that colour too; the general effect, in that glowing room, was of a mermaid under water—water reflecting the pink of sunset. Her pose was frankly voluptuous. I instinctively looked round for Christopher, but there was only Ilona on the floor beside her. Around them was all the mess that Ilona manages somehow, one would say, to exude before bedtime. She was absorbed in a paper cut-out. I

54

could see it now as she pulled it to its full scissors-man length.

"Look Liz—ten gollies in a row. Hand-in-hand!"

"Wonderful, darling."

They smiled at each other. It was an intimate, touching scene. No stranger, standing on the dark threshold as I did, would have taken them for anything but mother and daughter. Elizabeth's free hand was caressingly laid on the bulldog puppy's head. He was cuddled snug in a relaxed heap on her lap. Relaxed. I was far from that enviable state—strung up and exhausted at the same time. Threatened with neurasthenia? Perhaps it was this which gave rise to a sudden morbid fancy. It was as if I, lucky Jenny, had been stripped to the bone by the prevailing east wind, and was slowly dying. It was accompanied by the idiotic conviction that all I had of colour and warmth and wealth and love was being sucked from me in a maelstrom and drawn towards—no, drawn away *by*—Elizabeth who sat there so patiently smiling and serenely undemanding, so obviously fitted to receive it into her empty hands.

The hysterical nightmare sensation didn't last. Ilona turned her head and saw me, and sprang to her feet, upsetting the domestic scene centred on my twin.

"Mummy—look! Ten gollies, and not one of them broke!"

The bulldog puppy woke with a snort, and struggled from Elizabeth's lap to welcome me. Elizabeth herself was leaning forward anxiously, to draw me down beside her on the sofa.

"Jenny—you look awful, darling! Those frightful winds—and you've never quite thrown off that 'flu——"

Warmer now, I allowed myself to be fussed over, to have ten paper golliwogs draped round my neck, lei-fashion, to feel the toes of my right lizardskin shoe ravaged by rough destructive paws and tongue. I was the centre of it all again, though on the outskirts of my mind lingered a sensation of unease. I felt a little lightheaded. Heavens, how my head buzzed. I stared, confused, at the Shiraz spread beneath my feet. The deep mellow rose colour was broken by an inky design. A small fly crawled across the rose, pursued by the puppy, and disappeared into the black.

'Like that fly,' I thought—for heaven's sake, *what* was I thinking? A fly? No—'I am a seagull. . . .'

"Jenny, you do look odd, love; you're not feverish, by any chance? I'll ring for tea."

I heard my own voice say, slightly pettish and unreasonable: "But I don't *want* tea. I want a drink—"

"Jen, it's only half past five. And I bet you didn't have lunch, either; you must *eat* if you're to get well again."

As usual, neither of us heard Clayton's approach.

"You rang, Madam?"

Even in my lightheadedness I recognized that he addressed Elizabeth.

"Mrs. Emerson isn't well, Clayton, she—"

"I'm sorry to hear that, Madam." An obsequious sympathetic glance. Behind it, satisfaction.

"—and she's eaten nothing all day. Bring some fresh tea."

"Certainly, Madam."

As he reached the door I called after him: "No—I don't want tea, I'll have a drink. Clayton, you can bring the drinks tray now."

My twin looked at me. "Darling, you need *food*—"

"I need a drink," I said furiously, "damn it, do I give orders in my house, or not?"

There was a sort of soft sound from Clayton. Of surprise, I think. Like a pussybud bursting. Elizabeth looked stunned. And hurt. I was instantly the prey of compunction. As Clayton left the room I held out my hand towards her.

"Liz, I'm sorry—"

She looked away, and I was appalled at myself. How could I have reminded her of homelessness, when her action had been solely one of concern for me?

"Blind not to notice, wasn't I?" It was a stifled whisper. "I've worn out my welcome. I have, haven't I, Jenny?"

"Darling, what utter nonsense. You really mustn't take notice of my silly crossness after 'flu. I'm just beastly tired."

She leaned her forehead on her hand. It was a pale tall forehead, like a pre-Raphaelite maiden's. I got the impression of silent distress. 'The sedge is withered from the lake, and no birds sing.' But wasn't that *The Belle Dame Sans Merci?*

"What is it, Liz?"

56

"Nothing. Or rather—" her finger traced along the edge of the chimneypiece, and then her hand fell stiffly by her side. It was her left hand. The ring marks noticed there by George had faded quite away. "It's just that you've been good to me, you and George— and I don't want to trade on it."

"You know very well, Liz, we *both* want you here for as long as you choose to stay." At that moment, looking at her pretty, distressed face, I truly meant it. Though I felt a twinge of compunction when I spoke for George.

"No one on earth, who's happily married, wants relations with them always. Time I moved on."

"Oh *Lizabeth*—" said Ilona in an outraged tone.

"After all, I've my own life to cope with—"

I sat up straight on the sofa; here at last was the opening.

"—and that is?" I asked, casual as I could be. "Liz, you've never really told us *what* it is."

She stared at me almost as if I were her enemy. Or was that another sick fancy of mine? Her mouth opened on a round "Oh" which sounded imploring; or startled. There was an appearance of conflict in her face; then, just as she leaned towards me, and I felt sure at last I had her confidence, the telephone by us gave out its shrill commanding ring. Inwardly I cursed it.

Ilona was across the room and had the receiver off its hook.

"Hello . . . Oh, *Christopher*. Did you get the thank you letter for the chocolates, *darling* Christopher? *Oh.* Would you like Aunt Liz, she's here? Or Mummy?" The receiver was handed over to my twin who took it, I thought, with some relief. Ilona was frankly eavesdropping. I hoped my interest was less obvious.

When Elizabeth at last put down the receiver she said: "Christopher sent you his love, Jenny. He hoped both you and Geneviève were in top form."

"He saw us both today," I said tartly, "so he must know we're not."

Behind us Clayton had come back into the room with drinks. Elizabeth was looking at me wide-eyed, she seemed oblivious of him. "Jenny, you don't *mind* that Christopher wanted—no, but you couldn't, when you and George—"

Colour flooded up my throat. "Mind? My *dear* Elizabeth...."

Something on Clayton's tray fell over with a crash. We both stared at him, startled, and I thought how unlike him it was to be so clumsy.

"I'm sorry, Madam," his face was impassive, "the glass is fortunately intact."

"Oh, good. Give me a very large, very dry Martini, please, Clayton. No—a large Scotch—" I luxuriously stretched my hands towards the fire. "I could have killed everyone at the office today, Elizabeth. Murdered them one and all, with pleasure."

"And Christopher, too?"

Clayton brought the drink, and then began to make up the fire.

I smiled, cradling my whisky in my hand. "Heavens, most people want to murder Christopher. It's *de rigueur* in my world."

"Jenny, you do sound tough. Tough and tired and most unlike you ... perhaps it's all those pills."

"Vitamins and iron and hypophosphates. They'd hardly make me tired."

"Sleeping pills do—I'm sure they're awfully bad for you."

Again I felt that irritable flow of red mount up my face. What did it matter how Clayton thought of me? No business of his if I took an entire chemist's shop. He finished with the fire at last, and went away carrying the bullpup, whose suppertime it was.

"Now that's just fine and dandy, Liz," I said bitterly, "in one breath you've made Clayton think I've my eye on Christopher *and* that I'm drug-addicted into the bargain."

"Addicted?" she said sharply. "Why Jenny, what—" but was interrupted by a great roar of monkey laughter from Ilona. I'd forgotten her presence, little wretch. She was still dancing around singing, "Mummy's got her eye on Christopher!" when George came in and found us in an atmosphere not all concord.

"Daddy!" She flew to him and clasped him round the legs. "Mummy's got her eye on Christopher——"

"Oh, she has, has she?" George good-humouredly crossed the room to kiss me.

"I hate my family tonight." I was cross as any child as I hugged my glass pettishly to me. "I don't know which has been the greater pest—Ilona or Liz."

"Darling, that's rude." George disengaged one of my hands, and kissed it. "Drinks already? Early, aren't we?"

Elizabeth stood up; her usually pale face was pink, whether from annoyance or embarrassment I couldn't tell.

"Come on, sugar, we'll go off upstairs—we're unpopular."

"No, no, *no*—Daddy's only just got home."

"Hi—come on." Elizabeth held out a hand.

"No, thank you, Lizabeth, I think I'll stay."

Something flickered over Elizabeth's face, which I couldn't interpret. Pain? Annoyance? She said lightly: "Very well, then," and walked away from us out of the door and shut it carefully behind her. We all felt a bit mean, perhaps, though glad to be alone together. Ilona went back to her paper dolls. I put an arm round George's neck, my head on his shoulder, and was deliciously warm and comfortable and relaxed. I was never cross with George, which is something pleasant to remember.

6

Look like the innocent flower,
But be the serpent under it.
                    MACBETH

After that evening life went on much the same as usual for several weeks. Between me and Elizabeth things were ostensibly smooth, but below the surface deterioration had set in; I blamed myself, which made me extra nice to my twin. During her years away with Father she had developed that tiresome type of over-sensitivity which sees innuendoes where none exist, and turns chance crossness into a significant battle. When at her best—sweet and gay and delightful, playing with Ilona as if they were two children together—she could, like Father, charm the birds off trees; but there were other times, which grew more frequent, when she exhibited her prickly-pear dual nature. And after these moods subsided she would sit for hours in abstracted silence, on her face the look of someone—Haunted? Not perfectly—and yet, it troubled me. When I spoke of it to George he laughed, and said that Jenny was indulging the imagination of Geneviève.

I also mentioned it to Christopher. It was just before dinner-time, one evening in late February, when you get a few of those strange light days, forerunners of spring. There was that same odd restlessness in the air, the feverish sense that somewhere or other are wonderful things waiting to be done, and you must up and off and do them before it's too late. I felt Christopher's restlessness, too. Elizabeth was to dine with him; and now he walked up and down the drawing room, up and down. She was late, but he was not generally an impatient man. Eventually I begged him to sit down.

"For," I said, "you're getting on my nerves. It's worse than a leopard in the Zoo. I think it's you who must be haunted, not Liz."

He laughed, "Sorry, Jenny," and came to stand behind me, where I was arranging flowers in a vase. White narcissi, and my favourite pheasant-eyes. I handled their long sappy stalks with pleasure.

"It's a good smell, isn't it?" Even these days I didn't care much for silence from Christopher.

"It is. And the one you're wearing, Jenny."

"Molyneux's 'Vivre'."

"Goes nicely with spring."

"That's what I thought." There seemed no more to be said. I continued to snap and bend the stalks, and push the flowers into place. Easier to handle than most people.

"Isn't Elizabeth tiring of you yet? Or you of her?" It sounded the most casual of questions, but when I turned my head I saw the deep creased frown on his face. "Does she never speak of leaving you?" Was he anxious to hear that she would stay?

"She does, sometimes."

"But you wouldn't dream of letting her go just yet." His voice teased. I grinned back at him. For some reason he wasn't getting in my hair tonight.

"In two or three weeks she's taking a trip to Paris, anyway."

"And is that a good thing? Has having a twin sister—grown version—worked out well?"

"In some ways," I said; cautiously, for I must admit that sometimes I realized Providence knew what it was about when it robbed me of my twin in childhood. Never question Providence, my grandmother always said.

"You don't find her—disruptive in the home, Jenny?"

"No: it's not that, it's just—this *look*." I glanced at him sideways, wondering if he thought me stupidly fanciful; but he said absently: "The word, my love, is 'dead'—not 'haunted'." Which gave me a shock. He hardly sounded like the ardent lover George believed him to be. As though following my thoughts he added: "I gather George doesn't really go much on her?"

"Good heavens, did Liz say so? George is as good as gold with her, he—"

"That's what I really meant." He smiled widely at my outraged face. "Listen, love, you know most men couldn't resist. But I ought to know by now that George has something better. . . ."

His voice actually sounded sincere. Amazement made me stay quite still, the flowers limp in my hands.

"It seems a long time since I first tangled with you, Jenny. You and spring together." And he bent his head and kissed me. It was a long and thorough kiss, and my willpower was so sapped by surprise that I made no attempt to draw away. It would have seemed childish, besides—but George wouldn't have liked Christopher kissing me, and I was too stunned to notice if I did or not.

Out of the corner of my eye I saw a movement close at hand, and hastily drew back. Within a few feet of us stood Clayton, with the drinks.

"Excuse me, Madam; where would you like these?"

Flowers were scattered where the tray usually stood, and I stared down at them guiltily while my face burned. Christopher looked silently amused. I could have hit him.

"On the table by the fire." What did Clayton's opinion matter? I asked myself defiantly.

"Jenny? Christopher?"

She came lightly into the room, and it was as if the spring flowers scattered on the table had risen and come through the door. She bloomed; yet always I was conscious of her undercurrent of fear. 'O Proserpina! For the flowers now, that, frighted, thou lett'st fall, from Dis's wagon!'

"Why—don't *stare* at me, Jenny! You look as if you'd seen a . . . What's the matter?" Her voice trailed away. She looked uncertainly from Christopher to me. I was aware then, with extreme certainty, that she was in love; and I felt indignant. For did the brute care? Did he? It hadn't stopped him making a pass at the happily married woman that was me.

"Is there something wrong? Smuts on my nose?" She was uncertain, trying to fathom our reaction.

"You look glorious, Liz," I said sincerely. "You look just Christopher's cup of tea."

She stared at me then, and her hand went to her mouth. I spoke without thought, but to her my innocent remark was bitchiness. Christopher's known love of blondes. . . .

As Clayton passed me on his way out he gave me a sideways and easily-interpreted glance. ('Caught you out nicely, *Madam*.')

"If Jenny hadn't already said it—" Christopher took Elizabeth's hands in his.

"Your cup of tea, am I?" she said lightly. "How dull. I'd sooner be your glass of champagne."

"All that, and more. What's this scent you're wearing? Jenny has a good one, too."

"Jenny thinks it's time you both went away and left her in peace to do the flowers," I said. All things considered, I was thankful to see them go, and when George came through the door at last my world was whole again.

"Darling, are you both busy today?"

It was breakfast time, and three days later. Elizabeth, her hair in short pigtails behind her ears, was eager-eyed, and put her arms lovingly round my shoulders. The frost between us had evidently thawed.

"George has got this awful cold—I think you heard him say last night that he might just go down to the office this afternoon if he's at all better."

"Did I? I'd forgotten. Anyway, I meant Jenny and Geneviève."

"Either or both of us could take a day off, if necessary."

"Goody. There's an old Garbo film at Universe One—let's go. After lunch."

"Yes, do let's—I adore Garbo. Which is it?"

"*Marie Walewska*."

"If you'll excuse me, Madam," Clayton chipped in—he was lighting the spirit lamp beneath George's eggs and bacon on the sideboard—"but they're showing the same film just round the corner. At the Heraldic."

There was a hearty sneeze behind me. "You two nits going to stuff your heads with dreams?" asked George. "No, no," he croaked at Clayton, "take those eggs away—couldn't look at them. Couldn't swallow them, either. Bring me some whisky."

George believed strongly in the whisky cure; it does at least produce a pleasant haze in which misery can be forgotten.

"Lovey, do go to bed."

"Can't. There's someone I simply must see this afternoon, if I can get there."

"You look awful." Elizabeth considered him. "I'm sure you shouldn't go. Might be dangerous for you."

"Could be more risky not to, on this occasion."

They sounded as if they might start chipping at each other, so I hurriedly intervened: "Poor client. Hope his resistance is in order. Surely your clerk could deal?"

"He could, but better not. No, in this case, certainly better not. Don't fuss, Jenny. I'll take the car, and I shan't be long."

"On neat whisky and no food that *would* be dangerous."

"I might manage to eat at lunch time."

"Unless you promise, my darling, I won't go out with Liz."

"Jenny, I promise."

"What time does the Heraldic start?" I asked Clayton.

"Two-thirty, Madam. Usually."

"Oh sweetie, *sorry* to be a bore," said Elizabeth, "but please let's make it Universe One. The thing is, I must pick up some shoes in Bond Street first. I'll stand you lunch."

"Dear of you, Liz—but I must stay and watch over George and pamper him. Or he'll drive to the city in a whisky haze."

"She doesn't trust me, bitter blow. How can marriages survive on lack of trust?"

"Sweet George, I do trust you, but——"

"But I *will* eat a nice little lunch, and then you can have your day out with Liz."

Reluctantly I agreed.

After breakfast I went upstairs to my room. It was Clayton's day off, and Mrs. Jason was going out as well because her niece was in London for the day. Ilona would be lunching at school, and there were several things for me to arrange, and telephone calls to make. Elizabeth followed me up.

"Jenny, you're not happy about today? Look, I'll nip down to Bond Street this morning—don't wait lunch for me, I'll get myself a snack out somewhere. And I'll meet you at the Heraldic—when was it Clayton said? Half past two? Right. We'll have a slap-up lunch another day, Jenny. That's a promise. I'll tell Mrs. Jason you'll be in."

I was glad to have her so affectionate again, like a genuine twin. Things had been sticky the last three days. She had been withdrawn and on guard with me, and once I'm sure I heard her crying. If only Christopher could be induced to propose. and take her off abroad, we could all be happy.

I kissed her fondly: "Bless you, Liz, that's a good plan." And she smiled and went out, looking happier than she had for days.

I was busy all morning, at work on the odds and ends which crop up in a household like ours, even with a Clayton really in charge; and when these were done I put on the tape-recorder and played back Geneviève's latest material. Now and then I glanced out of the window and saw that dark clouds were rapidly climbing up the sky. In our little garden the sharp green forsythia buds were tossed by the sudden wind. The weather was odd for the time of year; first, unusually mild, and now the temperature had dropped until it held a touch of ice in it. Freak thunderstorms could happen in such weather, and I did hope we weren't in for one now. They do something dreadful to me—my heart goes thump, I almost cease to breathe, and I act so confused and strung-up that anyone who didn't know me would probably think it was a nervous breakdown. I find these reactions shaming but uncontrollable.

About quarter past one I went downstairs. Mrs. Jason and Clayton had already gone out, and I could hear from distant sneezes that George was in the dining room.

"Poor lovey," I breathed kindly down the back of his neck.

He jumped.

"Darling, your nerves!"

"Just didn't expect you, Jenny. Thought I was all alone in the house."

"We got reorganized. Didn't Elizabeth tell you?"

"She went out without my seeing her. You aren't laid for."
He got up and fetched me a plate from the sideboard.

"Unlike Mrs. Jason or Clayton to forget. How's your cold?"

65

"Much of a muchness."

"*Darling*, then must you——"

"Yes, Jenny, I absolutely must. It's one hell of a sticky mess, something I must see to personally." He hesitated. "Perhaps we'll have to talk it over, you and I, but not now."

"*We*?" I was amazed. George was always mum as an oyster on his clients' affairs, even with me.

He didn't answer. His nose and eyes were streaming, his sneezing virulent. I couldn't protest even when he helped himself to another large tot of whisky, but I could see that he ate something with it. I piled Dublin Bay prawns, in a richly-flavoured sauce, on to our plates. Mrs. Jason was good at cold food, and I was glad to see George eat so well in spite of his misery. But the whisky still sank steadily in its bottle.

"Darling George, I don't want you back with a drunk-while-driving charge. Shall I leave a message for Elizabeth, and drive you there myself?"

"Don't fuss, sweetie. Colds and whisky clear my head."

"Common delusion, they tell me."

"Sweetie, stop *fussing*."

I said soothingly: "Oh, *all right*—" And as I went round behind his chair on my way out (I would be late for Elizabeth), I bent and laid my face against the back of his neck, and kissed it.

"George, I love you very very much, so please take care of yourself. Promise?"

"I promise; and I love you, too." He twisted round in his chair and kissed me; he didn't look very appetizing with that cold, but I was never so blindingly aware of how much we meant to each other.

"Good-bye, my sentimental love. Enjoy yourself."

As I closed the front door a gust of wind blew my hair across my face: impatiently I pushed the strands back behind my ears, and turned up the collar of my Burberry. I glanced up at the sky and felt an ominous shrinking in my stomach. Right up above towered a tremendous thunderloft. Coal-black, with glittering edges, it raced across the ice-blue sky, like a wave about to break. There was a low, distinct rumble, and a pttt, pttt, pttt of rain-drops increased its rhythm all around me.

66

I hesitated. Should I go back? But what a coward Elizabeth would think me . . . I fumbled in my pocket for a headscarf, pulled it out, and tied it firmly over my hair. The cinema was only three streets away. I stuck my hands resolutely in my pockets and set out. Before I had gone two hundred yards the freak storm was on me in all its fury.

Horizontal icy rain tore at my unprotected face. The wind howled with the malevolence of an archaic god, and suddenly there was a flash of lightning, followed an instant later by thunder. Breathless from battling the wind, and from neurotic panic, I struggled on, slipping and stumbling on the streaming pavements in my high-heeled shoes. Cars slowed down, pedestrians had disappeared like rabbits into their burrows. I seemed to walk alone in a spiteful, rain-lashed whirlwind.

I paused, panting, and even against my closed eyelids the next flash was searingly white. The storm was right overhead. The light was that of murky twilight. Fighting down my irrational panic I struggled on. (*Was* it so irrational? After all, people *do* get struck by lightning.)

I reached the second street—no, the third, surely? Then the cinema was on the corner, just opposite. Incredibly, it wasn't; blinded by rain and fear I had come the wrong way. If I doubled back to the last street, and turned right again, I should make the side exit. . . .

Then it happened.

There was a curious sizzling splitting sound, a blue-white flame shot out of the sky, and I'll swear that I actually saw it zigzag as it hit the tree not twenty-five yards away.

Blindly, hysterically, I began to run.

That was a fool thing to do. Stiletto-heeled shoes aren't safe on a slippery pavement. Only a few yards and then the heel of my left shoe caught in a grating, and I went sprawling on to my face. When I dragged myself up my shoe lay in the gutter, but the heel had been wrenched from the sole and stood upright, securely wedged by itself in the grating. My left stocking was laddered, my knee was grazed and covered with blood. I was winded, shaken; and stood there shivering, my broken shoe in my hand, as I tried desperately to drag the trapped heel free.

"*Jenny*! Oh, poor you. . . ."

The voice appeared to float just above my head. I glanced up. A window had opened almost level with my face, and there peered out—oh, thankoffering!—the anxious pretty face of Marjorie Hellevan. Lost to all sense of direction, I had come finally to grief before the house of my oldest friends.

"I've fallen down," I revealed superfluously.

"You tell me!" Marjorie gave her seraphic grin. "Wait—I'll be with you."

The window snapped shut; after the briefest of intervals Marjorie appeared, wrapped in a hooded waterproof, on the steps.

"Leave it, you idiot," I heard her say. It was sound advice, the heel had no intention of coming. I left it there looking like a Salvador Dali detail, and limped into Marjorie's hall.

"You and your love of thunder!" She slammed the door. "What *were* you doing out in it, anyway?"

I explained.

"What a bore—I'm afraid you'll miss the flick. Bill can ring the cinema and leave a message for Elizabeth. I should think we'd better attend to that knee." Marjorie shouted instructions to her husband, and then led the way to her bathroom. Downstairs I could hear Bill—*Professor* Hellevan he was, these days—dial a number on the telephone. Later we found him in the drawing room, absorbed in an archaeological paper.

"Hello there, Jenny." He gave me a lazy smile.

"Hi, Bill."

"It must be Marjorie who's your lost twin—not Elizabeth. You two girls are so ridiculously alike."

"The blonde and the chestnut of it." Many people have remarked on the likeness between us. They generally add, in a fatuous way, that it must be because we both have a Hungarian ancestress: as if all Hungarians are as like as two peas in a pod. But it's a fact that if Marjorie were three inches taller and two thinner and had my colour hair you could hardly tell us apart.

"Did you fix Elizabeth, darling?"

"I did not, our line is dead."

"Oh damn." I was dismayed.

68

"Never mind. Stay and have a cosy afternoon with us, and you can whip down to the cinema later and meet her coming out."

"There's George . . ." I said uncertainly.

"Don't be a fusspot, Jenny," Bill scoffed at me.

"But he has this awful cold. He oughn't to go out."

"After all, your garage is in your house. He only has to get out of the car the other end. He won't thank you for fussing."

"That's true." Men never did. Though I wished that I could rid myself of this faint unease which haunted me. The Hellevans were both so kind. And George was determined, and nothing I could say would stop his going out. . . .

Against a troubled inner resistance I said reluctantly: "Right. I'd love to stay."

7

So quick bright things come to confusion.
A MIDSUMMER NIGHT'S DREAM

We had a pleasant afternoon. Bill put records on the player, and Marjorie and I toasted our toes at the fire and gossiped against a background of Segovia's Bach. We swapped stories about Ben, the Hellevans' eight-year-old son, and Ilona; I heard all about the Hellevans' holiday they were soon to take in France, and how dreadful Marjorie's new passport photograph was, and how cross Bill got with her when she would leave her travellers' cheques around, or worse still sign them in advance. Then we had tea, and later—as the storm had now quieted to mere mutter and drizzle—I put on my Burberry again, borrowed a pair of Marjorie's boots, and set off to the cinema to meet Elizabeth on her way out.

"At least you can't get *those* heels caught in a grating, you clot," Marjorie yelled after me.

By the time I reached the cinema my leg had stiffened, and I limped badly. Slowed up though I was, I still got there before the first house had disgorged its patrons. I was told that no one had left during the big film, so I waited in the foyer. There was little to look at, only some life-sized portraits of Marlon and Elvis and Adam, and a horse called Red. At last the inner swing doors swung, and a small knot of people emerged. This was followed by ribbon development. The Garbo revival must have caught on, or the thunderstorm had driven more people than usual inside. I stood against the wall, so it was easy enough to keep a watch for Elizabeth. The flood finally dwindled to a stream, then to the odd straggler or two, and there was still no sign of her. Now no one had come out for at least three minutes, and people were steadily going in—I almost joined them, but I was damned if I was going in just to sit round a cartoon with Elizabeth. I thought she might have worried about me in that horrible storm, and hurried out. Perhaps, after all, that was what had happened. Again I approached the box office.

"Would you kindly stand to one side, Madam, this is a queue."

70

"I don't want seats, I only want to make sure—"

"*If* you please, Madam—three-and-six, three-and-nine, four shillings, ten; thank you, Sir. How many, Madam? Two?"

"I simply want to ask—"

"Some people *are*—" said the blonde girl who had a blown-up hairdo and stood idle behind the brunette in the box office, "they really *are*."

It was at least ten minutes before I got their attention.

"I told you once, dear," said the brunette plaintively.

"Blonde," I persisted. "Very striking. In brown."

"Look, you just don't believe me, so why ask? I bin here all the time, haven't I, Glad?"

"That's right," agreed the blown-up blonde, "that's what she's paid for, and that's what she done, so no use casting perversions." She filed her nail to a dangerous point.

"I wasn't casting anything on anyone." I turned away. Better go home, where I should probably find Elizabeth waiting for me, snug behind a teapot. I was fed up with my afternoon. I only wanted my dear George, and another cup of tea. Or a drink. Strong.

In spite of that stiffened knee the way home seemed short after my roundabout route taken earlier. I turned the corner of our road; and stopped, and stared.

Outside our house stood two police cars, surrounded by a small subdued knot of spectators.

The police; that day when I was thirteen . . . What could possibly have happened to Elizabeth *now*?

That was the only thought in my mind as stumblingly, hampered by my painful knee, I began to run.

"Keep your head *down*, Mrs. Emerson."

I heard the authoritative words quite clearly, but their sense failed to register.

Someone put their hand on the back of my neck and forced my head down on to my knees. At last the chaotic darkness began to dissolve. I feared its going. Even in my shocked state I was dimly aware that its presence had been a kindness, a shield from something too terrible to contemplate.

Yet I must contemplate it, for the dark had cleared. I made a dizzying effort and, against the pressure of that hand, pushed myself upright. Someone put a glass to my lips and I gulped down the brandy.

A ring of faces surrounded me. Like a dream they advanced and receded before me with the strange soft floating motion of jellyfish on a lazy sea.

I said: "He's still alive?"

"Jenny." Elizabeth knelt beside me, and put her hand on mine. It was like being touched by an icicle. "There is a—a *hope*." I knew she lied.

"I must go to him. Now. At once."

The circle of faces was steadier. In my emotional state they reminded me of animals waiting for a kill. But this was nonsense. These faces were friendly to me. Or were they? Everything was blurred; extraordinary. How can you count on something simple when your whole life is reversed in minutes?

"Where. . . ."

"In hospital. St. Francis Xavier's. Tregonna Road." It was a voice I didn't know. The same voice which had said: "Keep your head down." An arm helped me to my feet. Voice and arm, I discovered later, belonged to Inspector Morell.

"Take me there," I said.

One thought at a time. One action at a time. Steady does it. Don't think too much, or the wolves of fear and horror will thrive in the abyss of hysteria and madness. My physical vision, since the brandy, seemed abnormally clear. In a detached way I noticed Elizabeth. Every pore on her face appeared to be sweating. It lent her skin the dank, moist, almost green colour of a dead lily. Her brown high-collared dress was dark round the neck with sweat. Her fair hair clung limp and close to her head. Her eyes, which stared so intently into mine, had a curious unfocused expression—was it shock? 'How horrible she looks,' I thought; and then, remembering Christopher's words: 'she looks dead'. But it wasn't, after all, Elizabeth who was dead—or dying; it was George.

A police car took me to the hospital. Elizabeth fetched a warm coat from my room. As she put it round my shoulders she made

72

an almost unbelievable remark. She whispered it, I suppose, but it seemed at the time to echo through the hall.

She said: "Did you love Christopher, then?"

I made no reply, just stared at her, and then walked past her, with Morell behind me. My thoughts were so with George that—God forgive me—I forgot even Ilona. They told me later that a policewoman went to the headmistress, who kept Ilona back on some pretext until Mrs. Jason could fetch her. Blessed Mrs. Jason! Without her calm and collectedness where would I have been?

Of course Elizabeth wanted to come with me, but I wouldn't allow it. She thought I might need someone, I can't imagine why. My world shared with George was in process of dissolution. I was locked irretrievably into the aloneness of despair. Even the presence of Ilona would have been a reminder of the bond now dissolving in the final rupture of death.

Even writing of that time has caused me such misery that I've described it badly, with confusion. Yet that was how it hit me then: painfully vivid, but confused. Perhaps I still cannot bear to face what happened to George. Still less now I know what really happened. At the time—that day and the next—all I realized, or all I took in, anyway, was this:

After I had left for the cinema George evidently continued to sit on in the dining room till the whisky was all finished. Then he went down to the kitchen, put the coffee-pot, prepared by Mrs. Jason, on the hot plate, and made himself a cup of strong black coffee. Later he went back upstairs to his dressing room, took down his overcoat and hat, picked up the car keys which were on my dressing table, and went down again, this time to the back of the house where our garage was. A door opened into it from the kitchen passage. He closed it behind him after turning on the light. Then, apparently fuddled by his cold and the whisky, he got straight into the car, switched on the engine, and passed clean out behind the wheel. Had the outer doors been slightly open, even ajar, he might have stood a chance, but with them shut the poisonous fumes. . . .

It was Elizabeth who found him. . . .

The police driver drove as if he watched Z cars every night of his life. I stared out of the window. It was getting dark. At the time I had an odd fancy that it would never be light again. Inspector Morell didn't speak until we were quite near the hospital. "Miss Lemprière was most worried that you didn't turn up at the cinema. We had just put out a call for you, Mrs. Emerson, when you came back."

"I must have missed her coming out."

"Oh?" He gave me rather an odd look, I thought, but I was in no state for explanations. That happy afternoon with Bill and Marjorie seemed very long ago.

The hospital was a huge grey stone building, as ugly and forbidding as only a Victorian hospital can be. 'Abandon Hope' should have been carved across its front. But I had abandoned it already, when Elizabeth knelt beside me on the floor and said: "There is a *hope*." Reverend Mother would have told me to pray, but I had got out of the habit years before. Anyway, it takes just as much practice as any other skill. There was no one to whom I could turn, except the medical staff somewhere within that grim grey building ahead of me.

A young nurse took us up to the fourth floor, and along a passage to a waiting-room. Morell had accompanied us, and I took it for silent sympathy on his part—it didn't strike me as odd that the police were sticking to me closer than a brother. Presently an Indian doctor came in and apologized for having kept me waiting. He explained that various things were being done for George, but I could see him soon. His manner was hurried, courteous and somehow blank. When I put the inevitable question he smoothly evaded a reply, but I saw the look he exchanged with Morell, which he thought I didn't see.

Soon afterwards the ward sister came and took me to the cubicle where George lay. Unlike the doctor she made no attempt to hide things from me, and there was pity both in her manner and her face.

A curtain divided the cubicle from the rest of the ward. There was a tubular chair near the bed, and I sat on this and stared at George's face and took his hand in mine. He was deeply unconscious, his breath came in stertorous gasps. Once,

74

when I pressed his hand, there was a very faint flicker of response, as if the strong tie between us somehow tugged him momentarily back from the far frontier where he wandered. That was the only sign, during the long hours while I waited by his bed. Even after all this time I could not bear to describe what he looked like. He died in that cold hour just before dawn.

Another man died in the ward that night. A young mechanic whose scooter had been in collision with a bus. I passed his widow on the way out, a pretty, fair-haired girl who looked no more than seventeen. We exchanged glances which contained not so much sympathy—we were both too drained for any such warm human emotion—but the sort of recognition that one ghost might give another. That is my last vivid memory of that night. The next hour remains the only one of which I've no recollection. Someone—presumably Morell—took me home. Our doctor was called, I was sedated and put to bed. The next thing I remember is waking some time on the following afternoon; looking, bewildered, at the clock beside my bed; and then the slow, inexorable, and anguished recollection of loss.

8

The worst is not,
So long as we can say, "This is the worst."
                                        KING LEAR

"There's a lot to be done."

I remember saying this to myself as if it could prove an antidote to the lethargy of drained despair. Yet when I wanted to get up out of bed and start, Elizabeth prevented me. I couldn't make her understand that I would prefer to be up, and deal with things myself, than lie there alone with the ever-recurring horror of my thoughts which began, 'If only I'd stayed at home and driven George myself—'

"There's Ilona. I shall have to break it to Ilona."

"Not today, Jenny. You just aren't up to it."

Idiotic phrase! As if one could ever be up to it. How do you tell a child that her adored father is dead, in a way which leaves no scar? Hopeless, but it had to be attempted. At present Ilona knew only that George was very ill. She had wanted to see George, and cried, and been told it was impossible; that even I wasn't seeing him that day. But it must be broken to her in the morning. One can try too hard to gloss things over with children: better a harsh reality than a belief that you can trust in no one.

"There's George's stepbrother. I ought to ring him up."

"Darling, he's been rung already."

I was astounded. "You didn't even know he existed!"

"Clayton knew."

Of course Clayton knew. Was there anything he didn't know? It was one of his main assets to George. . . .

A wave of grief swamped me again. I could not lie here and do nothing. The second she left me alone I got up and dressed. The face in the glass was a face I didn't know. Neither that of the diffident girl who had found Christopher too much to handle, nor George's lucky Jenny. That shocked, hollow-eyed, expressionless face, did it belong to me?

The bedroom was so tidy, without the masculine disorder

George strewed over it. It was unbearable. I went downstairs. Clayton met me in the passage and moved aside for me to pass. His manner was unctuous. Grief and sympathy sat as falsely on his shapeless features as on an undertaker's. To his condolences—I swear he'd rehearsed them before a glass—I could respond only with a weak smile, a shake of the head. He opened the drawing-room door for me as though ushering me into my tomb.

Morell stood by the hearth. He turned as I came in, and gave me a long cool look. The constraint of his manner seemed excessive.

"They never told me you were here."

I moved forward into the room. My limbs felt weak. The sedative had been strong, and I had to sit down hurriedly on the sofa. Where was Elizabeth? The police were one thing she might have dealt with for me. Then I remembered she had not known that I was getting up.

"How do you feel, Mrs. Emerson?"

What a fantastic thing human communication is! Did he expect me to launch into a long description?'

" 'I can't believe it's happened,' " I murmured, "isn't that what people say? I wish I felt like that."

"You are appalled?"

I stared at him. What *did* he expect? Where *was* Elizabeth? I got up to ring the bell. Clayton could bring tea, and fetch my sister.

"Just one moment, Mrs. Emerson. I should like a word with you. Undisturbed."

"Of course." I was bewildered, even a little angry. "If I can help you in any way—"

"I hope," he said in a soft voice which held a hint of—was it irony? "that you will help me, Mrs. Emerson."

I sat down again, and he sat opposite. "Tell me what I can do?"

"You seem very calm."

"I've been drugged," I said stiffly. "It's customary after shock, which also has a deadening effect. In case you didn't know."

"Of course." He put his fingers together like a lawyer, and

77

leaned forward. I realized suddenly that I was in the witness box. "Mrs. Emerson, I asked you just now if you were appalled by your husband's death?"

"Naturally."

"Naturally. You're a natural woman—you laugh when you're happy, cry when you're sad, that sort of thing?"

"Yes, I suppose so." I nearly added that I bit people when annoyed, but any spirited reaction petered out under the weight of the awful misery of George's death.

"So your self-control is all the more admirable now."

I made no reply. After a pause he added: "I have to advise you there will be an inquest on your husband's death."

"I suppose so."

"And a post-mortem is being carried out today. Afterwards his body may be moved wherever you wish."

This time I stared at him.

"But there was nothing physically wrong with George!"

"I see no reason to assume there was."

"He had a check-up three months ago—I made him—and he was perfectly fit then. I thought—you said—it was fumes from the exhaust that killed George—my husband."

"It was."

"Then——"

"There may, too, have been some subsidiary cause."

Again I stared. "But wouldn't Dr. Knowles—"

"Dr. Knowles was your husband's doctor, and your own?"

"Yes."

"Did he ever prescribe sleeping tablets for your husband?"

"For George?" I stumbled over his name. Should I ever speak it again without this stab of misery? "Good heavens, no. He always slept like a baby."

Morell gave a lopsided smile. "I don't know what you mean by that, Mrs. Emerson, I am a family man myself, and——"

"I mean he slept well."

"He never took tranquillizers?"

"Never."

"Now, Mrs. Emerson. You yourself had been sleeping badly, and—your doctor had had occasion to prescribe tablets for you?"

I couldn't imagine where this was leading. "Yes. Sodium amytal. Capsules."

"Ah. You had been on edge? Worried about something? But you're a healthy young woman, Mrs. Emerson, with a happy marriage, a child, plenty of money. Why did you need sleeping pills?"

He was needling me more with every word, but I felt too ill and miserable to fight back. "I'd had 'flu. I got run-down. I couldn't sleep. I was working quite hard, too."

He shot me a quick sideways glance. "No other reason?"

"What other reason could there be?"

"There are always reasons. Reasons which may not be apparent even to oneself. For instance—your sister was living in the house. There could have been friction."

"But there wasn't. Inspector Morell?"

"Yes?"

"I don't understand why you're asking me all these questions?"

He stared down at his hands, and frowned. "Be patient a moment longer. Tell me, where are your sleeping pills now?"

"In my dressing-table drawer."

"They are not, you know. We have them."

"But that's ridiculous——" I stopped. This whole conversation was like a sinister nightmare. "*You* . . . but why?"

"Because they were found not in *your* drawer, but in the drawer of the kitchen dresser. And because when your husband drank his coffee that afternoon, he swallowed with it a certain amount of sodium amytal. The drug, Mrs. Emerson, that was prescribed for *you*."

I don't quite know at what point the drift of his remarks began to penetrate my brain, which was abnormally slowed down by shock, and heavy sedation. But when they did, the drawing room seemed to darken and grow cold, and then to start a long slow slide away from me. I sat there, and willed myself not to faint. The very fact that Morell didn't offer to help me but merely watched me with the alert look of a terrier which sees a juicy bone, showed me, even in my dazed condition, that whatever had happened to George I was chief suspect on the list, either as instrument or cause. I hung on to the edge of the sofa, and the room came and went and only Morell's face seemed to be a constant, watching me.

Then I heard the drawing room door open, and quick foot-steps cross the room, and Elizabeth's voice saying: "But Jenny—you got up! What—what's the matter, darling? *Jenny*!"

The room only swayed now, and it was lighter. I said weakly: "It's . . . he said—" It was too preposterous.

Her arm went round me as she faced the Inspector angrily.

"How *could* you? She isn't fit for it—*Look* at her."

Morell was unperturbed. "Miss Lemprière, no one is ever fit for tragedy, that's the nature of it."

"It's bullying she's not fit for," she stormed, and I felt a flicker of gratitude for her backing of me, "surely the police could show a little human decency——"

"Neither suicide nor murder come beneath that heading."

"*Suicide or murder* . . ."

Just then Clayton opened the door. "Would you like tea brought in, Madam? For the Inspector too?"

"Thank you, but I'm on duty."

"We're not offering you *drink*, Inspector," said Elizabeth impatiently, "only a cup of tea. Mrs. Emerson and I could do with one. Bring the brandy too," she told Clayton.

"I don't need brandy, Liz."

"Darling, indeed you *do*."

"We have our duty, Miss Lemprière," Morell said stiffly; he seemed nettled. "However, I'll postpone the questions till both you ladies have had your cup of tea."

When Clayton returned with the tray there was a fussy, un-comfortable interlude. I could feel my nervous system getting ready to shake all over, but I wouldn't suggest that Elizabeth should pour out, and I managed quite creditably, aware that a certain amount of shakiness would be normal in the circum-stances. A good dollop of Hennessy's helped, though alcohol only put an unendurable edge on my misery at that time.

"Do you want to see us one by one?" I asked afterwards.

"You should insist on waiting for your lawyer, Jenny," put

in Elizabeth solicitously. I wished she wouldn't look so scared on my behalf. I felt it would only poke up Morell.

"I haven't anything to hide."

"Miss Lemprière may stay if she likes. Now, Mrs. Emerson, I'm afraid I have to ask it: do you know of any reason why your husband should commit suicide?"

"But it's mad!" I cried. "Of course he wouldn't have. . . . He was going to see an important client . . . Why, over lunch——"

I stopped. My last words seemed to have produced a curious change in my hearers. Elizabeth's left arm, which touched mine where she sat beside me on the sofa, went rigid. As for Morell, I could almost feel the terrier's ears begin to prick. The bone at last.

"Go on, Mrs. Emerson. Over lunch——"

I touched my face with my fingertips. They sweated. "He was so serious about this—this case, whatever it was," I faltered. "He said it was vital he should go himself."

"But you weren't expected to lunch in that day?"

"But of course I was! I stayed because my husband was unwell, and——" My words died away. I moistened my lips.

"Your manservant and cook agree that you arranged to be out."

"I altered it."

"You told them so?" Total disbelief.

"No."

"So no one knew of your—change of plan."

"Oh, yes." My tension relaxed. "I and my sister were going to lunch out together and go to Universe One. Because my husband wasn't well we altered it, so that I could lunch at home and then meet her at our local cinema where they were showing the same film." I half-turned towards Elizabeth in relief, "Tell him——"

I stopped. She had shrunk away from me against the sofa arm. Her face was as livid as it had been the day before, and when she spoke it was with obvious effort.

She said: "Jenny, I'm sorry. I had to tell him. I had to. I couldn't help it. I didn't know, you see. Oh, Jenny!" And she wept huge, unreal-looking tears, though her lids never once blinked. It was an extraordinary effect—as if a doll had cried.

I said: "Tell him *what*?"

"What was true, of course." She spoke on a whisper, as if mortally afraid to touch me. "That we were going to Universe One, but you didn't turn up. When you didn't come to lunch I thought you'd come to the cinema, and when you didn't come there, I thought the storm had held you up. It was such a bad storm, and there wasn't anywhere I could telephone, and. . . and so after the film I went home. And you'd had lunch—and—and George was *dead*. . . ." Her voice petered out. She licked her lips, and then whispered again: "I'm sorry. He asked me. I didn't know." She was shaking. Morell gave a satisfied nod.

Fear was in the room with me, an almost tangible presence. I made one last effort: "Elizabeth, you *can't* have forgotten that we changed the plan."

"Did you," put in Morell, "did you, in fact, Miss Lemprière, forget?"

"No," she said. "No." And with an agonized look at me, "There *was* no change of plan."

9

Methinks I see these things with parted eye,
When everything seems double.
A MIDSUMMER NIGHT'S DREAM

That was it. I couldn't shake her. Morell could almost be
heard baying in triumph, but I barely noticed. I was so held by
the accomplished performance beside me. You would have sworn
she was terrified by me, when in fact it was I—like someone who
has put out a hand for a flower and clutched a snake—who was
terrified by her. Whatever her reason for this deceit, her lying
was superb. Surely she spoke the truth. And, *ipso facto*, it was I
became the liar. I must have been almost punch-drunk by that
time. shock after shock. Morell, who had seen me rocked, came
in again on round two with a conversational uppercut.

"So in fact you told no one, Mrs. Emerson, that you had
changed your plans."

"I told my sister."

"Who denies it."

"She is either lying, or suffering from amnesia."

A fighting spirit had risen in me, which I didn't know I
possessed. For one short moment I thought 'Christopher would
approve,' and was amazed I should think of him at all.

"Let us put Miss Lemprière's veracity temporarily on one
side. You lunched at home. Your husband was seedy. You made
coffee for both of you, and then——"

"No," I interrupted, "I made no coffee. I was in a hurry
to get to the cinema. I left my husband still at the table."

"But you didn't turn up at *that* cinema, either. Or not until
afterwards."

"I had a fall." Instinctively my hand went to my grazed knee.
"It was raining, and I slipped." I explained about the Hellevans;
gave him the time of my arrival there. Morell gazed at me with
what appeared to be reproach. "But that was *quite* the wrong
direction," he said on a peevish note. "What were you thinking
of?"

"I wasn't thinking. I'm terrified by thunderstorms."

"I shall have to check on all this."

"Of course." I leaned back, exhausted. I could guess his thoughts. If I was with the Hellevans, then I could *not* have been in our garage when George's drugged coffee had sent him into that last long cold sleep. The suggestion of hounds moving in for the kill had perceptibly lessened. The quarry might still be in sight—had I an accomplice?—but now I had the heels of them, though hazed with fatigue. I was a rag doll over which someone had driven a steam roller. George had killed himself, or been killed. The words meant nothing. Elizabeth had lied. That meant nothing, either. I was no longer capable of feeling anything at all.

"I think I'd like to go back to bed."

He made no demur. I even think he was glad to see me go, weaving slightly as I went. Elizabeth got up and came uncertainly after me to the door. I shut it hard, between us, before she could follow me out.

Whatever was clarified for me later, I must here make it plain that the events which followed George's death seemed to me at the time an unrelated jumble of madhouse facts. I want also to underline that I was knocked almost silly by George's death. As it was then immediately hinted I had either murdered him or driven him to suicide, it may not seem odd that in the weeks following his death neither my mind nor actions were logical or even under my control. Otherwise much which happened might have been avoided . . . I might not, for a start, have grown so suspicious of the police. . . .

There was a great deal which may appear clumsy in the stage-managing of George's death; though this clumsiness was really a devious piece of skill. I imagined myself being framed for murder; yet nothing would have suited my—'enemies', do I call them? less than my serving a long spell in gaol. It was towards something different I was being shepherded with such delicate care.

Without my shocked state I might have realized that things unmentioned to me did not necessarily pass unseen. I might have dared to seek help where help would normally be found.

But I feared people might think me mad or cunning, and I began to act like a horse which eats locoweed and takes enormous bounds to clear a single blade of grass. My fear and reactions proved the greatest help to my opponents. They only had to lie low and wait for me to take a terrified bound in their direction. I was pretty well in the state of a person softened up by brainwashing, and this they counted on. I hope, before the tale of my stupidity unfolds, I have made it plain that my reasoning was no longer to be counted on, since George's death.

After that conversation with Morell I went back to my bedroom, and desperately tried to think. Too much that was impossible had happened. It was impossible George had died; impossible what Inspector Morell thought; impossible that anyone had first poisoned George with my tablets, which were—impossibly—in the kitchen drawer, and then caused his death by carbon monoxide poisoning. Impossible, too, that Elizabeth had lied. 'George died, Elizabeth lied' went on and on the silly words with nursery-rhyme insistence in my head. It was almost relief to hear Ilona's small pipe of a voice raised outside my door in argument with Mrs. Jason. It shows how far gone I was to call that a 'relief', for it meant a dreaded moment was here.

She sat on my lap, and I held her very close and told her as gently as I could that George had died. The effect was heartbreaking. It's a horrible thing to see a child's complete trust in life go for good; and I think it was then, while I held her small shivering body close to me, that I decided if George had really been murdered to deal with the killer by myself. It may not have been a good idea, but I still think it was excusable at the time.

We sat there a very long while; Ilona sobbing and myself too exhausted and bewildered to cry, cradling her in my arms. The light grew dim in the room. I didn't turn on a lamp. Ilona's sobbing gradually lessened, and she sank into exhausted sleep. I just sat there. No one came near us, though often the telephone pealed downstairs. (It had been disconnected by my bed.) Ilona was heavy on my lap. I shifted my position, and laid my head against hers. How appalled George would have been to see her cry so! Sitting there in the dark I began to think again, disjointedly; sometimes there was just a nagging sense of loss, and then my mind would start to throw up pictures, like stills from a film, of the day George died. With horror I realized how important it was for me to remember every least thing about that day.

One thing anyway stood out stark and clear: I could never forget that Elizabeth had suggested the altered plan which had taken me to the Heraldic. Elizabeth had suggested it. Elizabeth denied the alteration. 'George died, Elizabeth lied. . . .' So, on the face of it, if George's death had been somehow engineered, Elizabeth was to blame. Or had she forgotten—and then been afraid of the implications of her forgetting? Elizabeth a murderess—that didn't make sense: what could *she* stand to gain from George's death? But Elizabeth forgetting her own arrangements within an hour or so—that didn't make sense either. In fact I was back to where Elizabeth came in: she was a mystery; in order to understand her, more knowledge was needed. George had been pitifully, tragically right, and I should have made it my business to find out. My neglectfulness now seemed a crime, I couldn't bear to think of it.

Someone knocked softly on the door. I started, and put out a hand to the standard lamp beside me. Ilona stirred, and muttered as the light flicked on. I looked at the time. Half past six. The knocking came again—like the knocking in Macbeth. I was reluctant to answer. Clayton, Elizabeth, the Inspector——?

Tap, tap, tap.

"Come in." I didn't turn my head. Ilona did not wake as whoever it was stepped into the room.

"She's asleep," I said, "don't talk loudly—she's been terribly upset."

"Poor child," said Christopher's voice. "Poor Jenny, too."

I steadied myself with an effort. "I can't talk about it," I mumbled into Ilona's hair, "I can't." Once I began to cry I should never stop. Never. 'Thou'lt come no more, Never, never, never . . .' How hideously those words, remembered from schooldays, chimed with the truth of later life.

"You don't have to." His voice was very kind. He sat down on the bed behind me, and put out a hand so that it covered mine.

86

How often George and I had sat like that, at the end of a long day, talking things over, until he had put his arms round me, and there was no more talk.

It was impossible not to cry. With my head still against Ilona's I wept silently until her hair was wet and sticky with my tears. All the time Christopher sat beside me, quite silent, patting my hand. I cried till my temples throbbed, and I felt drier than a squeezed lemon. When I had finished we just sat there, and the only sound in the room was Ilona's heavy breathing.

After a while: "This idea that George could have committed suicide is madness," Christopher said. "To anyone who knew him. And the other thing seems equally impossible."

So the Inspector had talked to him. "Is he still here?"

"Who?"

"Morell."

"No. I've just seen him out. Jenny, there would be no possible motive for anyone to kill George?"

"None."

"So it must have been an accident?"

"But he took some of my sleeping pills."

"That's impossible, too. Except—how much whisky had he drunk?"

"A lot," I admitted, and I began to weep again. "If only I'd stayed, that afternoon. If only I'd driven him myself."

"Never think like that; cut it right out, before it becomes a habit. It's what people always say and think when there's been a tragedy—and I'm not sure you can circumvent fate, anyway." The words were kind, but he spoke almost mechanically, as if he didn't mean them.

"He wasn't in a state to drive. Anyone could have foreseen that. If—if what *did* happen," I stumbled on, "*hadn't* happened, he might still have had an accident."

"George was the best driver, even with a half bottle of whisky inside, of anyone I know."

It was no use saying it again, no use even thinking it, but I should have stayed. I changed the subject.

"Did Morell tell you that Elizabeth lied?"

Christopher stood up, and now frowned down at me.

"He said there was a difference in your statements—yes."

We had been close, a moment before. Now that was over. I couldn't guess what he thought. Nor ask which of us he believed.

"Look, Jenny my dear, I have to go. Got a dinner. Oh, and before I forget, Miss Starr and the office staff send all their sympathy. And John's written."

"Yes," I said dully.

"Shall you stay here for the present? I mean, after. . . ."

"Yes, of course. Where else would I go?"

"I don't know. I just thought that in a week's time I'm going to the country, to write in peace."

Christopher's aunt had died some years before and left him a house in Cumberland. Everyone expected him to sell it, but to their surprise he made full use of it, turning into a sort of bucolic squire on his holidays.

"You and Elizabeth and Ilona are welcome to join me. Give yourself a break before you face things again."

"Thanks." What did it matter where we were? "But the police may not let me go."

"There's no possible motive, as we've agreed, for George's death." Was there a query in his voice, or had I imagined it?

"There must be, since he died."

"I don't think they've ruled out the possibility of accident."

At his words the horrible picture I was holding in my mind—Elizabeth's face as she told her lies—began to break up as though someone had taken a hammer and cracked the surface. I must have imagined things. She was muddled, she had had a shock too; while I was temporarily unbalanced by grief. I stood up, still holding Ilona in my arms, and laid her gently on my bed.

"I'm going to put her to bed in here tonight."

"Good-bye, sad Jenny. Try to sleep. I'm so dreadfully sorry, my dear."

I had never known Christopher sweeter or kinder, and I felt so grateful to him.

He opened the door. There outside stood Clayton, holding a glass upon a tray. At sight of Ilona he hushed his voice.

"Miss Lemprière thought you might like a drink, Madam."

I took the glass, and watched Christopher walk away. Then I

grew aware that Clayton was watching me, a closed-in look of secret satisfaction on his face. I went back into my room and shut the door quietly. There was no motive for George's death. Christopher thought so; didn't he? To that I clung. But what, with a little help from other people, would the Inspector think?

The inquest was over; the jury returned an open verdict. What else could they do? There was not enough evidence to hang a dog, let alone a loving wife. The post-mortem showed that George had swallowed a small quantity of sodium amytal. It had been taken in coffee, and was probably enough, its effect increased by whisky, to confuse him. I learnt later that the bottle found in the kitchen drawer wasn't a fruitful clue. My prints were on it, as might have been expected, and others which were blurred. They could have been the chemist's. I don't know why Morell told me this. I was nonplussed by him. He had such a poker face. Was I chief suspect still, did someone else fill the bill, or did he think George took the amytal himself as a tranquillizer or for a more sinister reason? If the latter, surely he would have taken more.

The questions Morell asked me embraced the whole household, as well as Christopher, Lucy Starr, the office staff and George's secretary. Then he consulted a notebook. "I think that's everything, Mrs. Emerson, just now. You'll be available should we require your help again?" I understood it as a statement rather than a question, and thought it wise to broach the subject of Christopher's invitation. "We may not even want to accept, my sister and I, but if we do——"

"I see nothing against it. Unless something crops up in the meantime. Anyway, you would naturally leave us your address." He gave me a thin smile, and as he replaced the notebook in his pocket suddenly asked: "You knew Mr. Leyton in your childhood, I understand?"

"Yes."

"Ah." A brief sardonic glance. "He was the classical case of the boy next door?" If he knew, why ask?

"We *were* engaged once," I said as casually as I could, "but it didn't work out, for either of us."

"These things do happen. And then you met Mr. Emerson."

"Yes, at the dance where I'd just broken my engagement."

"Ah. It was you who broke it off?"

"Yes."

"Officially the woman always does, doesn't she?"

Before I could think of a satisfactory reply to this back-hander, he added: "And Mr. Leyton has never married. He's been squiring your sister round quite a lot lately?"

"He knew her too, when we were children."

"Early loyalties." Again that sour ironic smile, and then he went, leaving me discomforted. Christopher; Elizabeth; myself. Perhaps the police were unbiassed in their suspicions. It made one feel like Tom O' Bedlam—'By a knight of ghosts and shadows I summoned am to tourney . . .' Ilona, fatherless, mustn't grow up with the taint of unresolved suspicions in her home. . . .

I went back into the drawing room, and knelt down before the fire. My head ached. Oh Lord, how tired I was! And yet now was the very time when I should be on the alert, searching out the truth. The police didn't seem to know it; or they weren't talking. Somehow, somewhere, there must be a clue to what might have been no more than accident.

An ugly thought thrust its way up into my consciousness and brought anguish with it. Had George hidden something from me? Was there some dark reason why . . ? I couldn't bear even to contemplate it. If it were true, then everything about our relationship had been false, its foundations mere quicksand. George hadn't, of course, truly liked Elizabeth. Start then with her. . . .

There was a choice before me. I could tell her to go, making the excuse that I no longer felt fit for company. It wouldn't take much hinting from me to make her put forward her Paris visit. Our relationship had been too strained since I accused her of telling lies. *But*—if she went; there too went the chance to find out more about her. Wouldn't that be, in one way, a relief? To wipe it all out. The temptation was very great, and yet for Ilona's sake nothing must be glossed over; when Elizabeth left it could only be after all doubts about her had been resolved.

Even as I reached this decision I heard her cross the drawing

90

room behind me. She knelt down to put a caressing arm around my shoulders. "Jenny, we shouldn't be at odds now, you and I—"

My withdrawal was instinctive, and slight, but she felt it.

"Please don't, Jenny. You can't really believe I made up that cinema muddle on purpose? Such a *muddle*—it was a hideous, muddly day, and—Look Jenny, I didn't even tell Mrs. Jason to do lunch for you, after I left you that morning——"

"So you *do* now remember."

"Yes—well, I do remember we said something about it—"

"You mean to tell the Inspector, Liz?"

"If you want, Jenny, though it's a bit embarrassing now."

Somehow I felt better, with her admission. It just didn't occur to me to wonder if her offer was genuine. The fact that it was made seemed to put matters right. In an access of generosity I said: "I suppose it doesn't matter now—not all that much." I looked round. She looked young and lovely, if wan, and I could have sworn to her sincerity. As she kissed me there were tears in her eyes.

"They checked up on me pretty thoroughly, Jenny. Luckily the girl at Universe One box office saw me come out—though she couldn't remember selling me the ticket. But she knew she'd remember if I bought it half-way through the house, or anything —the manager said she was reliable." A small smile parted her lips. "Luck for me, wasn't it."

"They would have wanted a motive." I was amazed at the hardness and steadiness of my voice.

"And I had none, had I?" She put her head on one side, like a maddening sort of bird; in that second I knew with certainty that she was acting. "At least, I can't think of one. Jenny, I'm so glad everything's all right between us."

She went away, and I sat down wearily on the sofa. There was the puzzling cinema alibi; and motive, motive... What possible motive *could* she have had? She wouldn't gain money by George's death. She had hinted I was involved with Christopher, so there she'd gain nothing by freeing me. I was neither fool nor vain enough to suppose he still cared for me, but I was rich and we had been engaged ... and suggestions that I cared for him came

91

easily to her tongue: 'Jenny, you don't mind about me and Christopher—?'

Hadn't Clayton been present then? Clayton had seen Christopher kiss me. Had he told the police?

Elizabeth again, on the evening of George's death: 'So you did care for Christopher then—'

It wasn't possible that she thought I would kill George for Christopher's sake! Yet what else could make her say it—another act, like the one I caught her out in just now? And to what end?

Nothing made sense, there was no follow through. I should go mad if I sat here longer, thinking of the problem of my twin. The idea suddenly came to me that I might enlist Christopher's help. Somehow that lightened my spirits, till they darkened again at once before the thought of George's funeral next day. Wretchedness and confusion drove out the thought of Christopher. Tomorrow loomed like a blank forbidding wall, across which I could not see.

10

Time shall unfold what plighted cunning hides.
KING LEAR

The ill-wind proverb is surely a true one; the recurrent tragedies which overwhelm people and nations served to take the public mind off Geneviève's misfortunes. She herself was reported on long and indefinite holiday, while Jenny rated only a few paragraphs here and there. Even George's funeral passed almost unnoticed, except for one or two blurred photographs of me and Elizabeth side by side, both dressed in black. There was a mound of spring flowers on George's coffin. I have always found spring poignant, but in future it will be unbearable as well.

I remember being almost alone in the house, on the following afternoon. Elizabeth had realized my desire for solitude and taken herself off—where, I don't know. While Ilona had gone back to school, where they promised to keep a kindly eye on her, and let her do exactly as she liked. Mrs. Jason was probably asleep in the kitchen, her bulky form relaxed in her rocking-chair. It was Clayton's afternoon off, and I decided to give him notice soon. Two women and a little girl surely needed no more than Mrs. Jason and a cleaning woman to look after them.

I went up to the drawing room, thankful to be alone at last. But the room, so empty, the clock that ticked away time with such an inexorable, funereal tick—had it always sounded so threatening?—frightened me. I was alone. If I spoke, no one would answer. If I called, no one would come. If I rang George's office, as I so often had, for comfort—

I must be firm with myself. Life went on. I repeated it several times, finally aloud. Life didn't stop because your husband died and your heart broke. I had been insulated from misery for years. Now it was my turn to be one with the cancer patients and the mothers whose children died in fires. The great thing was to realize that life went on, to create an illusion that one's own life went on as well. Telephone someone, perhaps: Marjorie? I picked up the receiver; but on the pad beside me someone had scrawled an unimportant message, doodled a doodle. It was

93

George's handwriting. He had done that doodle two weeks ago. Ilona had laughed at it. I put down the receiver.

The cupboard beside me contained a rug, begun some time back while I chatted to George and Elizabeth in the evenings. I dragged it from the cupboard, and began a resolute attack with wool and needle. It was all quite simple, really. You did the next thing, then the next, like the first steps after illness. Soon the muscles would strengthen. Perhaps, in a few days, another series of articles for John. . . .

"I still think the pale lilac would have been better in your room, darling." That was what George had said, last time I was tatting, or whatever you call it. George was right—I must tell him so when . . . Perhaps the rug wasn't such a panacea, after all. It didn't occupy one's mind as well as well as one's fingers. Keep calm, though. It was early days yet. This sick feeling of agony couldn't possibly last—couldn't possibly——

I got unsteadily to my feet, whimpering, and put my face against the wall. This was the point when people began to bang their heads—on, on, on until the awful things that happened were drowned in insensibility. Oh God, I said. Oh God, oh God, oh God. . . . It wasn't a prayer, more like hate. Anyway, there was nothing and nobody there. No one to talk to, no one to hate. The room was as empty as a——

The whole room seemed to watch me. I began to walk round it, touching the furniture. I wanted to touch something familiar. For comfort. But there was no comfort in the hard smooth surface of a Queen Anne tallboy, none in the feel of brocade. A sense of shame tormented me. In my happiness I hadn't made much effort to comfort other people. Disaster had been unimportant, when it didn't happen to me. Now I was punished, and I prowled that room like a sick animal, until I felt insane. The one thing no one should ever have in a room was a clock. Its tick-tick was too like the rhythm of a human heart, and like a heart it stopped.

There was a snuffling sound outside the door, a high imperious whimper. It was Clemmie. "You've shut me out," said the whimper again. Thud. When the door was opened the little dog bounded into my arms, all fuss and lick. "Clemmie puppy, silly

94

little dog." I put my face against his muzzle, and he responded with squeals of joy. He hadn't been walked for days. Well, he should have one now, a long one, which would make me too tired to think at all. I snapped on his leash, picked up my bag and jacket, and shut behind us the door of that dreadful empty room.

The police still had our car, and local walks were too reminiscent of ones taken with George. So Clemmie and I took a taxi to Hyde Park; it wasn't cheering, though wildly beautiful, all spring flowers starting from the dark earth, and tight green buds, I used to walk there when I was growing up and spring made me all stupid and sentimental, as well as lonely. Yet that original loneliness had only been a half loneliness, because though I could guess at, I couldn't really *know* what I was missing. . . .

Firmly I turned my thoughts Clemmie-wards. He was so like a bounding ball that it was hard to keep up with him. We went down past the statue of Achilles, and along the Row, and crossed over into Kensington Gardens where are those little shady walks which lead eventually to the calm figure of Albert the Good, seated among imperial animals. Here we turned right and walked under the chestnuts behind the Flower Walk.

I was beginning to feel tired. The sun was low, a faint haze hung in the air, and the late afternoon was cold. At last we reached Kensington High Street. I looked for a taxi but there wasn't one; of course I'd forgotten we were so close to the Air Terminal.

We continued down Gloucester Road. Plenty of cars and buses, not a taxi in sight. Traffic jostled its way up Victoria Grove, so I turned up it too. Somewhere in the side streets we might be luckier. I turned left, ahead of me a taxi started to slow down. Oh joy, it was stopping—no; it turned another corner, still slowly, as if the driver was looking for a number. All at once I remembered this was home ground: there, still with the board outside which read TO BE SOLD, was my former home.

The taxi stopped and the fare descended. I slowed my steps, and hovered. A brisk little woman in high heels tat-tatted across the road. She wore an emerald green pillbox, and a fiery expression. I quickened my steps and raised my hand to the driver.

He had already nodded to me when Pillbox gave me a glance of fiery contempt, stepped to his offside window, and began to issue instructions in a parakeet voice.

"It's my taxi," I said, like a cross child.

She had a most venomous glance. "Oh no, I think *not*."

"I engaged you, isn't that true?" I appealed direct to Caesar, who announced that the ladies could share; if they had a mind to.

Pillbox snorted. "If this *lady's* going to Wimbledon—"

"This lady is going to Regents Park, in this taxi."

I had opened the door and almost won, when Clemmie defeated me. He saw a cat on the opposite side of the road, and leapt, voicing hideous intentions. The sudden strain on the leash unbalanced me. In that moment Pillbox pushed past me into the taxi, and triumphantly slammed the door; and the driver, with a shrug of indifference, drove away. Tears of annoyance filled my eyes. I smacked Clemmie with a hearty smack. He beamed and puffed. Everything was suddenly too much. As a last insult heavy drops of rain began to fall, and in a matter of seconds it was streaming down. I looked round forlornly for shelter, and saw that the door of my former home stood open. A young woman regarded me from the top step. She had a pleasant face, tight black jeans, a heavy sweater, and long rather unkempt hair. A small boy peered out from behind her trews. He licked at something round and shiny on a stick.

"Have you come to see the house?"

"I'm afraid not."

"No one ever does." She sounded full of gloom. "I thought you came in that taxi."

"Not me. I wanted it, but a sort of parakeet woman snatched it."

"How mean. Here, you're getting soaked. You'd better come in and shelter."

"I couldn't bother you—" The last thing I wanted on the day after George's funeral was a long tête-à-tête with a stranger.

"It's no bother. The kettle's on."

I must have taken a wavering step forward, because she said encouragingly: "Oh, good. It's a filthy day and I'm sick of my

96

own company. Come on in." She led the way into the house. Clemmie followed her, guided by the smell of food, and I followed Clemmie. The child considered me with an angelic stare and wiped his toffee apple on my leg.

"*Barney*"*!* The girl pushed him ahead of us towards the kitchen. It was odd to follow a stranger's back into that room though the decor was completely changed. Now the floor was covered in stone tiles, the ceiling was ginger, and three walls were red and one black. There was a delightful painting of some spiny blue fish propped against the stove, and vegetables and fruit littered the table.

"Oddly enough, I used to live here."

"Not here in this house? How strange. I wish you would again. I can't tell you how I hate the place. Here, do sit down."

I sat, thankfully, yet almost in a panic to get away.

"Why do you hate it so?"

"We die to live in the country, but we simply can't rid ourselves of this. Ian—that's my husband—bought it years ago when everyone said it was a bargain, but it's full of dry rot. The agents have stopped sending people, but today a Mrs. Macadam phoned to say she'd be along after four, so I heard the taxi and thought you were her."

The pleasant voice went on and on while I sat in a haze of misery and tried to listen. She didn't look the sort of woman who spills her troubles to strangers, but the house and the dry rot seemed to have got her down, or perhaps the continual talk of a very small child, with its endless repetition. Mercifully all I had to do was make sympathetic noises at intervals. Through my self-absorption I heard her complain that everything went wrong for them here, even the family planning failed to work.

"Ian's tried everything, so have I, but we might as well not have bothered. We've got six already, it may soon be seven."

"Goodness, you must be tired." I understood her depression.

"As a matter of fact I get stronger and stronger, it's just our luck in this house. If only I had kidneys they might abort me."

There seemed nothing to say. I could think of no recipe, offhand, to make her kidneys fail.

97

A huge cup of tea was placed in front of me. It was good tea, and I drank thirstily while Barney and Clemmie shared the toffee apple lick for lick beneath the table.

"Can you smell anything too awful? Have a scone."

I raised my head and sniffed. Ian's supper was highly gar-licked, and I remembered George telling me garlic was an aphrodisiac, and wondered if I ought to tell her so. Then I grew conscious of an underlying smell which got right at the back of my nose.

"You can, can't you? That's it: that's dry rot. They don't even need a surveyor." She gazed at me in sorrowful triumph.

"Where have you got it?"

"All over the basement, and upstairs too in a little room at the top. It's a most peculiar shape, like—oh, I forgot, you know it. Anyway, having the floor up hasn't improved it. We've got wood-beetle as well."

"Two and twenty misfortunes," I said absent-mindedly, biting into my scone. It was very good, floury and buttery. "That was my sister's room. At least, we shared the big one on the next floor down, but she claimed the other as a hideyhole. She used to shut herself up there and write stories."

"Did she, she sounds fun. I used to write a lot as a child too, but now I paint." She indicated the delightful fish. I made sounds of approval through my scone. Barney made a swipe at the painting with his toffee apple, added to the impasto, and gave a dark, angelic beam.

"You wouldn't care to see over the house, would you? We've altered quite a lot. Or would it make you feel like a ghost? You just *might* suddenly hear of someone who would buy it."

She sounded so wistful that I could hardly refuse. The effort not to think of George was killing me, but if we made a quick round I could edge my way to the front door. The rain had almost stopped.

"I'd love to see the house again and then, if you don't mind, I must fly. I have to fetch my daughter from her school."

The drawing room looked larger than I remembered it. The walls were hung with oils and gouaches signed Philippa Maddox. They were good. I noticed a street scene which included our

98

house. Rather tentatively I inquired if she exhibited. She mentioned one or two of the smaller well-known galleries.

"I'd very much like to buy the one with this house, if it's for sale."

"Would you really? What luck you came in out of the rain."

I wrote her a cheque then and there, although she protested that it didn't matter when she was paid, and we left the painting ready for me to collect, and climbed the stairs. The interior of the house still seemed to have grown; I suppose Mother liked clutter, whereas the Maddoxes preferred life simple, not to say stark. We examined the top floor, and then went up the few narrow steps which led to Elizabeth's former lair.

I peered into the room. The same wallpaper put there for Elizabeth still covered the walls. On the window seat lay a few dusty objects which I took to be Mrs. Maddox's children's toys.

"Goodness, I never thought of it till now, but those things must belong to you, unless some other child used this room once. You might like them for your daughter, they'll clean up all right. There's quite a good kaleidoscope amongst them."

"Where *did* you find them? I'm sure Ilona will be thrilled."

I picked my way gingerly across the exposed joists.

"They were underneath the flooring. There was a board loose in that corner. I suppose your sister had a private cache for pet possessions. Do you remember them?"

"Yes," I said thoughtfully, "I do."

"Well, you must have them, of course. And there was one other thing." She spoke over her shoulder as she led the way downstairs. "An old green diary. Perhaps you'd like to take that too. I'm afraid Ian was so enthralled at actually finding treasure in his house that he sawed through the lock, and we've both read it. Your sister had a peculiarly vivid imagination. Bit creepy, really."

I remembered Elizabeth's return and how, looking at our old home, she had said: "Did you ever find my diary?"

"What exactly do you mean?" I asked Mrs. Maddox now.

"Well, she can't have been very old, but she was a born Agatha Christie. A loss to the thriller trade."

I felt a bit odd, and clutched at the banisters. She looked surprised, and I saw the speculative look she gave my clothes. "I say, are you all right? You don't look very good to me. Are those clothes—you're not in mourning, are you? Sorry, I shouldn't have asked."

"I'm all right," I said weakly. "And yes, my—one of my family died."

She was watching me with some distress. Just then I was as eager to be away as she was probably eager to have me go.

"Look, I simply *must* hurry now. Thank you for showing me the house, and your paintings. And for tea. Oh, and for the toys. The picture's lovely." I stooped and gathered it up. "I shall hang it in my drawing room, you must come and see it there." She smiled politely, and I knew she would never come.

"Just hold on and I'll fetch the diary, and a carrier bag for those things. We'll ring the rank in the High for a taxi."

Cluttered with Clemmie, a carrier bag, and the painting, I was soon being driven homeward through the park. It was now real dusk, and by that light it was impossible to examine the diary; so I stowed it away in my bag, where Elizabeth wouldn't see it when I entered the house, if she happened to be around. It was possible, however, to examine the toys more carefully than before. I remembered them all, as I had recognized the kaleidoscope. There was a recorder, an animal puppet, a carved wood doll from Austria, a musical box which opened and revealed a bird that fluttered to the tune of a Viennese waltz.

They had been new when last I saw them; and they had all been mine; they had disappeared one by one, and each time I had been temporarily heartbroken. Each time Mother had scolded me for carelessness, and Elizabeth had smiled at me her gentle, sympathetic smile.

11

Was ever book containing such vile matter
So fairly bound?

ROMEO AND JULIET

I didn't get a chance to read the diary until I went to bed. I collected Ilona from school, and fancied that other parents looked at me furtively, and then away when I looked back; I began to wonder if someone had spread gossip about me and Christopher and George's death. That I was up and about as usual probably told against me, but was there much sense in going to bed over a sorrow that was likely to last me the rest of my life?

When we reached home Ilona received the kaleidoscope with subdued pleasure—dusted, it looked brand new, and it seemed unlikely Elizabeth would recognize it. The other things were put away at the back of my wardrobe. It was impossible to hide the picture, which was large, but I said vaguely that I'd bought it somewhere in Kensington. I said it to Morell, who was in the drawing room again with my twin. He obviously put it down to madness or criminal indifference, but I no longer cared. He went away soon afterwards, and Elizabeth was uncommunicative about his visit, and began to speak of other things.

"Jenny, wouldn't you let me have Ilona at night? You do need to get proper sleep."

"I like having her in with me, Liz. And if she needs comfort I'm the one to do it. Thanks all the same."

"If you're taking pills you won't hear her cry."

"They don't have all that effect on me. Perhaps Dr. Knowles has given me a placebo." 'Or perhaps,' said an inner voice, 'he no longer trusts you with the real thing.'

Elizabeth made no further demur. I found myself examining her pale pretty face, and wondered detachedly just what I had in the house with me. The diary might enlighten me. And tomorrow I meant to confide my troubles to Christopher. If he thought me mad, he would say so. If not, he would tell me what to do. It was as simple as that.

Ilona's bath took quite a time, because she had another bout of crying. At last, after I had rocked her in my arms for half an hour, her sobs subsided into hiccoughs, and I was able to get her into bed, the kaleidoscope still clutched to her chest. She looked so pathetic she almost finished me as well, except that I now seemed unable to cry. I felt like a tired monument of grey stone which had been weathered by centuries of storm.

John rang up while she was in the bath, and left a message to say there was a pile of mail and he would send round the nicer letters next day by Miss Starr; and not to worry with the answers, the office would deal with them. Clayton brought me the message. I hadn't yet given him notice, I thought that could be relegated to Elizabeth, she might as well be helpful.

We dined together, in silence. Afterwards I went straight to my room. A small bed had been put up for Ilona, and she was fast asleep on top of the kaleidoscope. She had one of George's photographs beside the bed. I couldn't bear to look at it just yet, but its presence seemed to comfort her. Beside it stood the thermos of hot chocolate that Clayton placed there now each night, in case I was wakeful.

Tonight I was glad of the diary: anything to take my mind off the present. I got into bed, shaded the lamp so that it wouldn't shine on Ilona's face, and settled down to find out what Elizabeth had written all those years ago. To hold the diary gave me an odd sense of emptiness—it was as if the time when I was contented on my own, or happy with George, had never happened.

The lock hung open where Ian Maddox had severed it. The pages were as clean as when Elizabeth had written in them, though the ink was a muddy mauve instead of blue. My twin had written minute descriptions of her days. I was able to read, at boring length, of a New Year's Eve party: Elizabeth had worn green. ('Mother wouldn't buy me a new dress, although Jenny managed to scorch her taffeta and got another one. It didn't suit her, she's still just as plain.') We had a buffet supper with chicken in aspic, and 'a delicious pud with rum and chocolate which we'll *never* see at home, because we can't afford cream. Or so Mother says.' Much of the diary was as dull as this, and the overall picture that appeared was of an Elizabeth bored to tears, whose boredom and reticence had given an impression of docility. There was also a strange, and to me now very apparent, streak of pure jealousy of myself.

I couldn't remember being conscious of this attitude at the time. I couldn't account for it, either. Surely, with Elizabeth's natural 'star quality', it was *I* who had suffered from comparisons? Reading on I could only believe that an unusual vanity and closed egotism had made the presence of any sister intolerable to her, even such a sister as a Jenny—admiring, unenterprising, and overshadowed. The derogatory remarks were too frequent to be missed. 'Jenny thought the essay I wrote "marvellous". She was pretty pleased with hers, but Sister John only gave her six. It wasn't original.'

'Reverend Mother mentioned my progress in dancing class, and praised Jenny's "exuberance"(!) in the reels. *I* thought she made an exhibition of herself. When she throws herself about like that I could sink through the floor.'

'Christopher's a nice boy, he's very serious, and talks of interesting things when Jenny isn't there.' Further on: 'I *like* Christopher. He bruised my arm when we were playing cricket, but he didn't mean to, and kissed me afterwards.' (She didn't tell *me* about that kiss.)

I read on, through January, February and March: these months had inspired only the dullest descriptions of routine school and home events. With one exception: 'Jenny's musical box has gone under the FB' (floor board?) In April we had our Easter holidays. We went to a matinée once, and to the Zoo. Elizabeth recorded with envy that: 'Maria Fanshawe and Peggy Egerton are off to Venice with their parents. Oh, *lucky* them. Our holiday will be Lyme Regis in late August. The nuns say we're lucky to have such a wonderful mother—if they but *knew*. We're not as poor as all that, it's just carefulness.' So she had liked Mother as little as she liked myself.

It was in April that Father made one of his rare visits of 'reasonable access', and I remembered the occasion—he had lunched us all at Scotts. In her diary Elizabeth referred to him as F: '*That man* is here again—it makes a change. Jenny thinks he's as wicked as sin, a prince of devils. I don't know *what* he is,

103

but at least he interests me. After lunch J. and M. went to the loo, but I sat on with F.—he'd whispered earlier he wanted to talk to me. Fun to hear that he thinks I'm the only one of the family who's good for anything; and he wants to keep in private touch with me, not through M. I said that I couldn't see how we'd go about it, Mother saw all our mail. He frowned, and said 'I arrange', and that I wasn't to tell Jenny. As if I would! Then he wanted to know what I felt about it, and I said it would be fun, like a liaison. He roared. Asked how I knew the word, then made me solemnly promise not to give him away. I promised, and he told me what to do. He has some pretty bright ideas.'

What the bright ideas were was unrecorded, but later they came out: 'April 23rd. Back at school, a prize bore, and awful holy talk from Reverend Mum on meaning of life. Chance of first letter from F. I got out of class before Jenny, hurried to the newsagent on the corner and asked the newsagent (little grumpy man) for a bar of chocolate, *and* if he had a letter for "Miss Alison Gray". Couldn't believe it when he said "yes". Ran all the way home, to hide upstairs to read my letter. F. is thorough, he sent stamps, and a ten-shilling note for writing paper. A jolly funny letter, all about Abroad. It made my mouth water. Sun and fun and no Reverend Mum. How, how, *how* can I *not* bore him, though? Heard Jenny come in, F.'s letter joined the musical box.'

Ilona gave a little snort, like a puppy. I put down the diary, and peered at her, but she slept on. I felt shaken. Good heavens, could one really live with a child for years and have no inkling what it was up to? For all I knew, Ilona, in a few years' time, might carry on a passionate correspondence with Christopher.

The next entries were short, and often made every other day. Elizabeth wrote to Father, and from then on the correspondence absorbed much of her spare time and energies. It was uncanny how like him she began to sound. It was as if he had mesmerized her. The way she expressed herself grew more mature, but she still had anguished doubts about her ability to entertain him, and evidently expressed them, for she reported his reply:

'F. says my letters delight him, that I show what the French call "*sensibilité*" and "a realistic approach to life". Also they are "très, très amusants", but he begs me to remember "fluent French is a passport to the good graces of people of breeding and intelligence everywhere, in such civilized society as remains". I've asked Mademoiselle to help me, and she's knocked sideways. Thinks it's due to her brilliance, poor thing.'

'July 18th. It's Lyme again. I believe Mother would like us to have buckets and spades. Jenny's delighted—she would be. Without F.'s letters think I'd die. I can't believe he's bad, but *if* he is give me wickedness every time. He's staying with a Madame Belle-Isle near Cannes. They seem to spend most of their time on the beach, massaging each other with oil. Strictly not for Rev. Mums. "*Elle veut fortement te voir, et je l'ai répondu pourquoi pas? Certainement, elle peut faire un court séjour ici. Qu'en penses-tu, chérie? Ça te plaira?*" Would it! I wrote back enthusiastically—in French.'

'August 10th. Raving mad at Mother. It's *hell* pretending I don't know what she's done to me. Mother's observant, she's already asked what's wrong—grown-ups can made you vomity with their deceit. Last letter from F. was quite downcast. He had asked Mother if I might join him for a holiday Abroad, but she evidently sent back a curt refusal, saying that till Jenny and I were sixteen the present arrangement of "reasonable access" was all she could allow. The slyness of it . . . The worst of it is, I'm ripe for Abroad. It would *develop* me. Between Jenny and me an enormous gulf has opened. She's backward. Or simple-minded.'

I began to think she was dead right.

'August 12th. Joy, joy, joy! *Another* letter. F. says not to worry —just to decide if I'd sooner live with him or Mother. And then he'll fix it! Good heavens, I don't have to *think*—though it gives me gooseflesh to think of leaving Mother *entirely*—what happens if I'm ill? Can't see F. at anyone's bedside. But otherwise. . . . Lyme on the 15th, just as well. Mother says I'm spotty, and she'll ban all these sweets from the newsagent. I'd better start a subscription to the *Catholic Girl* instead.'

We had been nursing the infant Machiavelli in our simple middle-class household without knowing it.

The diary was blank during the Lyme Regis fortnight, but was resumed abruptly on the 31st. 'Home again. Everyone says how brown we look, as if it was a *feat*. Jenny's delighted—sometimes I think it's my duty to broaden her mind—what will she do when she's taken out? Or won't she guess that's the major purpose of life till it's too late for anyone to be interested? She'd better be a nun, and do the praying for us both—I'll need a lot of prayers before *I'm* through. No letter from F. yet. Perhaps he's changed his mind? I'd go mad. Meanwhile the only comfort is Christopher. We've met in the garden each night, when Jenny thought me in the bath. He knows quite a lot, for a boy, but at least he's not rough. *Almost* told him about F. but held back. He might think it his duty to give me away.'

'September 5th. *Feux de joie! Sonnez, trompettes!* F. has arranged everything. I'm to be spirited away on Our Birthday—15th October next; details later. I shook all over at first. Not that it's *sad* to leave—M.'s so dull and upright, and does Jenny *exist*? All the same it alarms me, although part of me can't wait. The nuns don't seem so bad now, and even London looks gorgeous, all mist and golden light. I can't be homesick beforehand, surely? The worst thing will be leaving Christopher. I'm quite dirty without baths. I love Christopher, I certainly do, but perhaps it's just as well I'm going while I can still manage him. Anyway, there are plenty of boys Abroad. How will F. arrange my passport? He never said. . . .'

So Christopher's passion for blondes had begun early. I had been blinkered by my 'backwardness'. Ilona gave a little cough, and moved restlessly. I put my handkerchief over the lamp, to darken her side of the room. Present misery lay in wait for me, swamping me with agony for George, and with George's loss. It was an effort to read on.

Few of the later entries contained anything of interest. The plan for Elizabeth's abduction went ahead. It seemed that Father was deliberately vague about their destination—perhaps he didn't want her to know too much, should things go wrong. I felt sure, though, that he had somewhere further afield than France in mind. Elizabeth had wondered how he would get her a passport; I did not doubt that he had managed through some shady friend; the up-to-date photograph would have been the snag. It was too simple, really. On September 30th she recorded:

'F. says my photograph enlarged well. He's had it done from the tiny snapshot Mother took of Jenny and me a year ago. She sent it to him with our Christmas cards.'

On October 7th came the entry that fairly shook me. For once the contents of F.'s letter had shaken even Elizabeth:

'Something horrible has happened. I feel shattered. If only I dare confide in Christopher. At first it was all fun, like a boy's adventure story. Now it's spoilt, and sinister. Spent two days wondering if I'd write and say it's off, but that would be the end of me, with F. I *could* feign stupidity, make out that Mother cottoned on, somehow? Then I'd have to confide in her, and she'd write to him. She might even make a legal fuss, in case he tried anything again. And it would *wither* me to tell her. I simply can't. She'd never trust me again, nor would F. Lost both ways. He's *too* intelligent: he just kept this to the last because he knew how I'd react, and wanted to make me feel already committed. It's a let-down, really, I can't see it any other way. He may be fun, but he's as devilish and dishonest as everyone else. Even Jenny was right about it.

'When his letter came, with the little package in it, I couldn't think what he'd sent me. It was two packages really. One contained a sort of green powder, and the other a gingery one. I thought they were sedatives! But I wouldn't take stuff which looked like *that*, it might poison me. Then I read the letter. No question of "would I?" Just instructions. I was to put the green powder in Mother's food the night before, and give her the ginger one at breakfast—as if she was a dog. He swears blind it won't harm her, just put her out of action for the day. I'm green with funk. Anyway, Mother might not let us go without her, has he thought of that? Sometimes I believe his plan is harmless, no worse than a joke with sneezing powders. Then a ghastly thought creeps in.... And it would be *me* who'd done it, not him. It's like a nightmare, and I start to sweat. Then I see myself as plain dumb, it's imagination, that's all. As if any man would let his daughter do a thing like that. Surely if I can even *think* it of F. I can't want to go with him? And yet, though I have these nightmare suspicions, I *do* want to—very much. That shows how bad I am—birds of a feather. Can one help how one's born?'

'October 11th. Frantic note from F. Why haven't I replied? He must *know*, etc. . . .

'I dither. Try tossing coin. Heads I go. (Powder for M.) Tails I don't. Penny rolled under bed. Ominous? State of continual funk. Jenny bright and babyish all day, Mother snapping. Future gay and terrifying—or all the time like today. Tossed up again. Heads three times. Licked both powders four hours ago. Not dead yet.

'5 o'clock. Last minute decision. Wrote to F. Mother tried to stop me going out—said I must, must have evening paper with picture of dear little bear born in Zoo. Ran to post. Dropped letter in—felt my heart had stopped. Looked at powders again, and had inspiration: shall put green powder down loo, give M. ginger powder alone, and pray. *Pray*. Now it's up to God. Even Reverend Mother would be pleased with that.'

On the fifteenth came the last entry. I could remember her face, grave and preoccupied, as she had written it, sitting opposite me at the table.

'The Day. I've been sick several times. Made Jenny swear not to tell Mother. Can it be worth it? Half hope F. will have mild accident. Mother had powder in her porridge. She said, 'They even seem to be colouring porridge now,' but ate it. Now past eleven, and she doesn't look too good. Why did F. ever start this? I never thought it would be quite so horrid, though underneath I feel a kind of wild glee about Abroad. Said goodbye to Christopher last night, he didn't realize it. He was so sweet, and fairly restrained. Now I'm looking at Jenny across the table. Try to see her as he might: that hair could be pretty, but it's always in a mess. Big mouth, high cheekbones, slightly Eastern eyes—our Hungarian ancestress. It ought to be smashing, though she's just a dull baby. *The* only thing I mind about going is the thought that Christopher and Jenny might start something. No: Jenny's for a convent. She has no temperament. Almost feel sentimental about not seeing her again.

'Mother's just been sick upstairs. Too jittery to go on with this, so . . . Cross my fingers, and write here for the last time (I hope). Now for Abroad—and under the FB with this. *Dear* diary, as those clottish Victorians would have said, goodbye.'

12

What! wouldst thou have a serpent sting thee twice?

THE MERCHANT OF VENICE

I closed the diary. I was cold and dazed—Mrs. Maddox's words had prepared me, but what I hadn't foreseen was the cold egotism, the lies, vanity, and calculating appraisal of other people. I knew now past misunderstanding that in Elizabeth we had harboured the born criminal and adventuress. She hadn't known what the powder would do to Mother, yet she had gone ahead. She would do anything to get what she wanted——

A sense of wild panic filled me. I lay there, and gripped the sheets; my hands sweated. What *did* she want, why had she come back, was it mad to think that she had connived at George's death? If she hadn't foreseen he'd die, why had she drugged him? The unanswered questions just went round and round. *Was* it Elizabeth? What could she possibly hope to gain—or, what did someone else hope to gain? For it crossed my mind then that she might not be alone: perhaps she had lied when she told me Father was dead. . . .

I felt flayed by exhaustion, and overstrung. I got up, took two sleeping pills, and went back to bed. Sleep came while I was clutching George's pyjamas for comfort, as Ilona had clasped the kaleidoscope. The last conscious thought I had was that Elizabeth would never have risked setting me free anywhere near Christopher, unless she stood to gain more than she might—to her way of thinking—lose.

I woke next day glad that Miss Starr would be coming early, and I could send a message by her that I must see Christopher urgently. I would give him the diary to read. I didn't worry about what effect it might have on his feelings for Elizabeth. Her weaknesses weren't of the kind that easily rouse pity. They were negative strengths, evil ones. In the meantime I returned the diary to the back of my wardrobe, with the recovered toys, and dallied over my breakfast tray so that when Miss Starr arrived she found me alone upstairs. She gave me a compassionate look and suggested brusquely that I should hop back into bed.

"I'm all right, thank you."

"You don't look it, Mrs. Emerson. You look all in."

I tried to smile. "Staying in bed won't help. . . ."

"It might rest you."

I gave in, "But only till eleven," and she sat down on the end of the bed and drew a packet of letters from her bag.

"These are the ones we thought you'd like to see."

I thanked her, and sat nervously pleating the edge of the sheet between my fingers. There didn't seem anything to say.

"You poor child, you have had a bad time."

"Yes," I said dully, "and Ilona too."

Just then Clayton came in with coffee, and for once he was welcome. I still couldn't speak of George without bursts of tears. I think Miss Starr realized this, for she began to talk about the office.

"Mr. Anderson thinks Geneviève should take a long holiday, and then come back in a slightly different form."

I had forgotten Geneviève, my *doppelgänger*. "Just as he likes," I said listlessly. If he wanted to give her her *congé*, it was all one to me. I longed to ask what gossip, if any, Miss Starr had heard. Presumably the police had interviewed the office staff; but she was discreet, and I could tell nothing from her manner, which was always the same—kind, friendly and abrupt. However, just before she left she reopened her bag, and drew out a small clipping from a newspaper. Her manner was hesitant.

"Mrs. Emerson, I've been wondering whether I should let you see this or not. I don't want to seem too suspicious, nor to rouse suspicions in you. On the other hand—" she paused delicately.

"Go on."

"I think you ought to know that this was published. In spite of being definitely cut out by Mr. Anderson's orders."

I took the clipping and saw that it was from a Swiss paper, published in Zürich. I was looking at a transcription of the article that had appeared on Geneviève's private life as Jenny. Halfway down the second column someone had marked a paragraph in ink. It was the one firmly excised by Christopher from the original typescript, the one concerning the wealth which Grandfather's invention had brought me.

"Where did you get this?"

"It was in the Geneviève file. Mr. Anderson had asked for it, and as one of the new girls had messed it up I took everything out and put it straight again. This was stuck in amongst all the articles which were syndicated at the time. I nearly passed it over, then I saw it was marked. Mrs. Emerson, I can't imagine how they got it."

"Nor can I." So Elizabeth—or Father?—could have known about my fortune. In Miss Starr's mind this could only have been suspicion, in mine it was now certainty. Remembering the cold calculations in that diary——

"But who put it in the file? Who would have marked it?"

She shrugged. "You know the office—people in and out all the time, particularly in the records room. Literally anyone could have put it there. Someone outside, or someone in."

"Someone who was interested enough in my fortune to mark a paragraph about it. Someone perhaps who didn't know I had one until they saw the article?" I ventured, and wrinkled my brow. "It doesn't make sense, does it? Not if it was only by its being published abroad that someone noticed it. *Was* it marked in the office, then, or did someone send in the cutting from outside? And if so, to whom?"

"It was the only cutting from that week's paper, so presumably it was an office copy, as we get most of the foreign press. But that's only guesswork. Not everything we put out is filed."

"Then who would normally cut it out and put it in my file?"

"Any one of the office staff who had nothing better to do." Miss Starr gave a wintry smile. "It's a junior's job, though. I did quite a lot of it in my salad days."

The shock of George's death had certainly done something to my brain—the penny had taken a little while to drop: only someone who had seen the original typescript could have given it to the Swiss paper. I said so. "Or could it have been a mistake, were they the only paper to receive a *full* copy?"

"Quite impossible, I should say." Miss Starr spoke with vigour. "I retyped the MS. of the article myself, and that was the only copy which was sent out. The original, with all the corrections, is there in the file."

"Don't you generally see the foreign papers? Wouldn't you have noticed what had happened?" She was a fine linguist, and read French, Spanish, German and Italian with equal ease.

"Yes, I do. I couldn't think how I missed it, until I saw the date. I was on holiday then. Miss Darby took my place. Her languages aren't very adequate, and I don't suppose she checked every article right through. Now she's in America, so we can't check up on *her*! It might be possible to find out from the paper concerned how they got it, but the trouble is, the journalistic mind. We don't want to draw attention——" Again that delicate pause. I agreed, with fervour. "But, Mrs. Emerson, I'll do my best with a discreet question here and there. It may take time."

Time. The one thing I felt we no longer had. Again I wondered what rumours, if any, she had heard.

"I suppose there's been a lot of talk?" I ventured.

"You know the office—but Mr. Anderson has sat squarely on everything like a swan on its nest. Don't worry, my dear."

"So long as he isn't hatching it," I said dryly.

"He's a hundred per cent on your side," was all she said, but I felt a bit cheap to have questioned John's goodness to me, his integrity and his discretion. Why, after all, should anyone trust me? It was warming to know that he did.

"If you need any help, you've only to let him know."

I shook my head. Obscurity was all I wanted for the dark opinions I was forming. At least, for the moment. A newspaper office is not the best place to find it.

"Then I'll be off."

"Just a minute." Again I nervously pleated the sheet with my fingers. "I wanted to see Mr. Leyton, but not to make a *thing* of it. There's something I must ask him, and——"

"Good heavens, *how* could I forget——" She tapped her forehead with one finger. "What a mercy you mentioned him. Mr. Leyton sent you a message. I saw him this morning, before he left."

"*Left!*"

"Yes—He's gone to Paris on a job, but I can give you his telephone number." She was jotting it down as she spoke. "Here it is."

"Thanks." I took it, and put it in my bag, but hopelessly. I couldn't discuss this with him on the telephone, nor read him an entire diary. I hoped my dismay wasn't too apparent, or too odd.

"He's flying to Scotland, to see someone on his way back—and then motoring straight down to Cumberland. The message was that he hoped you and Ilona and Miss Lemprière would join him. He'll expect you, anyway, unless he hears to the contrary."

"Thanks," I said again. A great wave of lethargy swept over me. I felt threatened by a tide of ominous circumstance. Christopher, my one standby, was gone. Could I show the diary to Morell? Somehow the thought of explaining it was preposterous. Although light was thrown on Elizabeth, it might seem that I was trying to use her as a scapegoat. But that drugging of Mother —it was *too* coincidental; I should have to inform Morell, though I didn't relish it. He obviously disliked me and—after Clayton had tattled—he probably despised me as well.

Miss Starr interrupted my thoughts: "By the way—that cutting: don't worry about it, will you?"

"Oh no," I said idiotically. "Forewarned is forearmed."

"I wondered if I ought to bring it, but——" She picked up her bag and gloves hesitantly, and added: "You see—it always looked odd to me that, well, *she* turned up—and then, not so long afterwards—though it's libellous, isn't it, and one wonders what anyone could gain by *his*", again a delicate pause, "death."

"Nothing." My bitterness was acute. "It's all loss." And then the new misery I had to live with prompted me to inquire: "I'm afraid I never asked—how are *your* affairs?" As usual she looked drawn with fatigue. I noticed it now with shame.

"No difference," she drew on her gloves. "Mother none too good. We get along all right really, Mr. Anderson is so kind."

"I know he is." From my bag I drew out my cheque book. "And I'd like to help as well. Look, don't feel embarrassed, will you, but I would be so glad if—" I was talking too much and nervously.

She *was* embarrassed. Hideously. I didn't know that Miss Starr could look so discomposed. Her plain sad face went a deep mottled pink, her ears glowed. She couldn't even thank me, just scooted out of the door without a backward look or even a pat for Clemmie, whom she adored. I was awed by her extreme uprightness. Somehow I must find a different way to help her, but I was impressed by her reaction: it was, I thought, so Cranford, and rather sweet.

Later in the morning I did get up. To stay in bed only made me more restless with despair and misery than I was already, and at the other extreme waited the great tide of lethargy to drown me. So I got up, and did over my face very carefully. Under the present stress of things the Hungarian strain had grown more apparent. I looked melancholy-mad, like someone escaping from state police. I pulled a face at myself, but the result was alarming, and I hurriedly turned to the prosaic business of every day. I took a shopping bag, and went to the delicatessen, but while I bought tinned bamboo shoots, saffron and wild rice my brain was occupied with one problem: should I show Morell the diary? Could I risk a wait for Christopher instead? And all the time there was the nagging sensation that I was seeing everything just wrong, had been carefully encouraged to watch one part of the stage while the clever conjurer was busy elsewhere.

In the end I decided to tackle Morell. Directly on getting home I telephoned the police station. A polite young sergeant answered. Inspector Morell was out—was there a message? I felt my determination ooze away.

"I don't suppose the Inspector would be this way, some time?" Idiotic to be so nervous. "It's just that, ah, I wondered how things were going——" It must have sounded mad; yet I couldn't explain on the telephone.

"I see." I could almost hear his thoughts: 'Is it worth the Inspector's time . . . is this the preliminary to confession?'

"It's not truly important, Sergeant." Why had I said that? Of course it was.

He had made up his mind. "I'll ask the Inspector to look in on you, Mrs. Emerson."

"Oh, thanks . . ." I put down the receiver and turned, to find Elizabeth standing a little way off. She pushed her hair back from her forehead, and gave me an odd glance, hostile and pitying at the same time.

"Who was that?" Her voice was not so casual as she tried to make it. When had she come in? Could she have heard me say 'Sergeant'? I moved away, saying over my shoulder: "Just a little business matter I should have settled before now."

"Oh." She stood there with drooped head. She didn't believe me. I felt suddenly a need for open attack.

"Liz, is Father really dead?"

"But I told you he was." Her voice sounded plaintive.

"What did he die of—and where?"

"Goodness, Jenny, you never asked me all this before."

"I wasn't interested before." It was a mistake to say that, for she came back with: "Well, why are you interested *now*?"

I regretted opening my mouth. Father's problematical death was something else to be discussed with the Inspector. I tried to shrug away the subject. "Oh, I just wondered, that's all. You're so silent about him."

"I've been silent all along. It's not a pleasant subject to me." There was a slight jarring whine in her voice. "No—something made you wonder. What was it?"

Inside me an inner voice warned: shut up, change the subject, you fool: to rouse her suspicions now is the sheerest folly. Still I blundered on, cursing myself. "You lived with him all those years, and yet you never mention him. *Why*?"

She considered; not so much her reply, I think, as what lay behind my question. Her answer was in the shape of an appeal for sympathy—clever enough, unless you had seen the evidence I possessed.

"Jenny, you *knew* Father. How could you possibly imagine—" her soft lower lip quivered, "that I'd *want* to talk about him? How could you, with—" she gestured at the room, "all this, imagine what it was, being taken away like that. And staying with him, and the years—" she choked, wiped her hand across her eyes. "I hated him."

Admirable, I applauded inwardly. Now I could act too: "Poor Liz. Poor darling. Of course it must have been foul for you—"

She was no longer listening. I couldn't think what she was staring at, until I saw it, left there idly on the sofa by Ilona: the kaleidoscope. Elizabeth picked it up almost absently, yet I could feel rigid intent behind her scrutiny. I allowed myself to be forced by her silence into explanation.

"I got it for Ilona yesterday. She needs spoiling just now."

"Jenny dear, I'm sure she loved it—or was it self-indulgence? These things always fascinated you, didn't they?"

She raised it to her right eye, and I knew the colours swirling before her vision, as I knew the questions jostling in her mind. It was as if I myself were looking at the lemon crescents and purple stars—and the question-mark.

"You bought quite a lot yesterday, didn't you? Almost a spending spree. That picture of our old home, too."

I said she was shrewd. And me—my wits were certainly blunted by distress. It had been sheer idiocy to give the kaleidoscope to Ilona already.

Elizabeth and I stared sullenly at each other. Then a strange thing happened, the sort of sentimental trick that time and nostalgia play. Like Proust's madeleine the kaleidoscope brought back the past; and all at once I could no longer see my twin with later knowledge, only as the aloof superior being whom I had passionately tried to emulate. Tears came to my eyes, as if I were gazing at the sun. It only lasted a moment, and then I knew that I had lost the kind and innocent image for ever. I don't know what Elizabeth saw in my face, but her own expression softened.

She leaned forward and just touched her cheek to mine, lovingly. Neither of us mentioned the painting or the kaleidoscope again. We were back, ostensibly, on better terms.

13

... murder, though it have no tongue, will speak
With most miraculous organ.

HAMLET

It may have been strain, or perhaps I ate something: that's
what I thought at the time, anyway. The nausea came on after
luncheon, and I must have looked pretty peculiar, because
Elizabeth earnestly advised me to go and lie down, but I
refused.

"Honestly, you look rotten, Jenny. At least have a hottie to
clutch. I'll fetch you one."

"Clayton will do it," I said weakly; but she was gone from the
room already, though she took long enough coming back. The
afternoon passed very slowly; towards tea-time I began to suffer
from gripes in the stomach, and nausea came in great waves,
leaving me hot and cold by turns.

"I can't think why you *don't* give in, and go to bed." Elizabeth
looked at me closely. "Are you expecting someone, Jenny?"

"No," I lied weakly. Impossible to say now that I expected
Morell. Did she guess? She was acute enough. Anyway, I
realized all at once that I no longer felt up to an interview with
the Inspector; and I wasn't looking forward to presenting him
with that damning piece of evidence against my sister's character,
for I still had a grim conviction that I must protect myself
continually from his suspicions. Besides, it looked as if he wasn't
coming.

"Perhaps I will go to bed, after all."

"You really should. Will you want dinner, do you think?"

I shuddered, and shook my head.

"Not even something light—one of Mrs. Jason's fluffy
omelets?"

"*Please.*"

I barely got upstairs in time. Behind me I heard her call out:
"Clayton shall bring you a hot drink, later." Then I was in the
loo, and being very sick.

I crawled into bed like a sick animal. The attack seemed very

117

sudden. My temperature was below normal, yet I was shivering and aching—Mrs. Jason's cleanliness in the kitchen was impeccable, and so far as I knew there were no unusual gastric bugs going round. Alarm bells began to sound in my mind, and I remembered the diary, and Mother. How much had Elizabeth guessed of my activities? If Morell arrived I would confront him with the diary even if he came while I was being sick. Feeling dizzy I got out to fetch it from my wardrobe: it was no longer there. Elizabeth had taken a long while to get me that hot bottle. . . .

That was the moment when I first grew really afraid—for Ilona. You see, it hit me then, for the first time: the realization of why George had died. The improbable, wild conviction that it could only be like this. . . .

I sat there sweating, no longer from sickness, but from panic fear. Nothing would happen to Ilona while I lived—but how long *would* I live? A day; a night? Not so long? I thought grimly that all probabilities pointed to death within a few hours; though not from anything swallowed so far, for the pangs were no longer severe. Easy to guess that I was being kept out of the way in case the police called—Elizabeth had certainly overheard my telephone call. And yet there was little for my twin to fear now; with the diary gone any insinuation against her might bear the most sinister implications, and I couldn't unburden myself to the hostile Morell without some proof of what would otherwise carry the imprint of fantasy, of a disordered mind, or, more dreadfully, of the frantic efforts of a murderess to pin the blame elsewhere.

The longer I faced the situation, the more appalling seemed the aloneness of my crisis. It wasn't that I minded the thought of death; for myself I might have welcomed it. But somehow, and *alone*, I had to save Ilona from the evil game of chess being played around her. It must have been that apparently innocent little paragraph in a Swiss paper which had set the game in motion.

Alone. That was the word which made me shudder. For I simply wasn't up to it; what I lacked, and needed now, was a logical mind. It was Elizabeth who had been good at mathematics, not me. It was Elizabeth who had learned chess so well from Father—It was Elizabeth. . . .

I rocked myself to and fro in an effort to calm myself, gripping my arms tight round my knees. *Steady* . . . no blind panic. That was no way to protect Ilona—to admit defeat before the fight really began. At least I knew where I was now—or thought that I knew. And there was one thing I could promise my enemies: I was *not* going to 'commit suicide' that night.

It wasn't pleasant sitting there wondering how the attack would form . . . Drugs? Or a shot in the dark . . . No—because Ilona would be sleeping with me, and it would be no part of the plan that murder should be suspect *this* time. It must be a complex business to put a pistol to someone's head, and then arrange it to look like suicide. A more complex business, say, than the faking of a motive for George's wife to murder him.

Murder, and suicide from remorse. Just enough suspicion thrown on Jenny for her to take fright and kill herself. Though not enough evidence to lead her to the dock, and then to gaol, where she could never be hanged, only kept alive, a continual barrier to the acquisition of a fortune. But this way: this would bring a fortune to Ilona; and who better to look after her and administer the fortune than her loving next of kin, her kind Aunt Elizabeth? 'A little more than kin, and less than kind. . . .'

Here I came up against a snag. Elizabeth couldn't have known there was no legal guardian appointed for Ilona . . . could she? It would be laughable to suppose that staunch old Mr. Saunders, our family solicitor, would have told anyone about our wills as they now stood, unaltered since we had both made them years ago. And so the sinister case I had built against her fell to the ground. *Didn't it?* So I was just plain crazy; crazy as a coot. And yet——

And yet I knew, deep down inside, that I wasn't wrong. I ran over the sequence of events, in my mind: the marked passage in the Swiss paper, followed by Elizabeth's sudden reappearance. George's improbable 'suicide'; the cooking up of my 'interest' in Christopher; the lies about the cinema; the diary. It smelt of murder. And it smelt of murder due to happen again.

If only Christopher hadn't gone away! Impossible to convince

Morell without the diary, but I might have made Christopher believe. When had he ever found me untruthful? Then, too, Christopher was the only person apart from myself in a position to *know* I had no motive to kill George. Wasn't he? My hand went to my mouth. . . . Of course, that day he kissed me in the drawing room, I hadn't exactly hurried to push him away. Well, I was taken by surprise—and then Clayton came in. . . .

Another memory followed, unfolded from the depths of my consciousness like part of a paper chain which unfolds from a box as you pull the string. The thought of Clayton had raised it: a clear little picture of George and me at luncheon almost exactly a year ago; a vivid memory of a conversation which took place while Clayton hovered in and out of the room, the perfect unobtrusive manservant. I could remember every word:

"It's going to be a tremendous legal battle," said George, helping himself to salad.

"But surely he's bound to get guardianship of his own child?"

"Not necessarily; it's a fine point of law, d'you see. The old man's will by-passed him, and the money went to the child, *provided* the uncle or some suitable person stood guardian. No one expected the uncle to predecease the old man, but human nature discounts car and plane crashes—one just doesn't like to think of them in relation to oneself, that's all."

"I must say, it's a fascinating case, I've read every word. So has Marjorie. We feel that someone should get the poor little boy right away from his ravening relatives."

"So they should—if they can. I can't help being glad it's not my case. Two more unsuitable guardians than the father or the aunt can't be imagined—both blackguarding each other in public to try and keep control of a child *and* a fortune."

"And neither of them caring how much they damage the child."

"Exactly. Clayton, tell Mrs. Jason this is the best sauce she's ever made."

"I will, Sir."

"Talking of guardians, Jenny, I can't help feeling we've been remiss about Ilona. It's time something was put on paper about her."

"Oh sweetie, we don't ever fly together, you know we don't."

"We go by car together. Can't overlook that these days."

"How gloomy you are. Anyway, I once asked Marjorie and Bill and they'd love to look after her if anything happened to us."

"Something might happen to *them*, we might be in a multiple car crash together."

"Ilona, too. Who said I married an optimist? But George, we can't provide for *everything*."

"True. But we should have one legal guardian down on paper, anyway. It lessens an executor's difficulties."

"We'll see about it," I promised, "next time we add something to our wills. But not this very minute . . . with John hammering away at me about Geneviève's summer series."

"I don't suppose there's any hurry. Just let's bear it in mind."

And it had gone straight out of my mind until today. No doubt Clayton guessed that. We might have slipped into Mr. Saunders' office at any time when we were passing, but Clayton knew it wasn't like us to pay visits there without appointment. Clayton knew our habits just as well as he knew the running of our house. A duplicate of George's engagement book lay on his study desk upstairs. A duplicate of mine lay by the telephone so that anyone needing me could check on my movements, or make a necessary appointment for Jenny-Geveniève's double life.

I considered the possibility of Clayton and Elizabeth in league, and sweat ran faster down my spine. Had Clayton been planted in our household? Surely not—the marked newspaper cutting gave the lie to that idea; the source of information had come first from outside—and then what? Then perhaps Clayton had been approached for information? Been paid for it? My heart hammered in my chest. The sickness had left me very weak, but I must summon up my strength, and make a plan.

The carriage clock on the chimneypiece struck six. Ilona would be on the way home, bless her; feet dragging on the pavements as she made her way back to the home that was no longer a home, only a place which held a hidden, gathering threat. Growing fury shook me from head to foot. If Elizabeth had wanted money, I would have given it to her, willingly. But she was greedy. She wanted it all, just as she had wanted everything as a child, and resented my sharing it. Well, she was not going to get it. I had only to survive the night, and in the morning I would change my will. It was as simple as that. *And* I was not to be lured into 'committing suicide' either. I had only to be careful. Careful and clever, and not too much afraid.

It was plain now what to do. I mustn't try to sidestep. Things must be made easy, so very easy, for Elizabeth.

I put out my hand and rang the bell.

"You rang, Madam? Are we better?" Clayton's long pallid face oozed carefully prepared concern. (That was one of his dreadful little habits of speech. 'Are we better?' and: 'How is *our* cold today?')

"Not too good," I tried to make my voice more feeble.

"I'm sorry to hear that, Madam. What can I get you? Orange juice? Soda-water? A nice egg-flip, now?"

I shuddered. ('No, thanks very much. No more little doses of gripewater before the last big drugging takes place.' That would be late at night—in a hot drink? I was gambling on it, anyway.) "Simply couldn't face a thing." I moved weakly and pressed a hand on my stomach, now perfectly steady. "Not a thing. Such *pains*."

"Madam *has* been unfortunately lately." He clucked round me like a big soft hen. Patting in the blanket, stroking the sheet into place as if it were a cat. I felt really sick again, mesmerized by that disgusting hand, with its dry-ridged nails a shiny plastic-looking pink.

"I'd like another hot-water bottle, and please tell Mrs. Jason that I don't want anything to eat later."

"Not a *thing*?" His face expressed incredulous concern. "Madam will feel terrible by the morning if she doesn't eat."

('Madam will feel worse if she does.')

"I might have a delicious hot drink last thing." Watching him under my eyelashes I could see no change in his expression. "I'm sure Miss Lemprière will make it for me."

"Of *course* I will see to it for Madam."

('This touching devotion; faithful unto death. At least, till bedtime; perhaps the same thing.')

"If Miss Lemprière's busy Mrs. Jason could just see Ilona

has her bath, and get her in here to bed sooner than usual. We'll both have an early night."

"It's not my business, Madam, but I wonder you don't let Miss Lemprière have Ilona. You need all the rest you can get." There. Good old Clayton. In a moment he would have my head down on his bosomly chest, sobbing my little heart out. Kind, soft, poisonous old he wet-nurse.

"I like having her in here." I allowed my lower lip to tremble. "It's all got me down rather, tonight."

"I'm sure it has, Madam, I'm sure it must. I'm sure we must all ever so admire you for the way you've taken it."

He went away at last, giving a final sweaty pat to the eiderdown as he went. When I had my filled hot-water bottle and was left in peace I was able to relax a little. I hoped and believed that nothing would be tried just yet.

It was still light, though near the hour of dusk. Dusk outside and inside the house. I thought of George, but my carefully gathered courage began to ebb. So I thought of Christopher in Paris, and wondered what blonde he was giving the works to now. Strange, that he was ignorant of all this. What would he say when I told him? "Hysteria, Jenny darling; all women are too imaginative." Or would he just think me crazy with persecution mania? Without the diary as proof he could hardly be blamed.

Time passed slowly. Lying here I could keep track of my household by the sounds. There was Clayton's soft tread on the stairs; Elizabeth's brisker one as she went up and down to her room, music from the hi-fi in the drawing room as she opened and closed the door. Mrs. Jason's voice besought Ilona to dry herself properly, dear, do. All down the street, in houses both sides of us, similar sounds and activities must be taking place. It soothed me to think of it, but at the same time made the danger that threatened both more unreal and more appalling: as if Dr. No had appeared in the drawing room.

Perhaps, after all, it was stupid to fight. No fortune was worth Ilona's happiness—such as this was now George was dead and she had only me. Perhaps I should offer Elizabeth Grandfather's fortune, if she would go away and leave us both in peace. Geneviève could easily support us. But Elizabeth couldn't accept, that was obvious. What would people—what would Morell—think if I were suddenly dependent on a job? At the best, blackmail. At the worst——

My mind suddenly caught itself up with a jerk. *The tablets.* I must check if those new ones were still in my dressing-table drawer. I got out of bed, and fumbled for them. Here was the bottle just as I had last seen it, only space left for three or four tablets. Had I guessed wrong? Was something else, something unsuspected I could not guard against, to be the instrument of death? I turned the bottle round in my hand and carefully examined it, shaking the tablets out on to my hand. There were twenty-one, and I had taken four. That was correct. But surely these at the bottom of the bottle were rather large? Yes—eight were ordinary innocent tablets of aspirin.

I replaced them grimly in the bottle. No doubt they would be removed next day, before the police were summoned by my distracted sister. It was certain where the eight missing tablets would turn up: in my hot drink. Elizabeth's timing was admirable, so was the way she turned everything to account. There had been my call to Morell, for instance, most of which she must have overheard. (And why hadn't he come?) What else could explain it but a sudden guilty desire to confess? And then the testing wait had proved too long, my spirit had quailed, and on impulse I had taken action against myself, as I'd already taken action against George.

And there were other things to admire about Elizabeth: there was her foresight. If she had stood to gain directly by two deaths, suspicion must have fallen on her, after that sudden reappearance; but as a mere watcher over Ilona, who would suspect her? She was too clever to move fast, so it would surely be some time before the fortune was misused.

A sound of pattering footsteps in the passage, and Ilona ran into the room, followed by a skittish Clemmie. A shame to crush signs of better spirits, but I had to keep up my rôle.

"Darling, *hush*! Please, not so much row——"

"Oh, poor Mummy." She flung her small form into my arms. I held her tight.

"Better day, sweetie?"

"Mmmm." She was brave, now. She would never tell me that it had been a beast of a day. My heart filled with bitter indignation towards Elizabeth. Did she really intend the child to wake and find me unconscious in my bed? Such brutality seemed incredible. And yet, to convince, neither she nor Clayton must come to my room unsummoned. I think, if I had had the means of killing Elizabeth then, I would have cold-bloodedly done so. Mother love is a tremendous stiffener of the spine.

"Sweetheart, just tonight we'll banish Clemmie, I want a very quiet night, this once. Not his snuffles, only your snores and mine." I smiled into her pale face, and stroked her cheek. It was brutal to thwart her in any way. "Aunt Liz can take him down. Shall I read you a story?" I had seen her face pucker as her eye lit on George's photograph.

"Per-lease. Can I have *The Lion, the Witch and the Wardrobe?*"

As I opened it I wondered what had dictated her choice. The need for reassurance, for it to be reiterated that light will prevail? As I began to read, so I prayed that Ilona's choice of book was a sign to me, a tenuous promise that however dangerous our situation we should yet stumble somehow to survival. Ilona lay relaxed beside me, and whenever anything alarming happened in the story she gave a deep satisfied gurgle of delight.

"And that's the end of the chapter. Bed now, honeybee."

She flung her arms tight round my neck, and pressed her face into it.

"Ilona, *listen,* darling. Are you hearing me?"

Sniff.

"Please, sweetie, I know it's all awful, but try to think about the lion, try hard not to cry so much tonight——"

"Boooo——"

She quieted eventually, and I got her sad shivering form safely tucked up in bed. By the time she fell asleep I was exhausted, ready to cry myself. One look in the glass, however, and I could only feel cold satisfaction with the day's effects. That hollow-cheeked woman, with the drawn face and haunted eyes, she was a fit subject for what might be the night's events. I could not have looked more like a potential suicide.

14

I would not spend another such a night
Though 'twere to buy a world of happy days
RICHARD III

It was ten o'clock when Elizabeth brought my hot drink.

"There's heaven knows what in it," she whispered as she leant over me, and cast a look sideways at sleeping Ilona. "Brandy, the lot. Pretty potent stuff—do you loads of good."

(Heaven, or hell, knew what indeed.)

Mrs. Jason's step could be heard on the stairs. She was on her way to bed. Now she was just outside my door. Elizabeth raised her voice slightly, she spoke slow and very clear.

('*Admirable*,' I thought, 'throw it to the back of the gallery.')

"How rotten you look, poor Jenny. As if all the troubles of the world are on your mind."

"They are." (Make it easy, make it easy for Elizabeth.)

I began to drag myself out of bed.

"What is it, darling, tell me? I'll get it for you."

"My pills," I said loudly, "the sleeping ones."

"Don't take more than one, will you? Promise?" The hesitant note of anxiety; sisterly doubt.

"Two, perhaps. You've no idea what it's like, getting no sleep after all this." I allowed a note of hysteria into my voice. Mrs. Jason's steps diminished up the stairs. Elizabeth placed the bottle by the bed, and stood back as if to admire my finished portrait. Then she picked up Clemmie, and went away. Now I should be left alone all night.

Or so I gambled.

The whole chance I took for myself and Ilona was based on this assumption. Or was I wrong? There might be some other plan. Perhaps the nightcap beside me was only so little drugged as to send me into heavy sleep, when whatever evil was premeditated could be done. So I ought to provide myself with a weapon, and when the door opened quietly and the assassin crept towards my bed, must be prepared to act without hesitation or mercy. But I didn't really think this would be necessary, for they

126

would have had to deal with Ilona; and that would be undesirable—for some years.

Thoughtfully I put out my hand to touch the tumbler beside me. 'And in the cup an union shall he throw. . . .' 'Good Gertrude, do not drink. . . .' 'I will, my lord; I pray you, pardon me.'

If it weren't for Ilona, wouldn't I have given in? Almost I wanted to, without George. Here was no poison, but a peace-offering. No one could blame me if I took it. The cup might be innocent, the waking as usual. I put it to my lips, sipped, and sipped again. It wasn't unpleasant: alcoholic enough to hide a foreign taste—or very nearly. There was a faint dry bitterness, which might have gone unnoticed if unexpected.

Elizabeth must feel anxious now. Was she being sick in the loo, as she had on the day she drugged Mother, or was she too hardened for reactions? Throughout the long night ahead I must make no sound, for the enemy who might listen at my door must have her anxiety assuaged. Still, it was unreasonable to be too quiet. I need not have drunk the poison yet.

I slipped cautiously out of bed to find my weapon, a jagged-looking piece of bright-coloured stone which George had ridiculously insisted on bringing back from Turkey, a curious souvenir of our mountain expeditions. I remembered the day so well: the harsh blue sky, the kestrel making its expectant wheeling sweep above, the wild exhilaration which had seized us in that empty and austere landscape; and George finding the stone on the summit of the small crag where we stood, and saying, "Keep it, darling. We'll look at it when we're a nice tamed middle-aged couple, all safe and comfortable in town." Well, he couldn't have foreseen its future use, I thought grimly, as I wrapped it in one end of a handkerchief and twisted the other ends together, to keep it there and give myself a better hold. It came from a harsh land; it was as if it had brought into our civilized household something of the essence of that wild and alarming place where it had formed.

In my aloneness I was glad of that stone. And back in bed I kept my right hand over it. Not really a formidable weapon, but it might do for defence in a surprise attack.

I had plenty of time to think, that night. It wasn't safe to fall asleep. Now and then I began to doze, but each time a sense of danger jerked me back to consciousness. I lay and watched the moonlight move across the curtains. From the far distance came an owl's cry. The bird, probably in Regents Park, must be as lonely as I felt.

Enough of this self-pity. Reverend Mother would have said that no one ever was alone, however hard and dangerous the circumstance. Perhaps all these terrible things had come upon me because I had turned my back on my religion. But why should they touch Ilona? There would be an answer to that, too—they had an answer to everything. I tried to pray, but my mind felt rusty as an unoiled hinge; it was hard to concentrate. I tried to pray for George and Ilona, that one might find peace, and the other be protected. My words didn't feel as if they got anywhere, it was like speaking into a telephone when you know the line is dead. In the end all I did was lie there saying 'please God, protect Ilona, please protect Ilona,' over and over again. I didn't dare kneel; now, if ever, was a time when no sound must be made.

It was then I heard her on the stairs. First it was just a creak such as any oldish house gives out at night as wood expands or contracts; followed by another sound, nearer; as if someone had slipped on a step. And then I knew in cold certainty that there was someone outside my door.

Every muscle in my body tautened. My hand twisted on my makeshift weapon, and I found myself wondering coldly if I could use my arm muscles, they felt so rigid. Very cautiously I turned my head towards the door. A shaft of moonlight illumined it halfway up to just above the centre panel. There were bright glints of light on the faceted doorknob, and as I watched, the light flickered suddenly and winked at me. The handle had begun to turn.

Immediately I realized my mistake. No sound would be as bad to my murderer as the wrong sort of sound. Weren't the heavily drugged noisy? A real coma surely wasn't a soundless affair like Ilona's sleep. I breathed deep, and gave a little choke. Now the door slid open as quiet as a snake. I was in darkness, but the figure in the doorway was clearer than a ghost. All the same, I must be careful. I lowered my lids, and breathed as hoarse and rattling as I could.

It was a good thing I shut my eyes, for without warning a pencil of torchlight beamed straight home on my face. I could see the glare against my lids. They mustn't flicker. With an effort I kept them still, while a new panic formed in my mind. Did the cup stand where its untouched contents could be seen?

The next minute was amongst the worst of my life. The light had moved from my face, and there was no sound. I didn't dare open my eyes, and could only trust to luck that my snores and gulps were convincing—and that Ilona wouldn't wake. The door might still be open, or it might have shut without my hearing it. I didn't know if someone was now moving towards me with deadly intention in the dark. . . .

And then I knew we were safe, and my prayer had been answered. For the board creaked loudly on the stairs again, just as it had before. I opened my eyes, and where Elizabeth had stood a minute ago the moonlight shone reassuringly across the panels of the closed door.

"Wake up, darling! Ilona, *wake*———"

It seemed she would never hear my whisper; yet she mustn't be startled, or she might make a noise. Who else was awake in the house, I wondered; did murderers sleep with a good conscience on the nights their victims died? 'Sleep no more! Macbeth does murder sleep. . . .' That was only a play, even if Shakespeare had written it. How my mind was stuck on him tonight—today.

I put my right hand over Ilona's small mottled paw, and her eyes opened, and stared straight into mine.

"Listen, my darling—can you keep completely quiet, like a mouse, because I'm going to tell you something?"

A nod. Her eyes, still clouded with sleep, looked very serious at the thought of secrets at seven o'clock in the morning.

"Marjorie and Bill have asked us to breakfast, and as they've asked no one else we're going to creep out of the house quite silently, see?"

She lay there, and considered me. After this last night I hoped that I didn't look too alarming. "*Why* have they asked us to breakfast, Mummy? Can't we take Aunt Liz?"

A bell-like note had crept into her voice. I put my hand over her mouth.

"If you don't keep mum as mum, I won't take *you*——"

The feeble joke and threat together worked. At half past seven we were ready; I, in a suit, with my largest bag slung over my shoulder, Ilona brushed but unwashed.

"Now—dead silent till we're through the enemy lines, chum."

I opened the door, and listened. Clayton was in the dining room; I heard him shake out the breakfast cloth. Finger to my lips, I waited; Ilona dead silent at my side and in the spirit of the thing—the Lone Ranger, at least.

There was a rattle at the letterbox in the hall, the papers were pushed through and fell with a thump. A few seconds more and I heard Clayton emerge from the dining room, pick up the papers, and retreat into the back regions. For at least five minutes he would be busy with the headlines. I began to creep downstairs, and Ilona followed. We were at the front door, my hand was on it, when the thousand-to-one chance happened: the strap of my shoulder bag slipped—perhaps the prong wasn't properly through its hole— and, before I could salvage it, the bag fell noisily to the ground. . . .

"Oh, *Mummee*," breathed Ilona, and clapped her hand to her mouth. There we were, caught, like two living statues, and Clayton still as another, silhouetted against the kitchen light, the morning paper dangling from his hand. . . .

We all three stood and stared at one another. I felt paralyzed; Ilona certainly knew the secret was at an end, but even she got the sense of urgency, and was silent. As for Clayton—well, his face was in shadow, but surely this stricken dumbness on his part was more than the slight surprise he might feel because his employer and her daughter were slipping early from the house. I think he meditated swift action, but was hampered by Ilona's presence.

"Good morning, Madam. I didn't expect to see *you*. You're bright and early." His voice was unnecessarily loud. My hand was already on the doorknob, but it was like being in one of those awful dreams where everything slows down and you try to run from someone and your legs won't work. He took two quick steps towards us as if to intervene.

"We're going out," piped up Ilona.

Then the stairs creaked above us, as they had last night, and, my hand still on the doorknob as if frozen to it, and with safety within reach, I glanced up and saw Elizabeth, like a tall silent shadow on the landing. She was wrapped tight in a thin grey wrapper, and her bright hair fell to her shoulders. She looked more like a descending angel than a would-be murderess. This one moment I could imagine her harmless, and Clayton the perfect manservant hurrying to please. For all that, my mouth went dry. I knew myself at bay. The air shrieked with a heavy, tense vibration—I could almost swear it was audible, like wind in a telegraph wire. It was compounded of desperation, and shock, and fear—it spoke to me, as if I were an animal, of danger. *Kill.* . . .

I swear it was only Ilona's presence that made them hesitate a second too long. Then came salvation. There was the sound of a small truck pulling up outside, followed by the tuneless whistle of our milkman as he dumped four bottles on the doorstep. Elizabeth and Clayton froze. It was they who were living statues now, while Ilona, bless her, slipped forwards, raised the flap of the letterbox, and yelled hopefully through it: "Allie! How's-your-cat-that-had-kittens-on-Saturday? Did you keep one for me?"

Some large pork-sausage fingers pushed through the letterbox and wriggled within an inch of her nose.

"Sure did, Ilona. A lovely tortoiseshell maddermazell with three white paws and an orange one. But what's Clemmie going to say to her, eh? And what about yer Ma?"

"Ask her. She's here. We're coming out." She tugged at my hand, and I found the strength to turn the doorknob, and pull back the heavy door. Light drowned out the gloom of the hall. Ilona was in full chatter at my side. "It's only a *little* kitten, Mum, I could have it, couldn't I? And tortoiseshell—they're rare, Mum, they honestly are——"

I stood on the threshold of a world given back to us, and turned my head towards the hall. Beyond the reach of that wonderful light were the silent forms: Clayton in his decorous manservant's black, and Elizabeth, the tall grey wraith now three steps down from the top of the stairs. I looked at them; and they looked back at me with an inscrutable and beckoning terror, as Pluto must have looked at Eurydice when she turned her face towards the light.

My lips felt frozen into a smile. "Oh, you've got up, Liz. I've something to do very early, and I didn't want to wake you. I'll drop Ilona off at school on my way home." The flimsy explanation made no concession to probability. It took all my courage to add: "I shall be back to lunch."

She came one hesitant step further down the stairs. "Jenny— I'm sure you shouldn't rush about like this, so early. Let *me* take Ilona wherever it is; or Clayton."

"Good heavens no, my dear. I feel fine this morning, quite recovered. A fast day suits me—didn't even drink your posset; I fell asleep so heavily, and so soon." We were across the threshold, and Ilona skipped down the steps. Allie was apologizing to me about the kitten. If it was an entire litter I could still have flung my arms around his neck and kissed him.

"Thanks, Orpheus," I said, and: "we'd *love* to have her."

15

We have scotched the snake, not killed it
MACBETH

Marjorie's face was devoid of powder, and showed surprise. Her feet were thrust into Turkish slippers, and if anyone looked unready for early morning guests, it was she. All the way down the street I had wondered how to manage explanations, embarrassed as I was by Ilona's piercingly truthful gaze. Now she took it out of my hands: "You don't *look* ready for a breakfast party, Marjorie. I s'pose we're early—silly old Mum made us get up at *crack* of dawn."

"Did she, darling?" Marjorie gave me an anxious look, and shivered in the morning air. "You'd both better come along in, anyway."

Over Ilona's head I mouthed, "*Must* speak to you," and she responded with a reassuring nod and led the way indoors. Blessed Marjorie, my relief was intense. Even the incredible reason for our presence would be possible to explain. She was already smoothing things over for Ilona's benefit.

"Your silly old Mum has mussed up her dates, the invitation was for next week, poppet. But I bet your appetites have sharpened on the way, so I'm sure we can rustle up some breakfast. My Mrs. Jainey doesn't get here till nine, but come and have eggs and bacon. Bill isn't up yet."

She led us through to the kitchen but soon despatched Ilona to the drawing room with instructions to turn on the fire and give the white Pekinese puppies their puppy-mix.

"*Now*, Jenny, what is it? You look like a ghost on the verge of breakdown."

My laugh was strained. "So long as it's not a *mad* ghost."

"Don't be a fool, honey. Hurry up and tell, before Ilona comes romping back again."

"I can't hurry, it's a long story." I sat down and rested my head on my hands. They shook.

"Then you'd better tell it right from the start, while I cook these eggs, or your daughter will murder me."

"Murder!" A long shudder shook me from head to foot.

She gave me an odd look. "Is that what it is, then?"

So I told her, as well as I could, all that I thought and suspected, and had at last come to learn, about Elizabeth. Marjorie heard me through without interruption as she expertly manipulated the frying-pan, grill and coffee-pot. Then she said: "I believe you. I always thought it intensely fishy, that reappearance. And so did Bill. He couldn't bear her, you know. Neither of us could. Bill said she had two feet of surface charm, and underneath it all the chill of death. Seems he was right. That diary has a touch of the macabre."

"Had. I'm sure she got rid of it double quick."

"So she—or your precious Clayton—killed George. Or both—though the connection between them doesn't seem quite clear, *except* that he knew Ilona had no appointed guardian."

"I think she must have got in touch with him somehow *after* the news paragraph about me. He always hated me." Again I shuddered violently. "You do realize there could be another explanation of all this? That I've made the whole thing up. Twisted it to suit my book; that I'm mad as a hatter."

"You wouldn't suggest it, if you were."

"It could be my mad cunning. Isn't that what they're like?" I was trembling. Marjorie gave a half-smile, and shook her head.

"You aren't mad, Jenny. Relax. On the verge of hysterics, perhaps—and who wouldn't be?—but not mad. I think Elizabeth probably is—that diary! And you can't really look into her eyes. Had you noticed? I was told that once, by an eminent psychiatrist: that you can't really *see* into a mad person's eyes. Yours are as clear and normal as they ever were. Nothing would make me believe you could murder George."

"The Inspector thinks so."

"You *must* tell him everything, you know. How can he help you, unless you do?"

"Without the diary I've no proof of what she's like—of what she's capable. I did ask them to send him round, but he didn't come."

"He will. Then you send him on to see Mrs. Whatshername,

whose husband had read the diary to her. Wasn't Elizabeth's name in it?"

Blessed Marjorie! Relief brought me close to tears. Why hadn't *I* thought of so simple a step? Thank God for the curiosity of Ian Maddox.

"Why didn't I remember that?"

"Exhaustion, honey. And tell the Inspector about the marked paragraph in the Swiss paper, too."

"Yes. And there's one other thing to be done today. Please, Marjorie, don't say I mustn't. First I'm going to my lawyer, to make you and Bill Ilona's legal guardians in the event of anything happening to me, as you said we could. And then—then I'm going to leave you and Bill everything we possess, without mention of Ilona at all. Knowing you'd keep it for her. That will make her safe, double safe for now. And keeping her out of it will make you safe as well. Till this is all cleared up."

She didn't argue, simply nodded and gave me her affectionate smile. "You do that, Jenny. Though remember——" and the smile grew mischievous, "you might be tempting me and Bill to —oh Lord!"

"Go on—say it: to murder. Pretty, isn't it—that Grandfather's funny little inventions should have held the seed of this —this incredible poison in it."

"How corny can you get? Money is the root of all evil. Only a few people are big enough to handle money, or bear the lack of it."

I was silent. There was little I could claim in the way of achievement, except of a meretricious kind; if you counted out my success with George and Ilona. But George—oh, it was George, at least, who had been born for happiness; his kindly, loving nature had ensured it for him—no one could have said I tilled on thorny ground there . . . Marjorie was speaking again, and I hadn't heard a word: "—delighted to have had you here, but Ben's got a touch of what the doctor thinks is *real* 'flu, and I'd sooner not expose you both to it, you're so vulnerable just now. In a day or two he'll be all right—you know what he is, roaring temperature one day, playing games the next."

This was a blow. I meant to go back myself, and brave the snake, now that its fangs were drawn even if it wasn't scotched entirely. But I had counted on leaving Ilona at the Hellevans. It was the one place I thought possible for her then in her unhappiness.

Marjorie peered at me anxiously. "She had pneumonia last time, with 'flu, didn't she?"

"Yes."

"There's no one else you could visit?"

"With all *this* on my mind?" I said angrily; and then, "Sorry, darling. But at least may she stay here when I go to Cumberland? Christopher asked us, and it may give me a chance to do some Elizabeth-stalking."

"Of course she may. But you don't want to take too many risks yourself," she looked at me doubtfully. "You really should hand it all over to that Inspector. In the meantime, can't you take her to an hotel?"

"At the moment Elizabeth *thinks* that I guess what's wrong, she suspects, but she can't *know*. It's all chess and uncertainty. Given the chance, I might even pin George's murder on her. If I don't go back at all she may take fright—and flight."

Marjorie, I knew, would not have agreed with my distrust of the police. But should the Inspector visit Mrs. Maddox, and my story be backed up by Ian Maddox, it was still only guesswork on my part about George. Surely they would write it off as distraught imagining. No, it was my wits versus Elizabeth's. But till Marjorie could take Ilona, was it right to expose ourselves to whatever situation existed in my house? Yet almost obsessionally I wanted to find out the truth for George, after failing him so badly when he voiced his doubts about my twin. Surely, with the inheritance diverted, Ilona *must* be safe?

Marjorie spoke for me, when she said: "Of course, after this morning you'll have drawn her fangs. And you can lean heavily on the subject of Bill and me, she'll know you've talked to us, and she can't kill all London, so she must lie low. There's no other step she can take."

"Except revenge."

"It would bring ruin on herself, and she wouldn't gain. I don't think it's in her character. She's far too prudent."

"No, there's nothing she can do—with safety."

136

I think we both felt happier when we decided this. And, by the time Ilona was called in to breakfast, I could eat mine hungrily, relieved from any further presentiment of immediate danger.

Our street looked cheerful enough when I returned home. Daffodils, crocuses, and striped yellow and scarlet parrot tulips flared in the window boxes. The house—it would take time before I could look on it as 'mine' rather than 'ours'—looked no different from the rest: gaily painted and window-boxed, nothing ominous about it. No one could have guessed with what sensations of dread I turned my key in the lock and opened the front door. I almost expected to find Clayton and Elizabeth still where they had stood that morning—two grey, waiting forms, filled with evil determination, like the satanic governess and manservant in *The Turn of the Screw*.

The hall was unoccupied, the house light and airy. I could hear footsteps in the kitchen, and waited, tensed, for Clayton to appear, but it was only Mrs. Jason, her hair screwed up on top of her head in a Victorian knob, and on her face her usual kindly smile. "Well!" With sturdy hands she smoothed down her apron. "You took the start of us all this morning, Madam, and no mistake. You're better, I take it? That Ilona! Who'd have thought she could keep a still tongue for five seconds? Let alone five minutes."

"Yes, thanks, I'm better. I completely forgot until today that Mrs. Hellevan had asked us round to breakfast." It sounded unbelievable enough as I said it, but Mrs. Jason accepted it.

"She'd no call to get you up early like that, not after what you just been through. What's the telephone for, I'd like to know. That Clayton, he's gone out. Said there was something of the Master's at the cleaners you'd forgotten to collect." Mrs. Jason sniffed. "He's been gone all of an hour. Miss Lemprière hasn't rung though. She's in the drawing room."

So there was only one of them to deal with. Outside the drawing room I hesitated, but it seemed wise to go in at once and confront Elizabeth.

She was seated on the sofa, her hands clasped round her knees. Her long blonde hair, unknotted, fell in strands over her

137

shoulders. She had her eyes closed, and might have been in a semi-trance. The record-player was on, the music from *Scheherazade* wove its palpable dream, barbaric and sensuous, with Arabian Nights nostalgia. Elizabeth's absorption was too great, I thought coldly. Those hands clasping her knees were too tense for a dreamy state. If she wanted me to speak first, she could wait. I dropped into a chair opposite and sat silent, staring at her, while the music wove to its end. There was a click, then silence. Elizabeth opened her great eyes, yawned, and smiled with affectionate, easy warmth.

"Hello, Jenny. You seem better, I must say. You gave us all a jolt, getting up at that hour. Didn't know you *could*. . . ."

"I had to, sometimes, as Geneviève."

"Journalism, was it?" Her smile now mocked me. "John pulling the-show-must-go-on stuff, heartless beast?"

"It wasn't journalism. Or John."

"I refuse to make more guesses." She leaned back and shut her eyes. The pose was easy, her linked fingers still tense.

"You needn't guess. I came in here to tell you; you're always so interested, Liz dear, in plans for Ilona." Even to my own ears it sounded ironic.

Elizabeth yawned again, and gazed at her fingertips.

"My sweet Jenny, you're a marvellous mother. What *could* you be doing at that hour for the poor baby? I'm all agog."

I sorted words into careful sequence in my mind. (Casually does it.) "Poor Marjorie's in a flap because her child has 'flu. She's so busy during the day, the early morning seemed a good quiet time for both of us to get things straightened out. They may go abroad, you know, in two or three weeks."

"Jenny, I've now *quite* lost the thread!"

I watched her closely. "Before George—died, we talked things over and decided to appoint legal guardians for Ilona in case . . . anything ever happened to both of us."

Elizabeth sat very still. I consciously relaxed. "Now there's only me; and if *I* died, there's only you, Liz. But you'll marry, you might not always want to be bothered with a niece."

The protest was quick, and warm: "Idiotic Jenny! Why, I *adore* Ilona."

138

"Ummm. . . . It would depend quite a lot on the man you married. Anyway, as that's an unknown quantity, George and I fixed on Marjorie and Bill. Ilona loves Ben, and Marjorie wanted a daughter but can't have more children, so——" (Slowly—'mustn't babble.')

"A very wise move, Jenny dear." No hint of sarcasm in her voice. Could I possibly be wrong?

"Yes. I had to see the lawyer, anyway, this morning. So I got it all nicely fixed with Marjorie first; and Ilona saw the peke puppies, which took her mind off things."

"A tough time mothers have of it, don't they? Never able to put themselves first. Anyway, it doesn't seem to be *my* fate."

"Why not? You've been engaged once already, haven't you?"

"What made you say that, Jenny?"

"You'd worn a ring on your left hand when you first came to us. George noticed it."

"Oh, one up to George." She gave a bitter smile. "It wasn't —workable. I didn't even want to—discuss it." When she spoke George's name I felt an impulse to hit her.

"I made a new will, too, while I was about it. There'll be a more complex one later on. But just now I've simplified it by leaving everything to Marjorie and Bill." Did she give a little gasp? I couldn't be quite sure.

"You have? In trust for Ilona, I suppose?"

"No trust. I've simply explained everything to the Hellevans. You see, Grandfather's affairs were so complex; and now there's George's, and then—if Marjorie and Bill are ever needed— there'll be mine. It's too much to deal with now. So this way it's easy until I'm—well, ready to cope."

"And what did the stalwart lawyer say to that?"

"Oh, he approved. He's known Marjorie all her life."

"I see. Steel true, blade straight. Lucky in your friends, aren't you, Jenny? I suppose she's his niece?"

The remark was an awful revelation of how her mind worked. She must have seen something in my face, for she added quickly: "I only asked, Jenny, because you were always such an innocent."

"But growing less so every day."

She was silent, and I watched her curiously. By my reckoning she was already once a murderess, and had just failed to account for me. If she had succeeded, what had she planned for today? She would have sat there, I suppose, decorous in black; and then—grotesque thought—would Clayton have sat opposite, to discuss, in his unctuous soft voice, how the spoils should be acquired, and how divided? Not openly, perhaps, for there was still Mrs. Jason to be duped; so the bleak confederacy would have remained veiled beneath the façade of mistress and man-servant. Anyway, he might be merely her insignificant tool.

"Morell rang up," she said suddenly.

I stared. "Did he say why?" I certainly hoped not.

"Don't you know? *You* asked to see him."

I ignored this. "When is he coming? Today?"

She shrugged. "He meant to come in this morning. I told him you were out, that you'd be back to lunch."

I had to prompt her: "So what did he say to that?"

She gave me a sly look. "Nothing."

I couldn't challenge it, so I broached another subject: "Lucy Starr's coming here until you and I go to Cumberland, to Christopher."

It was her turn to stare. "I shouldn't have thought you wanted visitors just now! What a ghastly bore for us—for you."

"Lucy's different. She's—unobtrusive." My voice hardened. "She can sleep in George's dressing room, and work there too."

"*Work?*"

"Geneviève's not *dead and done for,* you know." I laughed, and she looked at me sharply. "I'm rich now, Liz, but money's uncertain stuff these days, it would be stupid to let slip that sort of highly-paid journalism while I've a child on my hands."

"You mean John expects fresh articles *now?*"

"Oh no, he's got a lot of material already. Lucy can work it over for me before we go away—that's why I've been generously lent her. Why, it's almost lunch time."

As we left the room the soft clear voice said behind me on a note of pure malice: "Bereavement seems to lend you energy, Jenny. I wonder why?"

Luncheon passed peaceably enough. Clayton served it, even more solicitously than usual. "I *was* sorry to be out so long this morning, Madam. You didn't need me, I hope? Such a *crush* everywhere. You can't say London's what it was." He held a dish of peas before me. His hand was shaking. Perhaps the sight of me still alive turned him up more than my corpse would have done. I thought suddenly that he would have made an excellent embalmer; Mr. Joyboy. How George would laugh, I must tell——

The spoon clattered from my hand.

"Do have more than that, Jenny. What will Christopher say, if I take you up there skin and bone?"

"He won't notice. Christopher's very tough."

"He'll notice *you*." She had parted her hair in the centre, and looped it back into a huge plaited knot. It lent her the look of a pale Florentine girl, quattrocento; fragile and elegiac.

Beautiful as a Botticelli. Clayton was watching her too. The tip of his tongue protruded between his lips, like a sly watcher. Titania and Bottom, I thought disgustedly. Did he want her? Of course he must. The thought was incredibly revolting, like watching an exquisite sticky flower trap a meat fly. The atmosphere of the house seemed contaminated by their presence.

"I'm not hungry," I said truthfully, and pushed away my plate.

By four o'clock that afternoon there was still no sign of the Inspector. I drifted about the house comforted by the thought of cosy Mrs. Jason belowstairs. At a quarter past four I went to my room and rang the police station. At least tonight Lucy Starr's comfortable presence would be installed next door in George's dressing room. There would be no more terrors in the dark. I was physically safe at the moment, and cruel unhappiness about George filled my mind; if I couldn't take positive action against his killer, I should go mad.

A young police sergeant answered. "Oh yes, Mrs. Emerson, Inspector Morell said you might ring—but you're late. It's past four."

"But I didn't know he was expecting *me* to ring."

"But you're ringing now." There was disbelief in his voice.

"I only wanted to know why he hadn't come in."

"The Inspector's been very busy. He explained to Miss Lemprière. He left a message with her to say that if it was important, would you ring here before three o'clock."

Damn Elizabeth! Would I never learn? "I'm afraid the message didn't reach me. May I speak to the Inspector now, please?"

"Sorry Madam. He left over an hour ago."

"When do you expect him in again?"

"Not for two or three days. Just one moment, Madam." The receiver went dead, then his hand must have slipped on the mouthpiece for someone's voice said quite clearly: ". . . too late to get him at the airport now."

"Airport!" I cried, dismayed. "He hasn't left the country?"

There was an annoyed exclamation, then: "You weren't supposed to be in on that, Madam. Keep it to yourself, if you please."

"But *has* he?"

There was no answer, only a disapproving silence, so of course I knew. My mind raced. What *should* I do now?

"We shall be keeping in touch with the Inspector; if it's at all urgent, Madam, we can send someone round to see you, and ——" But I had made up my mind while he spoke. How could I explain to some brisk young officer straight from training college who would simply look on me as paranoid? Probably he wouldn't even check with Ian Maddox before dismissing my tale. I would have stood a better chance with Morell, however strong his distrust of me.

"No thanks, it will keep till he's back."

"We'll have the Inspector ring you when he returns, Madam."

"Yes—and please ask him, this time, not to leave a message with *anyone*."

That sounded paranoid enough. As I rang off I realized that I should have reminded them about Cumberland; but just then Clayton came to say that Miss Starr was in the drawing room. Anyway, it was the Inspector's fault if they had forgotten Christopher's invitation. I went downstairs to find Lucy; at least the reinforcements—my second bulldog!—had arrived.

16

. . . melted into air, into thin air
THE TEMPEST

"I do love stations. They smell so nice."

Ilona clung tenaciously to my left hand. She wasn't usually a clinger, but she was still a pale subdued Ilona, who in some ways had temporarily reverted to babyhood.

"I don't." My left foot slipped on a piece of orange-skin. Under my right arm were papers and magazines; a train case, packed with games to amuse my daughter on the long journey north, was in my right hand. A smut blew into my eye, and tears streamed down my face, increased by the overpowering smell of fog which always seems to haunt railway stations.

A few feet away from me stood Elizabeth, immaculately pretty in a new suit, a silk scarf tied pirate-fashion round her head. I glanced at her desperately, and her face crumpled into a grin.

"Do *something* to your eye, Jenny! That gorgeous make-up you're wearing is on your cheekbones now."

"No free hand." I disengaged Ilona and dabbed at my face.

"The train standing at Platform Two is the ten thirty-five for Carlisle . . . calling at——"

"Come on, Mum!" Ilona urged me, "we'll never get good seats. Corner ones. Did you see that pigeon do something on that lady's hat. Won't she be surprised when—I *am* glad I'm coming too."

I couldn't agree, although our separation would have been hateful just now. Once Christopher was drawn into this a showdown lay ahead; and I wished Ilona well out of it. No good fretting, but reverses dogged my steps. Yesterday, just before I was due to take Ilona to the Hellevans, Marjorie had telephoned.

"Jenny, I do hate to let you down, darling, but the most awful thing's happened! It's Ben. You know he's been better, but this morning he felt rotten again, and when he got out of bed his legs just folded under him, he's semi-paralysed——" there was a gulp in Marjorie's voice, "—the doctor says he's had polio; so lightly it wasn't diagnosed in time."

"Oh sweetie, I *am* sorry. Poor you—and poor Ben." I heard myself make all the optimistic remarks which are meant to reassure.

"Yes, I know. Some people only get left with a limp." She sounded thoroughly woebegone. "But the thing is: Ilona. We can't possibly take her now—we're in quarantine ourselves."

"Listen, Marjorie, please don't start to worry about that too. She must come to Christopher's with me, that's all." Oh God, was it safe?

"Can't you leave her with Reverend Mother at the convent? They'd be sweet to her."

"Yes—but they haven't all that attention to lavish on a single child, they're so busy. Any other time I would."

"It *is* difficult."

It was; but this was obviously no time to bother Marjorie with my own problems, huge though they were. "Don't you fuss about us, honey, we'll be fine," I said, with false confidence. So here we were, Elizabeth, Ilona and I, on the way north together, the one thing which should have been avoided.

There was a crowd at the ticket barrier for Platform Two. Early holiday-makers, with bulging cases. A porter pushed his way past with a hand truck and more luggage. I found myself temporarily separated from Elizabeth and Ilona, and called out to them to wait. My eye streamed, I raised my left hand to dab at it again, and dropped a magazine. As I bent to retrieve it someone behind me rammed a large suitcase hard against my legs, and sent me sprawling forwards. I suppose my head came into contact with the truck's edge for there was a blinding pain, I heard myself cry out, and then the world erupted in a swirl of coloured lights and darkness, as if someone had shaken a kaleidoscope before my eyes.

When I came round I was propped up against the bookstall. My nose was pouring blood, and for two or three minutes I was completely dazed. All round me there were people's legs—it was like cows closing in on a dog, and my first conscious sensations were first of pain, and then of claustrophobia. A woman's voice was asking: "You all right, love?" Two St. John ambulance men had arrived with a stretcher, but I managed to haul myself upright and stood swaying, the centre of a fascinated crowd. Someone murmured that I ought to sue the railways, and the porter with the truck moved quickly away.

He needn't have worried. I wasn't interested in what had caused my accident. Neither Elizabeth nor Ilona was in sight. Perhaps they had passed through the ticket barrier without seeing what happened. But—Ilona hadn't got her ticket! *I* had it. Panic gripped me. *Could* she have slipped through somehow? Were they already on the train? Ignoring suggestions that I should go home or have a cup of tea, I began shakily pushing my way towards Platform Two.

"No, truly I'm all right," I assured a St. John's man who implored me to have a quiet lie down in case of concussion, "I've got to catch that train, my little girl may be on it."

"There weren't no little girl with you, Madam." He thought I was having hallucinations.

"She went ahead, with my sister." I shook him off at last. The clock stood at ten thirty-two.

The ticket collector gave me an offended glare. "No, Madam, I have *not* seen a little girl such as you describe. If she had no ticket it would have been contrary to regulations to allow her through. May I see *your* ticket, please?"

At last I reached the train. Up the steps and along the corridor, peering through door after door, even knocking on the lavatory doors, shouting: "Ilona, *where are you?*" while people stared, thinking me mad—as indeed I almost was, mad with fear. My eye streamed, my train case was lost, the side of my head was one large agonizing throb.

Now I was out on the platform at the other end, and running down it, peering in again at the windows, asking the guard, asking anyone: "A tall woman—blonde—in a headscarf—little girl with chestnut hair." No one had seen them. Then, just as the train started to move slowly from the station, a tall elderly woman who had been seeing someone off put out a hand and laid it on my arm.

"Excuse me, I overheard you questioning the guard——"
My spirits rose. "*Yes?*"
"Well, someone fainted by the barrier a little while ago, and"—

"Oh." I stared at her dully, dredged by disappointment. "Thank you, but that wasn't my child, or my sister. It was me—that was when I lost them both."

"Yes, my dear, but I'm telling you I saw her—a tall blonde woman in a scarf, with this noticeable child, chestnut-haired."

"Where?" I stammered. "Which way?"

She gestured. "*That* way. They hadn't gone far when the child turned and started to pull back. Then the woman bent over her, and then someone came between, but the next time I saw them the child was quite limp, being carried. I thought she'd been taken ill, poor little thing. Are you all right? You look very white, dear."

"Quite all right," I said mechanically. "And then?"

"They went over to the taxi rank. There was a long grey car. One of these private taxis, I suppose."

"And you're sure you actually *saw* them get into it?"

"Oh yes." Her tone was offended. "If it *was* your sister." Obviously she was beginning to think the whole thing odd.

"I'm sure it was. Forgive me, I must hurry—and thank you."

She called after me: "There was a man waiting for them."

"The chauffeur, you mean?" I stopped, arrested in my flight.

"No—someone in the back—I just got the impression of a man's form, it's not that I'm *inquisitive*, but I did *happen* to notice, because it seemed so odd; I said so to Gladys, that's my daughter, it's odd, I said, *two* people fainting, at one time——"

I was already out of earshot.

Through the ticket barrier, push through the crowd, run, run. ("Hi, where's the fire?") There was the taxi rank, but no long grey car anywhere in sight. I came to a halt, uncertain what to do, and then I saw the blue police box ahead of me like an answer to prayer; but were they kept locked? As I reached it a hand touched my arm, and I whirled round with an exclamation of relief that they had found me. But all I saw was the familiar fat white face of Clayton.

"Not that way, Madam. I mean, there's no call to turn nasty."

"*Where is she?*" I gulped out. My lungs laboured. "What have you done with her, you brute, where is she?"

His grip was painful, and held unpleasant authority. My

rising hysteria was quelled, though rage and misery and fear mounted in equal tension.

"That's better," he spoke softly like a sick-nurse, surveying my appalled face. "We do like to keep everything nice, don't we?"

"I'll do anything, give you anything you want," my voice rose again. "If you'll only bring her back."

"Ah, that's what I like to hear, Mrs. Emerson, so just remember to keep it quiet. That's if you want her back—lively. I'm sure the police can be very helpful, but some situations can only be solved by friends. Now suppose you and I take a nice taxi ride back to our house, without fuss, and at twelve o'clock you'll have a nice telephone call to take." He gave his thick catarrhal laugh, and the tip of his sharp tongue licked his lips as if he was savouring a pleasant meal.

The arrival home felt like a nightmare and distorted repetition of that arrival by taxi when Elizabeth had disappeared. I walked up the stairs with Clayton padding behind me like a jailer. Surely, I thought desperately, if the police weren't satisfied about George's death, they *must* have kept an eye on me and Elizabeth? But Morell had left the country—on another case, presumably—so they could have decided it was suicide. Or accident. And no obvious plain-clothes man had stepped forward to help me at the station.

In the drawing room I sank on to the nearest chair. My legs had ceased to hold me up. The house was sinister with silence. An early bee buzzed on a vase of flowers, but otherwise all was quiet. Mrs. Jason had gone home to her daughter, taking Clemmie with her.

Clayton stood just inside the door and looked at me, while I tried to control my frightened thoughts which ran to and fro like rabbits flushed from cover. I knew myself beaten, by the thought of a drugged and frightened Ilona; by fear of something worse.

"You just stay there, Madam, and rest. I'll bring you a drink. Would you like a plaster for your head?"

The combination of nurse with perfect manservant and jailer was sickening.

"No."

"Well, a nice little drink won't do us any harm."

He brought me brandy and soda on a tray, and offered it solicitously. "You and I shall be all alone in this house tonight, Madam. It's not always a nice job, working for others; I was often lonely, often had time to sit and think of the Master enjoying himself upstairs."

My spine instinctively stiffened. Clayton was as disgustingly cowardly as I'd always thought him, and a born sadist, too. He must never be allowed to see me beaten, it could prove fatal to Ilona, so I looked him coldly in the eyes, and like small active fish they shifted sideways.

"I don't know who employs you, Clayton—my sister, I suppose. But I do know you're in this for money. So don't push me too far—if anything happens to me or Ilona you'll get nothing."

"But I like power, too—I could have taught the Master some interesting tricks to show you," he gave me an unpleasant grin.

"You're a coward. Somebody else's little dog. You've never had the guts to make money by yourself," I retorted, coolly watching him. I didn't think I could make him more an enemy than he was already.

I had touched the nerve that made his reflexes kick. He lunged towards me, and his voice shrilled: "You—you bloody bitch! You and yours—eating us, eating us whole, that's what you done. Stealing from the people, stealing from those as is better than yourself, you . . . now you'll get yours, see?"

I put my hand on his chest and pushed him away from me. Taken off-balance he staggered and sprawled backwards against the sofa.

"Keep your distance, Clayton, or you won't find me helpful, whatever threats you use. Even my sister wouldn't threaten Ilona." I wished that was certainty. We glared at each other until he lowered his gaze, and stood there panting, sullen and subdued. Then he went and sat on the sofa, his head turned sulkily away. We were silent until prompt at noon the telephone rang. I jumped to my feet, but Clayton was before me. He grab-

148

bed the receiver, and with his other arm held me away. Someone spoke the other end, low and hurried, but I couldn't hear if it was a man or woman. Clayton grunted. I dug my fingers into his arm.

"It's *my* call—you said it would be for me." Impotent to stop him, I watched while he replaced the receiver. In spite of resolutions I couldn't conceal my frenzy for Ilona's safety. I shook and shook his arm.

"They've got clean away all right." His eyes gleamed, little raisin eyes in the puffed white pig-face. For one insane moment I thought of trying to win him over by offering him a gigantic reward. Then I knew it would be useless, like appealing to a gaboon viper. He hated us. He would never help us, even for a fortune. There was no grain of compassion in him anywhere.

"Did they say what I'm to do?" I shook his arm again. He tore himself free.

"Hey, don't do that, Mrs. Emerson! No use making a fuss. They've changed their minds, see? You'll get instructions, all right, but not by telephone—maybe they found it too dangerous. Maybe the line's unsafe." He seemed to brood a moment. "I'm to go get your instructions for you. There's an alteration somewhere."

"Then I'll come too." The bruised side of my head was a fiery agony, and pain throbbed all down my neck, but I hardly noticed, or cared. He was my last link with Elizabeth and—who else? Father? I had no intention of letting Clayton out of my sight.

"You'll do no such thing. You'll just stay here and wait."

"How do I know you'll come back?"

"Because they want something, see. You're to communicate with no one while I'm gone, or you'll regret it. So will that brat of yours. If there's so much as a whisper that you've talked to the police, that's cooked the goose. I'll be gone an hour, maybe two." He ruminated, then drew a small pillbox from his pocket. "We'll make assurance doubly sure. Where's your drink?"

"I'm not taking any drug. I give you my word that I won't communicate with anyone."

He tittered. "Your word—what was that worth, *even to*

George? Fond of kissing and cuddling with Mr. Leyton, weren't you, didn't stop there, I'll be——"

"Clayton, I've warned you once already. And I won't swallow that. You're wasting your time."

"If you don't I can't budge from this house, and you'll neither see nor hear from your daughter ever again; so——" he held out my glass, "better sit on the sofa, you'll be muzzy. . . ."

I hesitated, but he stood there in front of me, patient and solid as an ox. The spirit was fiery in my mouth. Utter hopelessness had me in its grip again. As I swallowed I thought only of Ilona. Perhaps they had other plans for her. Perhaps it was on Marjorie and Bill the screw would be put—or was that too complex? Perhaps this was my quietus . . . As I drifted off into a comfortable grey haze, I did not—selfishly—greatly care.

17

There was a bee humming in my head. Round and round it went, buzz, buzz, buzz. It tried to get towards the light. Then a clock chimed, ting, ting, ting—on and on. Something was wrong about the sound; and the drawing room was very dark. How odd that Clayton hadn't lit the fire, when I was cold, so cold. . . .

Then I was fully conscious, and it was like the day after George had died. Ilona had gone. The room was dark because dusk had come. *Clayton had not returned.*

I switched on a lamp and one glance at the clock made me realize what had subconsciously worried me about the chime. It was nine o'clock. Clayton should have been back hours ago. There was no intention of his return, he had merely guarded me while the getaway was made secure. Now not only was Ilona lost, but I had lost touch too with her abductors. Yet 'they' hadn't killed me, there must be a use for me; that surely meant contact sooner or later. Meanwhile the thought of Ilona tore at my heart. Had they drugged her, too? Where would she wake, and when? What story could Elizabeth contrive that wouldn't scare her?

I stood up dizzily, and only then noticed the envelope pinned to the sofa cushion. My shaking hands had difficulty in extracting the small cardboard folder. What was this, some cruel piece of mockery? It was a brochure printed to advertise a small hotel in Paris. 'Hotel *l'Etoile de Lorraine. Cuisine superbe. Propriétaire, Mdme Dumonde.*' An Odéon telephone number. There was a long description of the environs, and the beauties of the nearby Luxembourg gardens were dwelt on. The words '*Jardin du Luxembourg*' were heavily underlined in ink. The name of the hotel was also underlined. So too was the word 'Tuesday' in the list of times and days when the Luxembourg was open to the public.

Here, then, were the promised instructions, but they were vague enough. Evidently I was to go to Paris and stay at this small hotel. Then what? The Luxembourg gardens on Tuesday —or the palace itself? I held the folder beneath the lamp, and tried again. Amongst the fine print more underlinings were visible, this time in pencil. Secondary instructions? The words were: 'two', 'seat', and 'book'. Two o'clock was easy, it could only be afternoon. Well then, at two someone would leave a book on a seat in the garden and—more instructions in the book? It was a hideous travesty of a child's game of treasure hunt. Perhaps one should be thankful the clues were not in verse, I thought grimly.

After spending some time on the folder I could make nothing more of it. Then suddenly I realized there was something else on the sofa put there since I fell asleep: the evening paper. Across the front page sprawled words written in Clayton's spidery hand: 'Two items in the news will interest you.'

There could be nothing about Ilona, surely? A horrible dread, worse than anything yet experienced, overwhelmed me. I was so frantic with fear that at first I missed the paragraphs although both were marked in pencil, and it was only after a second exhaustive search of the paper that I discovered them. One read:

'Three Trapped in Burning House. Architect's Life in Danger. Fire broke out today in the Kensington home of Mr. and Mrs. Ian Maddox. Mr. Maddox (39) his wife Philippa (31) and their youngest child Barney (3) were trapped on the second floor by flames which spread quickly from the basement of their Regency house. Neighbours gave the alarm, and firemen fought the blaze for ninety minutes before it was brought under control. Mrs. Maddox, who is expecting another child, is in hospital suffering from minor burns. Rescued with Barney from a second floor window, she is said to have no idea how the fire started. Mr. Maddox's condition is reported serious, after he jumped to safety from a balcony.'

I read it twice, a third time. Even without the underlining pencil it would have seemed impossible coincidence. It was equally impossible to imagine that amongst his other sinister activities Clayton had skipped fatly from the house to raise a fire in the basement of our old home. My spine, already chilled with fear and shock, grew yet chillier. The shadow of Elizabeth seemed to grow and stretch, until it could darken the lives of strangers. Why had Clayton drawn my attention to that paragraph? God knows I was already threatened enough; but of course one fact hadn't occurred to me before, and now screamed up at me from the pencil-marked paper: I was not merely up against a murderess and her accomplices—but, at best, a gang, at worst an entire organization.

The other pencil-marked item laid any doubts to rest: 'King's Cross Tragedy. An unidentified man fell to his death before a train in the King's Cross underground today. The accident took place at ten-twenty, after morning rush hour crowds had thinned. The police have appealed for witnesses to come forward.'

Clayton could have utilized a coincidence to work still further on my nerves. But the time was odd—ten-twenty at King's Cross, a few minutes before I was knocked out and Ilona kidnapped. Who had been put out of 'their' way—someone who might have warned me? One of Morell's men? And if Morell's men were still on the job where were they now, when we most needed them? I daren't ring the police, because of Ilona. So why didn't they come to me—they couldn't surely suspect me of more complicity? Who, by this time, should be suspecting whom? Hysterical and overstrung I stared bleakly at the telephone, my only link with help. And yet to lift it might draw the wolfpack, the circle of watchers and watching eyes, closer to the camp-fire. My brain reeled. Impossible to add more than two and two together. After all, I knew the kidnappers; so why the elaborate precautions, the trail to Paris, when all that was needed was a blunt demand for ransom? I would have given all Grandfather's inheritance for Christopher's presence.

Christopher . . . hours ago he would have expected us on the ten thirty-five. It would be out of character for him to fuss, but surely even he would start wondering—might even telephone. Now I could look at the silent black instrument with a more friendly eye. Soon it was bound to ring, so I would plan what to say, but my brain buzzed from the drug, and instead I began idiotically to count. . . Before I'd reached ten, it would ring. My count reached twenty-five, and the instrument still sat there squat and silent, like a great ink blot of malignancy against the white book-case.

I began to prowl about the house, leaving doors open behind me so that I could hear the monster when it rang. Probably I was on the verge of insanity, because I remember talking wildly to myself, and to George. I implored him to forgive me, and held a whole one-sided conversation with accusing silence. In the room Elizabeth had occupied the distinctive scent she always wore still hung on the air. Her wardrobe door was open, and inside were some of her dresses, as well as her beautifully-cut evening coat. She must feel rich already, I thought grimly, to throw so much away. The drawer by her bed yielded nothing but face powder, stamps, an old comb, a paperback. As systematically as my muddled brain would allow I searched the room. It was clueless, at least to me. Morell might have done better. Was there any-where else he would have looked?

I pulled the wastepaper basket out from beside the writing table. Underneath face tissues and other rubbish was the crumpled orange telegram. 'Held up in Paris. Love, Christo-pher.' I turned it over and over in my hands. Held up in Paris. Held. So there would be no telephone call. No reason to expect us. No miraculous aid in the dark night of despair.

Paris. I scrabbled for the envelope and found it screwed into a ball. It was certainly addressed to Elizabeth. That was when another nightmare suspicion mushroomed into growth. Held up in Paris. *Hotel l'Etoile de Lorraine. Jardin du Luxembourg.* The marked paragraph in the office file, which had been released to a Swiss newspaper. *Christopher?*

It was morning. The sky was an opaque whitish grey, with a built-in glare. I had laid fully dressed on my bed all night, smoking cigarette after cigarette until the ashtray beside me was piled high with stubs, and the dirty smell of stale smoke hung over the room. Like a station.

At six I had risen, numb and exhausted, to make coffee in the kitchen. I sat at the table and looked at the sky and tried to keep my thoughts off Ilona, separated first from George, and then from me, and—oh Lord. I got up abruptly and moved about the

154

room. I must go to Paris that afternoon, if there was a seat on a plane. I wondered if 'they' would really keep an eye on me all the time, and thought it likely. The camp-fire feeling was on me again. If I looked out of the window, would someone take note of it? Some buddy of Clayton's, or one of Morell's men?

There were still things to do if I was to leave England, though my passport was in order and with it Jenny-Geneviève's last batch of travellers' cheques which she was due to use when the tragedy of George took place; no one had returned them to the bank. This made Paris easy. (Certainly Elizabeth, that able spy, must have known *how* easy.) As I packed a case, flinging in garments haphazard, I defiantly added some of Ilona's clothes. *Never doubt your luck.* At nine-thirty I picked up the receiver to telephone the airport, but the line was dead. That was when I noticed someone had cut the wires by the wall. Clayton was always thorough.

So they must expect me to go out, anyway to a telephone kiosk; and one or two purchases would be normal enough. There were small shops near Marjorie's where I often went. A glimpse, a mere glimmer of a wild plan crossed my mind. Hardly more than a confused idea. And yet somehow I felt, ridiculously, as though George had pointed out a way——

Outside the house I felt more normal and collected, less like a sufferer from fever. It was good to feel more in control as without looking about me I walked fast to the square where Marjorie lived. Her corner house stood sideways to the road. If you continued round the corner and past her front door you walked down a narrow street of houses of which Marjorie's was the first. On the corner of the next road to the left was the exact twin of her house, and a few yards down this road was a gate into gardens which stretched behind all the houses in her street. This gate, I knew, was often left ajar by the elderly gardener who worked there, while he shopped at the little stores opposite. I prayed fervently he might be there today.

I swung my shopping bag ostentatiously in my hand, and didn't look behind me. Here at last was Marjorie's house. I willed myself not to glance sideways at it, turned the corner,

walked sedately past the row of houses, turned the next corner—
and ran. There was one terrible moment when I thought the gate
locked, but it was only closed, and I had already shut it behind
me and was out of sight behind the lilacs when I heard the footsteps follow round the corner, and stop.

I waited, my heart pounding. Suppose the gardener, Marriott,
found me there, and called me by name? But luckily no Marriott
appeared, and after a minute or two the footsteps crossed the
road uncertainly towards the stores. When I judged it safe I
emerged from my lilacs and ran along the path to the back entrance of Marjorie's house.

I was almost ready to throw myself into Marjorie's arms and
sob childishly on her neck, but when the door opened it was Mrs.
Jainey, her daily woman, who stood there peering out at me.

"Oh, it's Mrs. Emerson. How ever did *you* get in, Madam?"

"Marriott left the gate open, as usual." I pushed past her into
the hall, eager for shelter even if now comparatively safe.

"Is anyone at home? How's Ben?"

"Ben, he mustn't try to walk—got a nurse with him, a proper
madam. My, Mrs. Emerson, you do look bad, hardly recognized
you, I didn't. Mrs. Hellevan's gone out to shop before the
doctor comes, and the Professor, he's lecturing this morning.
Will you wait? Like a cup of coffee?"

I pressed my fingers to my forehead. By rights I should go up
and visit Ben for five minutes, but for all I knew he was still
infectious, and I dared not risk it—nor was I feeling capable of
chattiness. And it would be dangerous to stay away too long, for
any watchers might start suspecting they hadn't been shaken off
the trail accidentally. "Coffee would be nice, Mrs. Jainey, if I
could have it quickly. I'm in a rush. But I suppose Mrs. Hellevan
might be back soon?"

Mrs. Jainey shook her head. "Only just left. Bound to be half
an hour, at least. Anyway, Mrs. Emerson, you go along to the
drawing room and I'll bring you a cup. Would you like a word
with Nurse? She'll tell you all about Ben, poor little soul."

"Oh no, thank you," I said hastily. "I mean, I'm sure he's in
good hands. I'll just write a note for Mrs. Hellevan."

In the drawing room I crossed straight to Marjorie's desk

156

and opened it. My fingers fumbled frantically through pigeon-holes. Suppose Marjorie had grown tidier, and locked everything important away, as Bill was always begging her to do? No—I gave a great sigh of relief, for my fingers had encountered something oblong and hard. I drew out her passport, stuffed with papers. Oh, thank God for the endearing idiocies of one's friends! Marjorie's travellers' cheques—I could guess how Bill would explode if he knew it—were folded neatly inside. Really, Marjorie needed her head examined—what I was about to do proved it. I slipped both passport and cheques into my bag, picked up her pen, and began to write a note. Mrs. Jainey came in with the coffee just as I finished.

"Started to rain. Coming down a treat."

"Oh dear, I shall get soaked."

"Fetch you one of her macs, Mrs. Emerson. *She* won't mind."

"Would you? And would you make absolutely sure she gets this the second she comes in?" I had written hurriedly:

Marj. darling,

The most dreadful thing has happened. I can't tell you what—or not in a letter, you might start feeling you should *do* something, and nobody can, nobody but me. Whatever you do don't start looking for me, don't come to the house, or phone the police. *Don't.* You and Bill won't be going abroad now, so I've borrowed your passport and travellers' cheques. I might even forge your signature—criminal proceedings, but what the hell.

Do forgive. So *very glad* to hear that Ben's getting on all right,

Love, as always,
Jenny.

After hesitation I added a troubled postscript. 'You might pray hard for Ilona and me—we'll need it.'

While Mrs. Jainey fetched a mackintosh I read through the note again. It wasn't satisfactory, but if there were none Bill would fuss, would certainly telephone the police when the loss of those cheques was discovered. I had misgivings, but I licked down the envelope firmly, and gave it into Mrs. Jainey's hands.

"Now I want to use the telephone. Is that all right?"

"Course it is, Madam. You go ahead. Let yourself out, can

you? That's right—then I'll be getting on with my work now."

I made a call to book myself on a late afternoon plane to Paris. Then I put on Marjorie's mackintosh with its matching headscarf—good enough semi-disguise in themselves, though half-way home I must find an opportunity to stow both away in my shopping bag, and return to the house dressed as I had set out. Now I felt irrationally better, having in however minor a fashion outmanoeuvred the enemy. For at any time, once I was abroad, Marjorie's identity could be assumed and Jenny could 'disappear'. If—as seemed likely from their behaviour—'they' wanted me in their hands as well as Ilona (without the danger and trouble of kidnapping me and with the appearance that I'd gone of my own free will), well, *I* now possessed the means of puzzling *them*; the hunted could become the hunter, and if they lost me their plans could be upset.

Ilona was probably safe until terms of release had been fulfilled. After that it would depend on Elizabeth's goodwill—had she any, even for a child? As for those others she was connected with—I shuddered. I was positive that, as soon as my visit to the Luxembourg gardens was over and the terms discovered, I must disappear and stalk the enemy before they could trap me. It was a plan, at least, if not a good one; but how I was to accomplish the second part of it I had no idea.

18

I am desperate of my fortunes if they check me here
OTHELLO

It was hot in Paris. Hot, hot, hot. Colour and movement and sizzling heat. The colour and movement haunted me like a continual reminder of Ilona's kaleidoscope. The voices round me were a million little drills picking at my nerves. I always loved Paris, with George. Now it was as if someone had turned the city upside down—a gallic Hieronymus Bosch, who had painted a Paris in hell for me in the colours of Renoir and spring. Under the pressure and misery, the aloneness and the fear for Ilona, single vision threatened to split into the hall of mirrors that is insanity.

Because my mind felt more like a late Picasso than anything else I groomed my surface with incessant care, in the hope that insanity wouldn't show. Perhaps the effect was odd, for people stared at me curiously when I spoke to them—humanity is quick to pick up the wavelength of desperation, and turns hostile towards it after the manner of a dog mistrusting fear.

As George's Jenny I was used to a continual response of warmth and love. Now an icy current was all around, bearing me away, and I was tempted to give up hope of recovering Ilona, and throw myself into the Seine. With the possibility of capture and ransom irrevocably gone, Elizabeth might be kind to my daughter. Or would the grim, incredible battle start all over again, with Bill and Marjorie, and with Ben as stakes? The prospects of nightmare had no end.

The Hotel l'Etoile de Lorraine was a dump. Little old ladies from the provinces crept in and out, mingling with several spotty students from America and Scandinavia bent on acquiring the aura of the Sorbonne, and some uninteresting middle-class French couples. I and my insanity must have seemed quite exotic company, like Gérard de Nerval and his lobster.

It was a relief when a later arrival drew the stares and whispered comments. She looked as out of place in that milieu as I felt. She was, I reckoned, Turkish or Persian, at any rate from

159

the Near East. Her figure was rounded, with a huge round bosom like the bosoms in erotic Indian carvings, and she had enormous quantities of black hair done in a heavy chignon. It was scraped back so hard from her forehead that it lifted the corners of her eyes, already slanted; harem eyes, George would have called them. As she paused by my table I noticed a faint delicious smell of tuberoses and something else indefinable—expensive, anyway. She cast a disdainful glance around the room, and asked me in French if the table next to mine was taken.

"*Non, Madame, ou je crois que non. . . .*"

She sat down with a rustle of petticoats, and made a face of enormous charm. "*Mon dieu, quel endroit! Si je l'avais connu, je l'aurais évité. Vous le trouvez tolérable, vous, Madame?*" She had a powerful personality; I felt myself reluctantly drawn into its orbit as if by a boa constrictor, although casual conversation was the last thing I wanted. I looked closely at her, with a vague idea that we had seen or met each other somewhere before.

"*Non, ce n'était pas mon choix.*"

"*Ah? Vous aussi? C'est mon frère à qui je dois cette catastrophe. Il a retenu ma chambre sans la voir—ces hommes! Vous n'êtes pas française, je crois?*"

"*Je suis anglaise.*"

"Ah? Rosbif, hotel Hilton, I speak it."

In spite of myself I smiled. "You know England?"

"So little. Very, very little."

"Hotel Hilton?"

"Ah, you laugh. That is good. When I come in, you are looking so sad, no? One must not, you know. Even if the crrrocodiles would eat, one must laugh or one ends——" she glanced round the dining room, caught my eye, and laughed.

"You speak English very well."

"Thank you. I am at finishing school once where are English, French, German—but I do not speak well, you are too kind."

I had finished my meal, and got up to go. This banal chatty companionship was intolerable. Ilona! Where was she—and dead, or alive? I gave my Eastern neighbour an abrupt good night and left. The girl at the reception desk was chatting in low tones with a porter as I passed, and both watched me in silence as I walked upstairs. While I shut the door of my narrow room, and carefully shot home the bolt, I wondered if any of the hotel staff were implicated in the kidnapping. Had I my watchers here, green eyes close to the camp-fire?

I lay on my bed and watched the rainy sky darkening to night, and found myself wondering bitterly where Christopher was now. With Elizabeth and Ilona, somewhere in the back premises of this very hotel? Did the roots of his treachery go deep into the past, to the days when Elizabeth wrote up her diary? Or was I quite wrong and was he safely back in England, puzzled by our non-appearance and innocent of the plots and counterplots which made havoc of my overwrought mind? I undressed and got into bed; but all that night, disturbed by the myriad loud voices of Paris as much as by the monstrous distortions of despair, I tossed and turned on the uncomfortable bed, until the rainy night lightened to a rainier dawn, and noises below in the hotel showed that its staff were up and preparing for another day.

During the morning I reconnoitred the Luxembourg gardens. It seemed sensible to check the number of seats where the expected book could be left. The instructions were so extra-ordinarily vague,—it might easily be picked up and taken before I could find it. I walked briskly, but even so it took time to make a thorough check. This drizzly day there were few people in the gardens, and none of them looked even mildly sinister. I was turning back towards the palace when a man came out of it and paused a moment to put up his umbrella. I caught only a glimpse before the umbrella hid his face entirely, but I could have sworn he was Christopher. I hesitated, uncertain, and he was away in long strides before I had made up my mind to follow. By the time I reached the gardens' entrance my quarry was getting into a car, which moved off into heavy traffic and was lost from view.

Furious with myself, I slowed my steps. If it *was* Christopher, to be confronted suddenly by me might have jerked out of him some unguarded remark. Perhaps he too had been reconnoitring the ground. It was odd to find how much I minded that Christopher was treacherous, perhaps worse: kidnapper, murderous accomplice. After all, I didn't like him very much. And then I saw that I was worse than slow—an absolute fool. Why I might have trailed him in a taxi to Ilona! I was standing there on the pavement and calling myself every sort of name, when an amused voice said behind me: "*Bonjour Madame*. You are sad again this morning, no?"

It was my friend of the night before. In the awful vacuum of that grey day and my stupidity I was almost cheered by her warmth and vitality. "It's a sad sort of day."

"Brm! You are right, yes; the more reason not to make it worse! Whatever happen I have always the feeling something better follow, and so it does. This is philosophy."

"I used to think so too. But life doesn't work out like that."

"No? You are right, of course—yet something here inside still tell me you are *wrong*. Let me tell your luck and say things will be better soon. Much, much better. Believe it, so it happen."

"I can only hope you're right." I forced a smile.

"Of course I am." She squeezed my arm. "Right from today, from this hour. . . . Now I shop. You will be in to *déjeuner*, no?"

"Yes," I said, and went my way, absurdly comforted; but I was not to see her then, for I lunched early, because of the rendezvous. Thoughts were my sole companions, and I don't want to harp on them, but they were grey. *Christopher*. It was an awful idea that he could be involved with this—it didn't really make sense. Christopher earned big money, which could have been bigger still if he were less fastidious about how he earned it. Well, there were two other classical motives, power and love, and I examined them both. Power went with money, so he could have had *that* before, too. Which left love. Perhaps he had Elizabeth in his blood, since their mutual experiments in childhood. It was no comfort to feel myself up against Christopher. Like Elizabeth he had always beaten me at everything, chess included.

Before going out again I checked over all my things. No one had obviously searched my room, but an expert could have done it without leaving traces. As part of the Marjorie disguise I had brought to Paris the light-coloured wig which I wore at parties last year. It was stuffed inside the dirty-linen basket in my room, and covered by a towel and a filthy shirt. It was a risk, but probably no one would bother to look there unless they were search-

162

ing for something specific. Marjorie's passport and travellers' cheques were in the bag I always carried with me. These amateur efforts to provide myself with a second identity were pretty infantile, I thought gloomily, as I put on more lipstick, and set off for the Luxembourg again.

I toured the gardens in record time. People stared as I passed them at a fast trot, and I forced myself to slacken speed. The last thing I wanted was to be conspicuous.

There was no book on any bench.

By half past two that was certain. By three I was frantic, pacing the gardens like a tiger, and biting my nails. I even examined the litter bins in case someone else had found the book and thrown it away. An official began to look at me too closely, and I went to sit on one of the benches and tried to calm down. I was now so scared for Ilona that it was hardly possible to breathe or think. This was a dead end; failure. My quarry had hidden itself. Perhaps Christopher had seen me earlier and thought me there to prepare an ambush. Did I dare try and reach him through the office? I simply couldn't decide. Not while I was suffering from this terrible fear that 'they' didn't mean me to recover Ilona; she had been taken for some reason more crooked even than ransom, perhaps merely to lead *me* into a trap. It made nonsense—but so did everything else.

"I had *déjeuner* out, after all."

I looked up, startled. She stood there with that friendly smile on her face, a huge shopping basket clasped in her hands. She plumped herself down merrily on the seat beside me.

" 'Ow tired I am, *chérie* I exhaust myself with all this silly shopping! Look—shoes, scent, and a 'eav-en-ly do you say? blouse? *Je suis toquée.* I, who have too much dress already—but you look so sad, again."

"You didn't buy a book?" something compelled me to say.

"Books? Me?" She gave me her sharp, gay glance, and the silly suspicion died. "*Chérie*, a book is about so much use to me as an old lady to a young man! You return to the Etoile, eh?" For I had risen. "Now? I think it is for a young man you are troubled—a young man who does not come."

"You could put it that way."

163

"Could I? Ah, it is too bad—and you so pretty, you find yourself another; they are all the same, men."

I was in no mood for her facile consolements, my mind was fully bent on my child.

"—you would be so good, take it for me?"

"I'm sorry, I didn't hear what you said."

"The basket—if you go to the hotel? I am expected out—but not with this!—to Passy, and I have not really time. . . ."

I was champing to go, and almost tore the basket from her. While she was speaking I had decided to ring up Christopher.

"You are too kind. How lucky that we met. You leave it with the porter, yes? The name is Madame Ankar, Room 11. Thank you, *chérie*, a thousand times. Oh, and the chocolates, they are for you. To cheer you." She waved a hand airily, and was gone.

I lumped that wretched basket with me to the nearest telephone kiosk, and rang the *Subscriber's* Paris office.

"Monsieur Leyton? He's not in the office, Madame. He's not even expected in. He finished here two days ago—we think he's back in England now."

"Do you know where he stayed, in Paris?"

"Please hold on a moment."

She found me the hotel name. I recognized it as one of his favourite haunts on the Left Bank. I telephoned, but the porter told me Christopher had checked out two days ago. Dully I put down the receiver, picked up Madame Ankar's basket, and trudged wearily back to the hotel thinking that this cat-and-mouse business left one stunned and helpless. It made Morell's methods seem straightforward. I wondered briefly what steps, if any, the police had taken about my absence—it would almost be relief to find Morell in my room, and pour the whole impossible story into his unbelieving ear. The porter crossed the hall just as I entered it. I handed over my burden, then relayed the message.

"*Mais, Madame!*" He threw up his hands. Madame Ankar had left, she had left that day! Before twelve. Her room was now occupied by a *commis voyageur* from Nevers. I gazed at him in stupefaction. Was he *sure*—positive?

"*Mais certainement!, Madame!*" Jean, here, he added, had brought down her luggage. He volunteered to see if they had an address in the office, but the receptionist didn't know where Madame had gone. Somewhere in Paris, that was all. I was altogether sick of Madame Ankar. They had better keep the basket, and let her claim it if and when she returned.

"*C'était pas Madame Ankar,*" piped up the larger page.

"*Mais, que dis-tu, Pierre? C'est ridicule!*"

The child sagely shook his head. "*C'est Mademoiselle Khahn. Je l'ai vue, moi, mille fois, dans le beau monde.*"

The porter grinned, and whispered in my ear that Pierre had worked in a famous hotel, and been kicked out for impertinence.

"*Les Khahn, ce sont des plus riches, des millionaires, d'Alexandrie,*" volunteered Pierre, treating us to his greater knowledge of the world.

"Certainly, that was why she stayed at L'Etoile!" scoffed the porter. But the child was right. I knew now where I had seen her. A year ago, in Paris, before a fashionable masked ball, and dining in a glittering Eastern octet. They had been pointed out to me as fabulously rich, particularly the eldest brother. Deep inside me a chord of unease and excitement was struck. The false name, the too-casual encounter, the friendly overtures . . . *the box of chocolates which 'Madame Ankar' had bought for me.* The porter delved into the bag and found them. I was shaking. The little group in the hall gazed after me as I mounted the stairs.

Inside my room I locked the door behind me, and tore the wrappings from the chocolate box. Beneath the top layer of sweets was a book—a six-shilling paperback: Durrell's *Justine.* I stared at it blankly. The first part of the Alexandria Quartet? I turned the pages, and as I flipped them over saw that a strip of paper with my name typewritten on it was pasted on the flyleaf.

I sat down on the bed and went through that book page by page, paragraph by paragraph. No pencil marks; nothing. I went through it three times, and ended no wiser than before. Tears ran down my face, I could have thrown the book on the floor and jumped on it. Why should any kidnapper take so much trouble—for the sake of mockery? It was like a ridiculous yet terrible charade; and I was the stupidest guest at the party, unable to complete the words spelt out for me. There was an ugly long-drawn-out type of cruelty behind the game; and hatred behind it, too. And what made it uglier still was that the stakes were a child, my courageous and loving Ilona.... 'Madame Ankar's' charm was totally corrupt—the memory of her warm sympathy made me feel physically sick. Madame—no, Mademoiselle. Mademoiselle Khahn, from Alexandria. The *Alexandria* Quartet—was this the clue? Was *that* where they had taken Ilona? And so this clumsy machinery had been brought into action to trail me right across Europe after her, to a country I didn't know, where we had neither relatives nor friends, where I could be hounded down with no danger to my enemies . . . But to what profit?

It was like dealing with the insane. Perhaps the master brain— was it Elizabeth's?—*was* mad; or perhaps, which seemed as likely, the significance of the fantastic pattern being woven round me hadn't yet appeared. Each time a new factor entered, it made nonsense of the rest.

' "*Les Khahn, ce sont des plus riches, des millionaires. . . .*" '

Money hadn't been mentioned as ransom but what else did I possess which could have tempted anyone? As for unbalanced hatred, it could hardly permeate an entire gang. My exhausted mind went round and round the puzzle. Perhaps *I* was insane, locked away, while day by day I imagined the things which seemed to happen round me. Perhaps Ilona was happily at play in the nursery of the Regents Park house, George at work in his office. . . .

There was a knock on the door.

My nerves jumped. My voice was higher than usual. "*Entrez.*"

The last person I expected to see glaring darkly at me from the doorway was Christopher. He looked pale and untidy in a green-grey machintosh. I had never seen him shabby before. He was scowling, and his lower lip jutted out in a way I recognized: it usually meant he was about to fight for a lost cause, and be very rude. The Nicholas syndrome well to the fore, I told myself. I felt exactly like a lost cause of the most hopeless kind, but seeing his face and sensing his antagonism I was pretty sure his lost cause wasn't me.

"What are you doing here, Jenny?" he said abruptly.

166

"Staying," I replied coldly.

He shut the door, and placed his back against it; his shoulders were hunched and his head thrust forward. He continued to stare at me like a bull about to charge, until I began to feel furious myself. And when his next unforgivable words were: "Where's Ilona?" the fury came uppermost.

"*You* should know," I cried, jumping up and facing him. "How dare *you* ask *me* that?"

"Oh, come off the histrionics, Jenny," he said coolly, "as an act it's just not good enough. Liz was always dual as twin monkeys, but you nicely presented yourself as the candid one."

I was totally bewildered. The temper and scorn seemed to be genuine—something else too: anxiety? But I knew how sharp he was; it was possible that I was being goaded with a purpose —run ragged. When I thought of Ilona, I couldn't restrain my temper.

"You sound as if you've just made the round of the bars, Christopher! The only reason I don't call the porter to have you thrown out, is that I *think* you know who has Ilona."

"Oh, very clever, Jenny. A pity I taught you chess, but you never beat me, don't forget. As to knowing who has Ilona, we both know that, although my knowledge isn't so detailed as yours. I'm working in the dark, while you're very much in the light—if you care to call it that. My dear, if you want my opinion, you're a double-dealing murderous little bitch—and the only reason I'm trying to drag *you* back from your dubious friends is your daughter. I liked George, most men did, and Ilona takes after him. If she'd taken after *you* I wouldn't raise a finger to save either of you. As it is I can hardly expect a medal from Interpol—or anyone else."

I was so furious by now that I hardly heard what he said. "It's a pretty effective smokescreen you're putting up," I stammered, "though not good enough. *You* wired Elizabeth you were held up in Paris—why? Why not wire *me*? And who tipped them off in the first place that Grandfather's grand-daughter was worth a deal? Funny, the way a Swiss newspaper got hold of that article, wasn't it? The marked clipping in the file—I suppose you know nothing of all *that*, either."

167

"Hold it, Jenny. I haven't the least idea what you mean. That's a pretty effective smokescreen, as you call it, too."

"The whole bloody thing is nothing *but* smokescreens," I retorted wearily, "layers and layers of them. I don't know who to trust any longer, and none of you trust me. All I want is Ilona. It's the only thing I care about, now."

He raised an eyebrow, cynically. "Who's been holding out what bait to you, Jenny, and for how long, I wonder? And how did he get hold of you in the first place, I'd like to know?"

"*I* wonder who 'he' is. You evidently know, I don't. And you knew where to find me, too, in this frightful hole. Explain that away if you can."

"I don't consider it needs explanation."

"Exactly. So what particular squalid bargain have *you* been sent to strike?"

He was watching me with a slightly puzzled air. "Bargains don't come into it here, Jenny, you should know that. Even if you've been sold the whole complex with built-in reactor set."

I was silent. The thing was beyond me. At last I said: "What is it you—they—want in exchange for Ilona?"

He went and stood by the window, and I waited impatiently for him to speak. At last he said casually, "Mind if I smoke?"

It was too much. So coolly infuriating—deliberately so?—that I found myself lunging out at him, hammering at him desperately with my fists, and sobbing hysterically that he must get Ilona back, he must, he *must*—He seized my wrists in both hands, and held me away from him.

"Hush, Jenny, hush. Someone will hear you——"

"I don't care if they do—I'll get you arrested—you're the lowest form of animal life. Did you come to report back—to shove me closer to the brink—to sneer and peer, and dangle Ilona's safety in front of me like a juicy carrot . . . *Damn* you, how I hate you. You, and Elizabeth too . . . Right back in that d-diary you were under her thumb. . . ." I gasped for breath as if I'd dived deep under water and come up drowning. We were face to face, antagonists, but now my enemy wore an air of bewilderment. More, he seemed shaken.

"What *do* you mean, Jenny? *Her* diary? Either you're a consummate actress or—But you must have been that, all along."

His hands dropped from my arms. We just stood and looked at each other. Both of us worn and neither of us trusting. Then he did an odd thing, he put up his hand again and stroked my head gently, as if he comforted Ilona. To this unexpected tenderness I returned deep-seated resistance. As dual as twin monkeys. That was where we both stood with each other.

"Jenny, I can't help you, unless you confide in me."

"You can tell me where to find Ilona," I answered obstinately.

He sighed, looked at me sideways a moment longer, and turned away shaking his head. "You always were an exasperating woman, in spite of those eyes—it must be that chin." He had reached the door, and added—I thought at random—"What d'you know of a couple called Jim and Dorothea Arkroyd?"

"*Who?* I never heard of anyone called that." I said wearily.

"No?" He looked thoroughly sceptical. "I'll give you a telephone number, Jenny." He took a slip of paper from his pocket and handed it over. "This one. If you decide to talk, ring up and—if I'm not there—leave a message that the weather will be better on Tuesday, and I'll come round. If you have any wild ideas of making a break by yourself, forget them. An iron fist doesn't unclench that easily. Another point worth consideration—there's no record of how Mrs. Maclean liked it, when she got there. Good-bye."

A quick look up and down the corridor, and he was gone, as I opened my mouth to ask what the hell he meant. I had got nothing out of him about Ilona; but if Christopher was in the game, his certainly wasn't the master hand. 'Jim and Dorothea Arkroyd'. Yes—the names were dimly familiar . . . but how? 'Who's been holding out what bait to you, and for how long?' And that puzzling mention of Mrs. Maclean. . . .

My knees felt shaky. I sat down on the chair. It was impossible that innocents like George and myself had stumbled into something political; something which took no account of ordinary people's lives, but ground everything in its juggernaut path to powder. *Ilona.* I shivered violently. What was a child's life to such people? Christopher couldn't be serious, he was only trying to muddle me, direct my attention the wrong way. . . . It was the kaleidoscope again, cunningly displayed.

The copy of *Justine* lay in front of me. Had Christopher noticed it? Most probably he had known it would be there. I put out my hand to open the book that might help me to my child, but some inner reluctance held me back. And instead I fell on my knees, and prayed.

19

Conceal me what I am; and be my aid
For such disguise as, haply, shall become
The form of my intent.

TWELFTH NIGHT

That night was the worst I ever spent; the message that stood
out for me in *Justine* was another terror; another prod; another
ill-defined threat. I was still nearer madness when, by three
o'clock in the morning, I had skipped through the book and
reminded myself of its contents. One thread of plot alone
concerned me, I guessed: Justine's search for her lost daughter
through the child brothels of Alexandria. This, then, was the
implied threat. And still it was all oblique; still no exact
demand, nor directions that could result in blessed action, in
Ilona's return.

Not surprisingly, I hardly slept. And I woke late, bedevilled
by black inescapable horror, and roused by a banging on the
door. I sat up in bed and muttered a hoarse: "*Entrez . . .*"

It was the chambermaid, duster in one hand, in the other
a white envelope together with a small package. She had found
them outside, she explained, propped against my door. I felt
she was lying, and that someone had tipped her heavily to deliver
them; but I could get nothing out of her before she left the
room.

My fingers trembled. I half-expected Christopher's writing,
or Elizabeth's. But in the classic tradition of ransom notes
there were only printed words cut from a newspaper and pasted
to spell out a short but melodramatic message on a sheet of card.
"She is safe and well—at present. We shall make contact later
in Rue Doubara at the House of Palms. Ask for Ibrahim."

My hands fumbled at the package, and discovered a thick
wad of Egyptian notes, tucked into a passport. I examined it,
and got another minor shock—the passport was an Egyptian one,
made out in the name of Marian Said. The details were my own,
so was the photograph—that excellent photograph taken for the
Subscriber last year, which had so pleased George. The slant

171

of my cheekbones and eyes was accentuated, and I could have passed for European or Europeanized Middle East. The name chosen seemed to hint at a mixed marriage.

There was a plane ticket, too; I didn't have to look twice at the destination, while I wondered who had acquired the photograph: Christopher? He must be in Paris to watch my steps, to push me further along the line 'they' wished me to tread all on my own; and—perhaps—arrange that a fictitious passport was planted outside my door. On impulse I examined my luggage. The pocket where I kept my own passport was empty.

My heart thudded, the blood drummed in my temples. How efficiently I was being herded towards the corral! Simply and without fuss I had been robbed of my own identity, and given another. I had only to move where I was told on the chessboard, and some invisible parody of a benign Santa Claus would hand out another mystery gift. To anyone watching I must seem no tormented fish on a hook, but a docile actress collaborating with a skilled director. Fortunately there was one thing the director didn't know: in my bag was my flimsy third identity in the shape of Marjorie's passport. It was—I hastily reassured myself— still there.

As I dressed and made up I thought of my next action, but thought was a slow business. This continual administration of small shocks plus sleeplessness, grief, and overriding anxiety for Ilona, had given me an awful sensation as if part of my brain were paralysed or in deep freeze. To take any decision was agony —for in this numbness I might have overlooked something important which would be plain to anyone else. When I remembered Mademoiselle Khahn's deliberate kindness, I wondered if 'they' were subjecting me to Pavlov's theories.

It seemed that the first thing to be done was to shake off Christopher, or any other watcher, while I tried to get Marjorie's Egyptian visa. My flight—Marian Said's flight—wasn't scheduled till later in the day, but that day must be my own. It seems fantastic now, but in that curious time of isolated action my mind tended to drift away from thoughts of Ilona. It was probably one of nature's safety valves coming into play.

Haunted constantly by her suffering or her death, my disintegration must have been complete. . . .

I looked in the glass. The oval of my face was blurred, and I tried to blink away the mistiness, but it was useless. Continual sleeplessness. . . . I turned away and picked up my bag. One of my two cases must be sacrificed. The zippered train case was the best, and I crammed everything in that it would hold, though most of my spare garments had to be ruthlessly discarded. The blonde Marjorie wig was essential, but took up a lot of room. I hesitated over *Justine*, and decided against it. To look at it again would be a repetition of hell. It went into the other case, along with the clothes, and to them I pinned an envelope containing money for my bill. With the case still there, no one would suspect me of doing a flit. I flung my travelling coat over my arm, to hide the train case, and went downstairs. A brief nod at the porter, and the Etoile was left behind. To shake off Christopher would be another matter, but even if he kept track of me at the airport I would get rid of him in Egypt at the very first opportunity.

The Bouf Mich' traffic was at a standstill by the lights. A taxi idled on the far side. I strolled across and, as the lights changed, thumbed the driver: "Galeries Lafayette." We drove off to a chorus of furious hootings, while I peered cautiously out of the back window. If the little man staring disconsolately after us from the safety of the pavement was a watcher, then he was lost. He too thumbed a cab, but it was hired.

"*Vite*," I begged my rescuer, "*je suis en retard*."

"*Volontiers, Madame!*" And we almost left the ground.

At the store the '*Dames*' was empty except for one woman fussing with her hat before a glass. I locked myself in the loo and made the changeover into my improvised disguise, turning the reversible coat from blue tweed to its white linen other side, and carefully pulling on the blonde wig. There was a pair of flat-heeled shoes in the train case, and by changing to them I altered my height. Now the fussy woman with the hat could be heard having a good cough. I waited what seemed an interminable time, but at last the door shut as she went out. I pulled the plug noisily and emerged to find only an attendant, whose indifferent glance gave me reassurance. I wiped off make-up and applied some suited to a blonde—lighter lipstick and pale powderbase, and a slight downward pencilling at the corners of the eyes to change their shape from tilt to round. Marjorie's face looked back at me from the glass. I walked out of the store more confidently than when I went in.

The Egyptian Consulate could prove a stumbling block. It seemed unlikely that a visa would be given at once, and, if not, I should have to try and 'buy' one in the underworld of Alexandria, which opened up a whole nightmare future of pitfalls. Success seemed highly unlikely, in spite of the money kindly provided by my enemies. But to be without papers or, worse, to be stuck with 'Marian Said's', would be fatal.

At first my efforts met with a complete block. I sat and stared at a man who looked like a large sallow mule, and told the story of a sick friend. I enlarged on her despair—she must travel on to Paris, she couldn't travel alone. I was the only person who could fetch her.

"She might employ a nurse," he suggested with simple malice.

"She was unable to find a suitable one," I responded coldly.

All the time I was in a fever in case he asked for some proof of the improbable story; and in the end I felt that I was pressing my luck too far, and gave in.

"You will leave your passport, Madame?"

"No good," I said, "it will be too late." Then I had the brainwave. Many of Bill's colleagues were eminent scholars, and there was one he knew quite well, from Egypt, who lived in Paris. We had met at a dinner. He was tall and nice and disarmingly young. One knew instinctively he was the sort of man who would know and be known by everyone. I took a deep breath, and plunged: "You know Monsieur X?"

A head was raised on the other side of the room. There was a sudden movement, a speculative glance. Risking everything I pressed home the point: "My husband knows him well. He's a friend of ours—and of your Consul. If you would telephone him. . . ." I was conscious of close scrutiny from somewhere on my left, and tried to relax. Someone walked soundlessly from the room. I stood up, as if to go, and was waved back to my seat again.

"If you would be good enough to wait a few minutes, Madame?"

The clock ticked on. I stared at my gloves, trusting that my face looked serene, though inwardly I was frantic. I visualized Monsieur X entering the room, his face when he saw me, and the inside of the Palais de Justice. I still don't know if they telephoned him, or if the mere mention of his name produced results, but when I left a visa was promised by five o'clock, and no one had even inquired if I had a Jewish parent.

Here was success, and I began to feel hopefully that I might take on Ilona's captors yet: pitiful amateur's pretensions. If I'd been a genuine spy it would surely have struck me by now that Morell and, by extension, the British police force, even perhaps Interpol, had been strangely off the scene since the time before Ilona's kidnapping at King's Cross.

At the airport it was like acting in a film—by rights I should have met a stranger here, *Figaro* folded beneath his arm as identification. But—ostensibly—there was no one to meet 'Marian Said'. In a cowardly way I would have been glad to see even Christopher just then, for I was mournfully aware of suppressed panic, and loss of identity—my dual personality was no longer Jenny-Geneviève but Marjorie-Marian Said.

I sat docile as a puppet in the seat booked for me, and turned the pages of *Paris Match*. In the train case above my head the blonde Marjorie wig was plumped out round my nightdress and covered with a sweater. Luckily the customs officer had chalked the case without doing more than lift the lid and peer inside: my versatile blonde splendour hadn't been advertised in public. Marjorie's passport, freshly visaed, was stuck down inside the back of my girdle. It felt like a Victorian poker stiffening my spine. It would lack an entry stamp, of course. That must be remedied I couldn't begin to imagine how. The identity I wore already, that of Marian Said, was a precarious thing.

So dissociated had I felt since leaving the Egyptian Consulate at five o'clock, that I had acted in a way which surprised myself: by entering a public callbox, and dialling the number given me by Christopher. It was a senseless act, this communing with an enemy, born of need for communication with someone who knew me as myself, however much I might be disapproved of or despised. The number rang and rang. I was about to give up when a woman's voice answered: "*Allô—allô.*"

"*Je veux parler avec Monsieur Leyton.*"

"*Votre nom, Madame? . . . Un instant. . . .*"

In a panic again I almost decided to hang up, when Christopher's voice, ugly with what sounded like fatigue, came on the line. "Jenny? This is a surprise—a good one. I thought you weren't going to ring. How's the weather your end?"

"The weather?" I said stupidly, "oh, fine. The sun's out."

"I hoped it would be better on Tuesday."

"On Tuesday? Oh yes, I see. . . . No . . . I don't think it will. It's not very likely, is it? I mean, it looks set all right to me."

"Why did you bother to ring, then?"

I was silent.

"*Jenny?* Has something happened? You haven't been back to your room all day."

"How do you know that?" I countered quickly.

"Have you? Where are you, Jenny? Where are you *now?*"

"In a callbox. I've been—shopping."

"*Shopping* . . . yet you expect me to believe——" He broke off, was silent, then resumed: "Look, I want to see you again. I *must.*" His voice sounded different, and I couldn't analyse the change.

"But you can't. *You* know you can't." Yes, Christopher of all people must know. I nearly said that no doubt he'd see me at the airport, but perhaps 'they' hadn't told him I was leaving Paris? Didn't he know they had taken Ilona farther away? Perhaps Elizabeth trusted him as little with her innermost secrets as she had when she wrote that diary. *I* wouldn't enlighten him, anyway. I would sooner deal with Elizabeth alone.

"How do I know? Oh Lord, we're always at cross purposes. . . ."

"Come tonight," I said.

176

"Tonight? To the hotel, you mean?"

"Oh yes, of course. To my room. After half past eight." I was convinced he had guessed I wouldn't be returning. . . .

"But Jenny, I don't call this satisfactory. I'd sooner see you now, if you'll only tell me where to come, and then. . . ." He was being expansive, almost conciliatory. I had a strong, illogical conviction that I was being held while someone tracked me down.

"I *can't* see you now. Good-bye." I rammed down the receiver and bolted, not without regret for my last lifeline to the treacherous familiar. In the first available *Dames* I changed from blonde Marjorie to high-heeled Marian; shaking, and scolding myself for stupidity. How *could* Christopher trail me to a callbox? He had no way of doing it, and certainly neither he nor anyone else would ever find out that I had spent the day as Marjorie.

I had always loved flying, so it was odd to set out with sensations of dread; hardly a premonition, more certainty of disaster. It seemed unlikely 'they' meant me to return; or Ilona. It also seemed more and more certain that I must be under surveillance of some kind—this only struck me after my visa euphoria had subsided: I mean police surveillance, not my sinister watchers—'they' might be conserving themselves till I reached my destination. Morell, I recalled, had left England. When I considered those who might be hunting me, officially or unofficially, the Marjorie stratagem seemed the height of feebleness, a child's conviction that fancy dress can totally disguise. 'You didn't know it was me, did you? What am I *now*?' 'Pork, I should think,' I muttered bitterly to myself. Any one of the people on this plane might be my shadow.

France was far below now, wreathed in cloud. 'There's no record,' Christopher had said, 'of how Mrs. Maclean liked it, when she got there.' Only one thing was sure about this life, for everyone—it didn't do to be too much afraid. I straightened my spine, feeling Marjorie's passport dig into it. There was no record, either, of how George had liked it when he died. Not on this earth, anyhow.

The city's personality was extravagant—a schizoid city, the

langueur and disorder of the East underlying the slick commercial modernity of Europe; the cosmopolitan chatter of tongues bewildered my unattuned ears. I put up at an hotel on the front overlooking that great sweep of bay, the Western Harbour, which the Greeks had called Eunostos—'safe return'. Would this for me prove irony—or prophecy? But I found it all too easy to remember that in this city the god had abandoned Antony.

No one had guided me here, nowhere on the journey had a hand touched my elbow, a voice whispered in my ear. If Ilona was truly tucked away in this brilliant yet moribund city, no hand was stretched out to bring me to her. I was conspicuously left alone. Conspicuous was the word. It was as if someone had planted me on a stage, turned on a spotlight, and left me there to act out a part I didn't know; though there was, of course, the stagey message that told me to find Ibrahim, which I hesitated to use, for instinct decreed I *must* somehow discover Ilona's whereabouts without falling myself into our enemies' hands. Yet I could not rationalize this feeling, nor begin to understand why 'they' should want to trap me too.

Feverish with longing for Ilona, I wandered aimlessly into the city's open squares. It was simple misery to look at the family parties squatting on the grass, and remember that I'd once been part of a happy family myself. The small children were gorging themselves on roast monkey-nuts, salted almonds and dried melon seeds, and clamouring round the sherbet-seller with his long-spouted jug—how eagerly Ilona would have joined them! Once or twice I started forward almost convinced I had caught sight of Elizabeth feeding sherbet to a little girl with copper hair.

Always I was disappointed. Yet in one way I was rewarded, for it was during this desperate evening walk that I thought I saw Christopher again; no more than a glimpse of a familiar-looking figure about two hundred yards away, whom I lost almost immediately in the crowd. Even then I felt a lift of spirits which was purely superstitious. Christopher had been in Paris, and there I discovered 'Madame Ankar's' identity. Perhaps in Alexandria the riddle of the Khahns' connection with Ilona's

178

disappearance would be solved. I returned more cheerfully to my hotel.

One of the Italian porters, sour-faced and inquisitive, was on duty. He spoke fluent English, so I decided to plunge: a step must be taken some time, before anyone could wonder why I hadn't looked up Ibrahim. Casually I asked the Italian if he knew the Khahn family, and where they lived.

He looked at me with amazement, and said that *everyone* knew where the Khahn lived, they were not people to hide themselves.

"Not me. That's why I'm asking you."

"Ah yes, Signora, of course! You are new to Alexandria, I think?" He paused, but I did not volunteer information.

"It is the old lady's residence the Signora desires?"

"Do they all live together?"

He laughed as if I'd made an exquisitely funny joke.

"Ah, the Signora is not serious! The old lady lives alone. But there are the children of her husband's other wives (they are Moslem, naturally), and many of their children, too. At one time we could count at least fifteen residences. Now things are very changed. . . ." He sketched a gesture which implied the dissolution of a whole world.

"I've no idea which one," I said desperately.

"The eldest son of the eldest son is called Harif. The richest of all the Khahn, or so he used to be. Now there are rumours—you understand, Signora, that Alexandria is a city of rumours, they flow continually like the water in the bay. . . ." He fixed me with a beady glance. In the world of the Khahn, said that glance, I, would be pretty small beer. "The old lady's residence—she who is Harif's grandmother—is very fine, and in the guidebook. It is rumoured she was to be turned out to make way for offices of the new régime, but the President had pity, because of her great age."

He darted to his cubbyhole and returned with a thin green paperbound book, which he pressed into my hand. "The guidebook. Very fine pictures of Alexandria." I tipped him, and the volubility redoubled. It wasn't necessary to dig, just to listen.

"The claws of all these peoples is cut, *non è vero?* The Khahn, they kept always a bit apart, so now no one knows quite how they stand." He gave a glance over his shoulder, looked back at me, and whispered: "The Government——"

"I suppose so."

"The riches, they were always fabulous. Less fabulous today, as I tell you, but still to us——" he bracketed himself with me in another expressive gesture, "enormous; if we are right, and not this cruel rumour which says"—again he looked over his shoulder, exaggerating the conspiratorial act for my enjoyment, "the Khahn are ruined. This may be so, it may be not. There is still the big cars, and the display." 'And the tips——' I thought, reminded of how dangerous my interest was. Perhaps the Khahn frequented this gaudy building—perhaps Guiseppe would hint that an Englishwoman had been snooping. It might be wiser to break off the conversation, but he was in full spate.

"Harif, he was not always popular—not like the old man, his grandfather, who was very good, very much beloved. There was nothing definite, rumours, that was all: yes, rumours. Business deals a little too clever, associates a little too sharp. Not that this means much in Alex; but the family is old, and proud. They say it was a relief to his parents when he set up on his own, out in the Western Rabat. His father, a weak man, was glad to see him go, though there too there were rumours."

"Of what?" I ventured.

"He had a name, Signora, a bad one, for women."

"Surely that's usual enough."

"Not in this way, though I would not wish to soil the Signora's ears! Suffice it to say he was not always discreet about his—tastes." A drip of moisture had formed at the corner of his lip. I saw it with distaste. He leaned his elbows on the desk, and a concupiscent smile spread from ear to ear. "Oh, he was deservedly interesting to his friends, was Harif. And to his steward who was not even Alexandrian, but French."

"French?" I said nonchalantly, conscious of walking on dangerous ground. "What was this Frenchman's name?"

"It began, I think, with a B——"

"Steward," I said thoughtfully, "an unusual occupation for a Frenchman, surely?"

"Nothing is unusual, here in Alexandria. And we have many

180

people who are happier outside their own country. Here we do not ask questions—we know the answers! Now I recollect: the name was Barfleur."

A slight tingle went down my spine. Was it no more than a coincidence that Father's family had come from the environs of Barfleur, in Manche? I said, still more nonchalantly: "Oh, *Barfleur*. Why, I *think* I met his daughter once—he did have a daughter?"

"Most certainly he had a daughter! *Bellissima!*—though penniless. And that is why it made sensation—was not popular——"

I leaned forward eagerly, but the hotel manager was approaching. Guiseppe forgot me at once and hurried forward. Still clutching the paperbound guidebook in my hand I turned slowly away, digesting the importance of this news. It would be wiser to leave things, for the moment. I could probe no more without drawing attention to myself.

20

They fool me to the top of my bent.
HAMLET

I was running down a long corridor. It was hot, and my head throbbed; my eyes smarted. It was as though I were running from a fire, but my limbs were lead, I dragged them along, moving first one then the other like blocks of wood. If I wasn't hoarse, I could shout for help—I woke. It was broad daylight. My right hand still clutched the guidebook. I was shivering violently, and the dream sensations were real: throbbing head, smarting eyes, and a throat which felt parched. Turning my head with an effort I could see the clock on the mantelpiece. Ten. I dragged myself from bed on limbs which would scarcely stand.

Oh God—don't let me be ill *now*. Yet even as I sipped a glass of water and tried to pretend away the sensations, I knew gloomily this prayer wouldn't be answered. It was only something infectious which made one feel like this. 'Flu, or measles or —or something worse, like smallpox. I stared in horror at my reflection. My face looked swollen. It blurred and wavered. Slowly, painfully, I began to dress.

The day was hot, and outside the air was dust-filled and smelly. The glare made me flinch, and I went back vaguely into the shelter of the hotel. My head pounded. Guiseppe was coming towards me, consternation in his face.

"Signora! Signora—you are not well——" His hand under my elbow steered me towards a chair. "You should be in bed, Signora. Let me telephone the doctor." I could hear him thinking: 'This woman has brought infection to the hotel'—in one moment he would call the manager.

"It's nothing," I croaked. "Just a touch of the sun—it's hotter here than I expected."

"That is all——?" He continued to stare at me.

I forced my aching back upright. "Yes—there's nothing to fuss about. Tell me, Harif Khahn—you were going to tell me where he lived?"

"You are not going out *now*?"

182

"Of course not," I lied. "I'll perhaps rest on my bed a little. All the same I should like the address."

"A pleasure, Signora." He took an envelope from his pocket and wrote something on it. "There. You will find everyone knows it. Now, Signora, let me send an iced drink to your room, and telephone the doctor. There is an Englishman all the English like."

I rose. "Truly, I don't need him." As he hesitated I murmured: "*Truly*. And I'd be thankful for that drink immediately."

"Certainly, Signora." He intercepted a page and gave the order. While his back was turned I walked fast out of the door. I looked back and Guiseppe was staring after me, horrified. He made a step as if to follow, and then I saw him turn briskly and trot towards the manager's office. Quickly I put as much space as possible between me and the hotel.

Goodness, how I longed for that drink! With every step my head pounded, my throat grew sorer by the minute. I had no clear idea what I meant to do. The drums of fever throbbed in my head, impeding thought. The envelope with Harif Khahn's address was in my hand. I squinted down at it—he lived at Mersa; that would be a long taxi drive—if I could get a taxi. The alternative was the unreal-sounding House of Palms; and Ibrahim. And, presumably, the waiting trap.

Ilona. The trap. Ilona. The trap . . . Ilona. I started to walk fast, faster, my feet kept time to the throbbing in my head. The sun was blazing down, the traffic sounds insistent; the blare of horns, the street cries, all seemed to mock me. I peered again at the envelope, but my eyes blurred and I couldn't read. Were there *no* taxis in Alexandria? I wouldn't recognize one if I saw it. . . .

A formidable object moved towards me, swaying and dipping. I could still recognize something as large as a tram, I thought with pride. I got on, and slumped back on the nearest seat. Everything was now all right. Through a fog a dark face stared at me, coming and going with part of the universal mockery. "Ras-el-tin," said a voice, "Ras-el-tin? *Ras-el-tin?*" Perhaps it thought me a deaf-mute. "Ilona," I said, and ruffled in my bag for money. It was taken, and I was left in such peace as physical misery allowed me. That tram swooped and swayed like a bloody seagull. . . .

"Ras-el-tin." I sat slumped with my eyes shut, smiling to myself. Here we were. 'They' would now bring me Ilona. . . .

"*Ras-el-tin.*" Someone was urging me up, dragging me by the elbow. An indignant dark face hovered over mine. Staggering like a new-born giraffe I got off the tram. The sun hit me a blow between the eyes. I walked forward, someone walking into sea. Every step moved mountains away in front of me. Eventually I stopped, everything circling round me as if I were a spinning top coming slowly to rest, and keeled over gently and finally on my side. There was a babble of seagull sounds, they swooped, their hostile wings blocked out the day, and I sank firmly and inconsiderately away from them, down, down to the bottom of a coal-black sea.

It was a large cool place I was in. A barracks of a place with ugly green walls going up, up to greyish distance. When I was conscious enough to care, I turned my head to examine my surroundings. Of course—I was in hospital. A large ward with many beds, most of them occupied by depressed-looking mounds. A young Arab doctor in a white coat stood by my side, hypodermic in hand.

"Ah—mis-sus Elvan, mis-sus Elvan," he repeated carefully and apologetically. I blinked at him, wondering why he called me that, and he advanced the hypodermic to my arm, and I shifted away again on a white cool tide out to sea, out towards the horizon beyond which I should find Ilona. . . .

Three days later I surfaced properly; horrified by my weakness, by loss of time. From a sour-looking nurse who spoke monosyllabic English I learnt that my illness was the brand of acute tonsillitis which attacks unacclimatized visitors to the North African coast, combined with a touch of the sun; the Alexandrian sun, at that. I felt awful enough—totally depleted; although my throat was better and my headache mild though apparently permanent.

The basilisk nurse came to administer the tablets which had replaced injections. I opened my mouth to ask if my hotel knew where I was, and shut it again. Who knew which of my enemies might not have caught up with me there as I slept? 'Missus Elvan', the doctor had called me. With any luck the hotel's missing occupant, Marian Said, had gone unconnected with Mrs. Hellevan, emergency patient in this gloomy place. With luck, again, Marjorie's passport in my bag had earned me a breathing-space. Medical people might not notice the lack of entry stamp.

But this hospital was no place to be stuck in, and I was glad when the young doctor told me next day that they were transferring me that afternoon. He was examining my throat at the time, with a torch. I made a croaking interrogative sound, but he gave no details, and I realized he spoke little English. Anyway, there was probably a different place for Europeans, or people who weren't too sick. It couldn't, I thought looking round me, be more depressing than this, which seemed pre-Nightingale. And I would ask no questions, or it might bring on someone to question *me*. I could only keep my mouth shut, and hope I should soon be fit enough to resume my desperate search. I smiled up at the doctor, and he smiled back, giving a deferential little bow which surprised me.

"Three oh-clock. Three," he repeated, holding up three fingers. "You ready, then come. Pri-vate am-bu-lence." He drew a small English dictionary out of his pocket, consulted it, repeated the word 'am-bu-lence' with evident pride, and went away.

'Oh Lord, *private*. . . . .' I told myself dismally, recalling the none too large store of notes 'they' had provided. I could see myself trying to soften a stony British Consul with a false passport sans entry stamp. ('*And* I've another at the hotel, in a different name, but stamped'. . . !) I wondered gloomily how much private medicine cost here; hopes of recovering my child alone diminished and diminished. . . . Oh *Ilona*. I closed my eyes.

Just before three the basilisk nurse brought my pills, and then dressed me as I sat weakly on the side of the bed with my head swimming. She did it efficiently, as if I were a large child she particularly disliked, gave me my shoes and bag to hold, said:

"They soon, with stretcher," and drifted away up the ward. Nothing had been said about payment, no one had asked for my address. It seemed odd, unless these things would be regulated where I was going. That must be it. Here was another breathing-space for which I was truly thankful. In the meantime I followed my policy of a shut mouth.

At about four (punctuality was evidently *not* an Alexandrian virtue) the ward door swung, and the ambulance men appeared. They looked rather tatty, and the stretcher, poised on an operation trolley, was none too clean. But they rolled me on to it quite efficiently, deposited my shoes and bag on my feet, and we moved off, the basilisk nurse walking at my side; down a corridor, into a lift, out again, along another corridor, and through a large entrance where a small blue ambulance was waiting on the gravel, backed up to receive me. They slid me in like a jelly on to a shelf, and proceeded to strap me down with what I thought unnecessary zeal—unless the driver was particularly dangerous. The nurse had faded away with the trolley, but just before the back doors were closed the little doctor appeared, framed against the burning sunlight. He raised a dark hand in merry farewell.

"Goo-oodbye, mis-sus Elvan. Now you be pleasant with friends." Perhaps he imagined all Europeans liked each other. I waved him good-bye, and murmured my thanks. The stretcher-bearers joined me inside, and the little ambulance trundled away. The loud purr of its engine was quite soothing, so I relaxed and wondered how far the new hospital was, and how long it would be before I could get out of it to resume my search for Ilona. I didn't dare think of the melodramatic threat which had been levelled at my child. I was determined to live only in the present, to reserve my strength for her rescue. We drove a long way and I grew sleepy, although the stretcher straps irksomely cut into me. I tried to explain my discomfort to the attendants, but failed. They merely smiled and shook their heads.

Eventually the ambulance drew up, the doors were opened, and my stretcher released. I was glad to move my arms freely again, but my relief was shortlived; for one of the attendants promptly engulfed me in a heavy blanket, while the other

186

expertly readjusted the straps so that I was pinned to the stretcher and lay there muffled up and helpless like Tom Kitten. I felt like a criminal for dispatch, or a lunatic in a straitjacket, and began to struggle feebly as the stretcher was swiftly swung out into the street; a narrow dusty street, where the closeness of the almost blank walls could only allow room for one vehicle to pass.

Above one wall I could see a mass of palm fronds, rustling their scimitar-sharp leaves in the hot wind. They looked sullen and thick, as if made of rusty green mackintosh with tattered edges. Straight in front of me was a narrow dark doorway, from which emerged a conjunction of unattractive smells. As I felt myself carried helplessly towards it a feeling of unimaginable horror overcame me, as if nameless evil brooded beyond, waiting for me, its dark octopus fingers reaching outwards in a blind and horrible groping. Who *were* these 'ambulance men'—and where was I? But I knew. The palms rustled like gossips retailing open secrets. Palms . . . and 'Ibrahim': to whom I had been so neatly brought, since I hadn't come of my own free will.

As I was taken through that nightmare entrance I opened my mouth to give one despairing scream, in a feeble hope that someone, anyone, would hear and report it (*in noisy Alexandria!*). But, before I could utter one cry, a fold of blanket was hastily drawn up over my face, and a hand brutally clamped it down over my mouth and nose, and held it there. I was borne struggling into that horrible place, and up a flight of what were evidently steepish stairs. In the distance there were voices, the bagpipe drone of some strange instrument, a young woman's laugh. Then these sounds were cut off abruptly by a door shutting. My stretcher was deposited ungently, and my two attendants clattered out of the room, leaving me alone with the blanket still folded over my face as if I were a mere bundle of goods, an object of total disregard.

I don't think—not even on that night in England when Elizabeth and Clayton had conspired to murder me—I have ever been so much afraid.

I lay there, scared and sweating, for what felt like hours. Now and then I struggled weakly, like a trussed fowl, but each time caused the blanket to rearrange itself in a more fiendishly smothering way; I was so afraid of being stifled that eventually I lay quite still, only conscious of the unsteady hammer of my heart. After a while I became paralysingly aware of someone in the room with me. I hadn't heard anyone come in, but all the same I *knew*. I shrank away from the enveloping blanket, trying hard and ridiculously to make myself invisible, unnoticed. Whoever was near me was standing by my head, in dead silence. And then two cruel hands descended, pressing the blanket smoothly down over my mouth and nose with a horrible suggestiveness. I gulped and fought for air, it was like drowning. And then suddenly I was released, and the covering drawn back from my face. It was Elizabeth who bent over me, her fair hair swinging down almost to touch me. She put a hand on my forehead, and gave a little amused giggle as I automatically winced away.

"There, Jenny dear, that was just to teach you a lesson, and to do as you're told. Be good, and you won't ever need lesson two—nor will Ilona."

I couldn't speak, not even to ask about my child. Elizabeth moved away and sat down on the end of the bed where I was lying, and gazed at me intently.

"I suppose you're wondering how we got on to where you were, poor simple Jenny. Well, if you *will* wander about the town delirious, with Khahn's address clutched in your hand like a signpost! Of course the hospital rang us up. . . . And I guessed from their description it was you misusing Marjorie's name. Your little doctor was sweet, he was delighted to find you were one of our oldest friends—we said we'd send a private ambulance for you, and not to mention that you weren't going to another hospital, or you'd start to worry about being a nuisance. It must have sounded excruciatingly odd, but they'll swallow anything here, with a big enough tip. You'll find out. *Anything*. . . ." Her blue gaze swept over me with humiliating amusement, and then she giggled again. "You know, Jenny, you look just so damned funny, like that. Do you want to be let out?"

I only wanted to murder her, and I wouldn't give her the satisfaction of replying. So I stared stolidly at the ceiling, where a small green gecko looked back at me in apparent surprise. It evidently thought I looked damned funny too.

"Oh Jenny, you are a *bore*. Don't start sulking, like you used to when we were children, or I'll come and tickle you up again." She rose and came over to me. All my muscles tensed. She stood there looking down at me, and for a moment the mask of gaiety vanished and I could almost feel the black despairing hatred seep out of her towards me, a fog of loathing—the 'deadness' described by Christopher. Then she smiled, and flicked me across the face hard and contemptuously with the back of her hand.

"You haven't even asked about your precious child! D'you know, Jenny, I don't think you care for her as much as the good mother act you put on implied? Isn't all this frisking about after her just part of an enormous guilt complex—because of Christopher?"

Still I didn't reply, for silence evidently goaded her, and if she really lost her temper I might learn more. As well, I felt unpleasantly weak and dizzy, and wanted to reserve my strength. She gave a short laugh. "Anyway, you'll be glad to know that we don't mean to deprive you of *him*." She spoke viciously, jabbing out each syllable as if it were a sharp weapon aimed at me.

I spoke at last. To my own ears my voice sounded weak and tremulous—the voice of the hunted. "I don't care about Christopher, Elizabeth. You're welcome to him."

"Just don't keep lying to me. Just don't lie, that's all." She was walking restlessly about the room, her hands gripped together, her knuckles showing white. "You certainly won't get away with that one. Why, Clayton found out——" She faced me again. "Very convenient, getting work in Christopher's offices, wasn't it? And all those old rumours, you weren't too happy about breaking it off——"

"Clayton's wrong." My voice was stronger. "At least, not at the time, I wasn't, but——"

"Look, Jenny, we'll get on better—*you'll* do better, if you stop giving me that one man, one girl, act about George. I know what you felt about Christopher. See? I *know*." She rubbed her hand wearily across her eyes. "All I *don't* really know is what he felt about *you*. And that, my dear, is what we're going to find out."

I stared at her, puzzled. She was obsessed by thoughts of Christopher. Certainly she was projecting her own feelings on to me. If I hadn't looked on her with such distaste I could have pitied her. She looked torn in pieces. If I was in one hell, she was in another. But her obsession was not going to allow me light on mine. So I had to say it: "Ilona?"

"What?" She put her hands up to her forehead, and knuckled the sides of it, staring at me like one drugged, her eyes large and beseeching in her thin face. In some indefinable way she had aged since I last saw her. I could see her easily as a skull, with blue living eyes still in its sockets. "Oh yes—Ilona." She appeared to be thinking; and then, with resolve, she began to undo the straps which bound me. "I'm just warning you, Jenny, don't try anything on, see? Outside this door is the most villainous-looking Negro you ever saw, with the sharpest knife. He enjoys using it, too. . . ."

The last strap was undone. Temporarily I was too stiff to move. Like a competent nurse she heaved me up and swung me round so that my legs, their circulation agonizingly restored, dangled over the edge of the bed. I felt like a puppet glove.

"Just you sit *there*. . . ." She cocked her head sideways, listening for something. I rubbed at my wrists. I couldn't hear whatever she was so intent on. All at once she moved over to the window, undid the catch, and pushed at the semi-closed outer shutters so that one of them swung wide. The light was intense, ominous. All I could hear was the continual rustle of palms, the strident noises of Alexandria.

"Ahmed!"

A man's voice rose in reply. So there was another of them below—I might have known the window would be guarded. Elizabeth spoke rapidly, in what I took to be Arabic. Question and answer succeeded each other. Over her shoulder she said to me: "She's always in some trouble or other. . . ."

"She"? I raised my head, and stopped rubbing. Elizabeth was silent, as though she wanted me to listen too. Then I heard it quite clearly—the subdued and muffled sound of a child's sobs.

190

My sister leant out of the window. "Oh, for heaven's sake! What's the matter *now*?" There was no answer, only the sound of renewed and hopeless sobbing. Ilona. Every mother knows her own child, her ear is even attuned to the difference in a baby's wail. I called her name, but so feebly that she didn't hear. Painfully I dragged myself off the bed, just as Elizabeth said: "Go back to Ayesha at once; at *once*, d'you hear?" And slammed the shutters so that we stood in semi-darkness; I paralysingly aware of my weakness, knowing I couldn't possibly fight her at that moment, and she as immovably in my way as the Bargee when we were children.

"Unfortunately," she said evenly, "Ayesha isn't always very good-tempered. And Ilona is the most disobedient little brat— how could you ever have produced such a rebel hellcat, Jenny? You were always as meek as a pie. Here, you'd better get back on that bed—why, you're shaking, you're shaking all over like a leaf. . . ."

In a horrible parody of solicitousness, which reminded me of Clayton, she put her arm round me; and half-carried me back to the bed, where I collapsed panting on my side. "You just lie there, you lie there and rest. I'll get you some milk and brandy, and when you're better and stronger—why, we'll have another little talk." Her hand rested lightly on my hair, in a motherly way. Her touch was sickening to me, but I didn't even have the strength to push it off.

21

. . . the bloody book of law
You shall yourself read in the bitter letter
After your own sense. . . .

OTHELLO

Whatever they were reserving me for, the next two days they treated me quite kindly. I was uneasily reminded of a turkey fattened for Christmas. I wasn't allowed to leave my room (any more than the turkey's allowed out of its pen), and one glimpse of the 'villainous-looking Negro' decided me against rashness. And I wasn't allowed to see and speak to Ilona—Elizabeth rebutted the suggestion with scornful impatience.

"For goodness' sake, Jenny! She's quite quiet and docile at the moment—d'you want to poke her up? Just remember, my dear, that whether you're to be finally parted or not depends entirely on your co-operation."

At least it didn't seem to depend, at the moment, on my murder. Evidently the tune was changed in some way since her savage determination on that night in London. For all that, the comparatively clement treatment made me almost more uneasy than before; and the thought of Ilona 'quiet and docile' tore at my heart. But I set my will firmly on survival, in spite of our situation. Survival for myself and Ilona. I repeated it to myself a hundred times a day. I forbade myself to think either of my child's misery, or my own. I slept at night from sheer exhaustion, and ate everything they brought me, so that I should be fitter for resistance. If this were the Pavlov softening-up treatment once more, I was determined to withstand it. At least I was helped by knowing Ilona was alive.

Now and then I heard her voice in the distance, although Elizabeth never let her near my window again, in pursuance of her policy of keeping us well apart. 'Ayesha' looked after me, in silence. An ill-fed Arab girl with a pock-marked face and a spiteful mouth. I soon gave up trying to extract information from her.

I don't know if it was the result of so much strain, followed by

192

illness, but I was in a curious state at this time. It was as if a complete curtain had descended between me and reality, shutting out all fear. It may have been self-hypnotism; I don't know. But I would lie for hours dreamy and relaxed on my bed, thinking of nothing, only conscious of the palms' rustling, and of the pervading heat, and listening all the time for Ilona's voice. And then, on the third morning, all was changed. I woke with my skin practically crawling with apprehension. I knew, as an animal knows, that something was planned for today. And as time passed and no one brought me anything to eat, and the silence grew more absolute, my mouth became dry not only for lack of water, but from fear.

Even the palms outside the window were perfectly still, as though they waited on events inside the house. I'm sure horrible things had happened here before. The aura of evil was unmistakable. Now, as I painfully emerged from detachment, I could feel it flowing towards me, an insidious current of malignancy.

About noon, when the heat was extreme and my mouth bone-dry from thirst, I heard voices outside my door. One was Elizabeth's. The other was a man's, unknown to me. I stood up, the better to take what instinct said was coming, and when they entered the room forced myself to appear calm and unafraid.

Elizabeth was even more drawn than two days ago; her skin sagged, there were circles round her eyes, and sometimes one of her lids gave a heavy, convulsive twitch, as though she winked at me. At first I couldn't understand what was wrong with her— after all, she was in the winning position—until I saw at last that she, too, was afraid. Afraid as I had only once seen her: at the Hilton, the day she reappeared; and—when I looked at her companion—I knew it was for the same reason: this was the man who had sat opposite us then, and stared me mockingly out of countenance.

At close quarters I thought him even more unpleasant than before. There was only one chair in the room, and he made straight for it and sat down, leaving Elizabeth to lean against the wall. I also sat—on the bed, and returned his stare with one blank as I could make it. He certainly realized my instinctive defiance and chalked it up against me, for I saw him chew the end

193

of his small moustache reflectively, and his hard little eyes looked me over as though I were indeed a fattened turkey. Otherwise he ignored me, and spoke only to Elizabeth.

"She appears not to have suffered from her—stay." He sounded as though he regretted it.

"You said to look after her."

"I meant, to take care she did not get away. You're a fool."

Elizabeth gave me a look of pure hate, which I interpreted as regret for lost opportunities. "Harif, I assure you——' Her voice was low and hesitant. So this was Mademoiselle Khahn's eldest brother, the one with money and power and vicious tastes, the one who had had a steward called Barfleur——

He made a gesture to silence her. "No names." Then he eyed me reflectively. They were the hardest, deadest eyes I had ever looked into, and after three minutes of staring I knew just why Clayton would never have succeeded as a top criminal. There is a hierarchy in evil, just as in other things, and I had no doubt on which rung Harif perched. It was the most merciless face, with its downturned lips and stony eyes, I had ever seen. Add to it sensuality, and you get a simple sum—sadism. The expression would have made anyone's fortune in Hitlerite Germany.

"You said she was the plain one—but I find her striking; unusual, in spite of her—er—vicissitudes. She looks to have more temperament. You haven't worn well, my dear, it's been a disappointment. And you've taken little trouble, just lately. Ah well—I'm not complaining. Zaina is certain she's *enceinte*—she tells me she is positive it is a son." He yawned, and Elizabeth stared straight ahead, avoiding both his eye and mine. Now I noticed for the first time that she was wearing rings on both hands, as George had mentioned. An incredible suspicion began to stir in me— But now Harif was giving me the pleasure of his mocking attention.

"I hope you've enjoyed your reception here, Madame?"

"The food has been good," I said politely, "but I'm thirsty, they forgot my breakfast."

"Ah, listen to this! They forgot her breakfast, poor girl. Well, my dear, we shall also forget your breakfast. We have more

194

important matters to remember. You are going to write a little letter for us. Not so?"

"No one's told me," I said. "It depends."

His easy lolling attitude was deceptive. I hardly saw him move. The blow caught me unprepared on the side of the face, and sent me crashing back against the wall. Then he took me by the shoulder and dragged me up facing him, and slapped me again and again rhythmically, first across one side of the head and then the other. I tried to defend myself, but it was like opposing an iron machine set in flailing motion. I heard Elizabeth give a little scream. It sounded more like excitement than shock. By the time Harif had done, my self-control had gone. Tears poured from my eyes, and I made no attempt to stop them. It was all I could do to force myself to sit upright. He walked over to the window and stood with his back to me as if I'd ceased to exist; as I felt I had. This was what it meant to be looked on as an object.

"I trust that has put an end to foolishness. Give her the paper, now. Show her exactly what she is to write."

Elizabeth crossed to me and placed pad and pencil beside me, together with a piece of typewritten paper. I bent my head, and through my tears read the message; the incoherent, disjointed, and cleverly-phrased *cri de coeur:*

Christopher,

I didn't know what I was getting into, they fooled me so. Please come—*please.* Help Ilona, even if you won't help me any more. We're locked up here. They've beaten me up, and I don't know how long they'll let us live. You can trust Ibrahim, who brings this, but he's weak, he won't dare act alone. Promise him anything you like—*anything.* I'll pay.

Oh, please come. *Quickly*——

JENNY

I stared down at the treacherous little note. Elizabeth was forcing the pen into my hand, closing my fingers over it. "You see, we know now where he is, in Alexandria. He couldn't keep away." She was flushed and panting. There was something masochistic about her pleasure, she leant on the feelings she thought Christopher had for me, as though they were a sore tooth.

"But—but he's already on your side!" I said baldly.

"Your views on Mr. Leyton's allegiances are not of the slightest interest to us." Harif turned round and bared his teeth at me. One corner of his moustache was wet with saliva where he had chewed it. "Hurry and write."

"I won't." It took all my courage to say it, now I knew what I was asking for. I had meant to speak firmly, but it came out in an alarmed mouse's squeak.

Harif gave me a gentle, and for that reason all the more terrifying, smile. "This is admirable! I see you have a passion to be an Odette." I winced. "Listen, my dear, I do not mean to waste my time, or anyone else's, by allowing you such a narcissistic amusement. It might be a pleasure, some other time; just now I am busy. You will write that letter. At once. If you do not, I shall send for your child. And if I have to send for her, she will suffer in a very unpleasant way, whether you write or whether you don't. You have three minutes to make up your mind if I mean what I say."

He meant it. I had no doubts of that. I didn't know whether Christopher deserved what I was doing to him, or not; whether he had double-crossed them, or double-crossed me. But I had inescapably drawn the Judas part. With a shaking hand I traced a copy of the note. When I had done Harif picked it up and studied it intently, then passed it to Elizabeth. "Excellent. The shakiness is easily explained by the beating-up—it really adds confirmation." I stared at him, and saw something flicker, a sort of mixture of greed and excitement, at the back of his eyes.

"Did I say I was busy? Perhaps not so busy I cannot spare a *little* time to make at least some part of that note true. . . ."

He took a step towards me. I put up my hands to ward him off, knowing it was useless, and over his shoulder saw Elizabeth's look of anticipation merge into one of pleasure. Harif was silent, precise, and scientific. He didn't waste a movement. Towards the end he was panting, with enjoyment. At least I had managed not to do more than moan a little, before I passed out cleanly, and very thankfully, on the floor.

It was dark when I came round, to the sound of my own moans. I was one large pain from head to foot. It was a wonder to me that so many brave women could ever have endured repeated violence, repeated beatings-up. There and then I humbly decided I would never make a spy.

It was hard to tell if it was dark because the sun had set, or because someone had closed the shutters; but there was no light filtering in, so I assumed it must be late. I managed to struggle up on to my elbows, but the effort made me moan again. And then, terrifyingly, a hand came out of the dark and touched my face, very gingerly, like a blind person trying to identify me. I drew in my breath with a gasp, my heart palpitated. A voice well-known to me said, very quietly: "*Jenny*——"

"*Christopher*. It's—it's not you—it can't be—why, they were going to get you, they made me——" I stopped, remembering that note. And I understood. Bitterly. "They *have* got you. You're—you're in the trap—as well."

"Lower your voice. Whisper."

"*Sorry*." I whispered it. I felt the bed give beneath his weight as he sat down on it, and found my hand.

"No—we're not yet both in the bag. Where have they got Ilona?"

"I don't know," I said shakily.

"I suppose she's the reason why——"

"Yes," I said, quickly, "that's why." I didn't know if he would believe me, or not. "They—they threatened to do all sorts of horrible things."

"Poor Jenny. But don't worry. I guessed the note was pure myth."

"It wasn't all pure myth." I heard the break in my voice.

"I know." Christopher's voice was hard. "So they did really beat you up——"

"What do you think I was moaning for," I whispered, again shakily. Out of the dark Christopher's arms went round me, and I collapsed into them like a child into a nurse's, shaking and shuddering. His face was pressed against my hair, and I could feel the anger in him. Somehow it put guts into me again, and I drew a bit away. He let me go.

197

"Sorry—you haven't told me how you got here."

"I followed Ibrahim." I gave a muffled exclamation. "Oh, don't worry—I put on a beautiful, zealous act with our thoughtful chum. We worked out the best way for me to come and get you; at eleven he was going to let me in. He and some charming oh-so-trustworthy confederate were going to help me spirit you and Ilona away, for much gold. I've just come a bit earlier than they expected, that's all." His voice was grim; and he sounded worried, I thought. "We have an hour, to get you and Ilona out of here. Can you move, all right?"

"I can try," I said, with no conviction.

"That's the spirit. And talking of spirits, have some of this." His fingers groped for my mouth, and pressed the brandy flask to it. I gulped willingly. It was amazing how much better it made me feel. It also made my bruised head throb like the devil.

"They haven't broken any bones, have they, Jenny?" There was acute anxiety in his voice.

"I'm *pretty* sure not." Cautiously I tested my limbs. They were stiff and painful, that was all.

"Who was it beat you up?"

"A man called Harif."

"*Harif!* I *see.* Now everything falls into place at last." *I* didn't see that it did, but the way he said it made me feel that Harif might find a reckoning. I hoped it would be a nasty one. Then I remembered something:

"*Christopher* . . . what about the guard?"

"What guard?"

"On the door—my door."

"There wasn't one—there's one in the garden. He's not quite so active as he was."

"But there *was* one on my door—a Negro."

"My dear, they may have expected you to try and get away before, but not after whatever threats they made against Ilona. Or in your state, alone. Probably another reason the guard's withdrawn is because they're starting to bait the trap."

My spine crawled. "You mean—they've guessed you'd come earlier."

"They may have—they may not. It could be."

198

"Which way *did* you get in, then?"

"There's a little window at the end of the passage. Through there. Ibrahim had obligingly mapped out your room for me—but not, unfortunately, Ilona's. He said evasively it was difficult to describe, he must show me."

"Then it *is* the trap—now." With both hands I pushed Christopher away from me, hard. "You must go—you must. Get some help for us, but get out of here, at once——"

"Steady."

His hand was on my arm, soothing me down. "I've done my best, at short notice, but the trouble was I didn't dare make contacts openly, and the chap I wanted was out. He'll be there tonight—I left a message. We can only hope it will be sooner, not later."

"Please Christopher, I know you must go."

"If I do, and my—friends—don't come, I don't know how much time you and Ilona will have left." It was baldly put, and in an odd way it steadied me.

"Why are you trusting me now," I whispered, "when you didn't before? And when everything looks much blacker against me than it did?"

"Come to that, why are you trusting *me*?"

"I don't know," I said honestly.

He laughed, softly. "Needs must, when the devil drives. For devil, read Harif."

"Yes, but *why*...."

His hand closed over mine. "No time for. explanations Jenny. If we've declared a truce, can you walk?" I felt his arm round me, pulling me up. I did my best to help myself and, muttering darkly, managed to stand upright. Each step across the room was painful. Christopher guided me over to the door. "Good—not bad progress." I leant against the wall and recovered my breath. Christopher kept his arm round me, while he spoke low in my ear: "These seedy dwellings haven't electric light, as you've seen—only oil lamps. There's one at the end of this corridor. The house is only one storey. Plainly and logically, Ilona isn't this end, or you'd have heard her.

"Now, when you come to the stairs you go down a few, and

then up, and along another corridor opposite this. It's all in darkness, but it's my belief that's where they've got her. We have to find out. Are you sure you can manage, Jenny? Because I'll need you."

"Oh yes." God knows how, but I was determined to manage.

"Good. Your job will be to hang on to Ilona, keep her quiet, and if possible get her back to the passage window."

"What happens," I asked in a small voice, "if anyone comes?" Sweat prickled on my spine.

His voice was grim. "I've got a gun—with silencer, all complete. But you don't want to worry about that, Jenny, you just keep your thoughts on Ilona and deal with her, whatever happens. See?"

"I see. And I'm not worrying," I added solemnly, "how could you ever think such a thing?"

"Oh, you darling——" I could hear laughter in his voice. He tightened his left arm round me, opened the door, and listened. The corridor was dim, the oil lamp burned low. All was still. Ominously still. Christopher pulled me out after him and we began, very cautiously, to traverse the corridor. Downstairs I could just hear a faint hum of voices, which grew gradually louder as we reached the stairs. He paused a moment but was evidently reassured, for he motioned me on.

We walked carefully into darkness, guided only by a distant crack of light beneath a door. I was finding movement easier now; and the thought that Ilona might be behind that door put strength into me. We reached it, and I heard Christopher's hand move softly over the surface, seeking for the handle. He had pushed me back against the wall—I guessed that he wanted me out of the line of fire, if we were surprised. He found the handle, and turned it cautiously. I drew in my breath—suppose the door was locked? But, amazingly—if they *were* holding Ilona prisoner here—it wasn't. And then, as the door swung open, and light from the oil lamp by the bed illumined everything, I saw *why* it wasn't: Ilona was sprawled higgledy-piggledy on the bed, her long lashes dark on her cheeks, her breathing very slow and heavy and deep. I was certain, even before close examination, that she was drugged. I was across the room and leaning over her, my cheek pressed to hers, before I heard Christopher behind me softly close the door. He stood with his back to it, looking worried.

"Is she doped?"

"I think so." I slid my hand down her arm, found her pulse, which beat slow and heavy—but strong. I rolled back the lid of one eye, and peered at the pupil. She didn't even stir beneath my hand.

"Yes—she's doped, all right."

"In one way that's not a bad thing—but you won't be able to carry her." He looked nonplussed. "You'll have to take the gun, Jenny. Can you shoot—ever shot anything?"

"A rabbit—once; when I was fifteen."

"Kill it?"

"No—just blew the fur off its trousers."

"If there's action, we'll need more than Harif's trousers to pin on the stabledoor." He came over to the bed, and looked down at Ilona. "No time to waste." He handed me the gun. "Drugs run right through this case, don't they? Right back to that diary. . . ." I gave him an odd look, but he didn't appear to notice it. "Now, here we go. . . ."

I remember reading once that all men instinctively spit on their hands before lifting heavy loads. I'll swear Christopher spat on his before lifting Ilona off that bed; she was a dead weight, all right. I couldn't keep my eyes off her face, which I'd never really thought to see again. Her cheeks had a waxy pallor they never had before, like the pallor of Victorian wax dolls. Her chestnut curls were dark with sweat. Her full, half-open lips were pale, too, as pale as the sculptured lips of Michelangelo's Boy David. Because of my obsessive tenderness for her, I failed us all dismally. I never heard the turning of the doorhandle.

Christopher did, though. With Ilona in his arms he whipped round just as the door opened. With the awful fatality of nightmare I saw it was Elizabeth who stood there, peering in on us uncertainly. I couldn't see if anyone stood behind her, but I thought not. I raised the gun automatically in my unaccustomed hand, and heard Christopher beside me say, after a split second's pause: "*Shoot*, Jenny. Damn you, darling—*shoot*. . . ."

I couldn't. I knew it, even as I pointed that wicked-looking instrument at my sister. All our lives depended on it, yet it was as if my hand had gone numb, or my brain frozen; as though 'they' had drugged me, as they'd drugged Ilona. And Elizabeth didn't seem afraid. She looked extremely odd, her eyes wide and blank and staring, saliva at the corners of her mouth. Her skin was sweating too; and yet I knew instinctively it wasn't caused by fear. Not fear of me, anyhow.

"*Jenny*," said Christopher urgently.

"I can't," I muttered, "you must see I can't——"

Elizabeth pushed the door further open and walked into the room, paying no attention at all to the gun in my hand. She was right, of course. I couldn't possibly have shot her, any more than I'd really meant to kill that rabbit, but I don't think she reasoned it out. Something was wrong with her, and she was as indifferent to the situation's lethal side as a zombie would have been. She spoke to Christopher with an air of bewilderment, ignoring me: "Are you taking her away? He won't let you, you know. He won't let anyone do anything he doesn't want them to—only Zaina."

Her voice, hitherto monotonously uninflected, dropped on the last word. She looked at me piteously, as though I could explain everything she didn't understand. Murderous, treacherous, I knew her to be; now she was empty, too. She stood there in our path, blocking our way, her hands slack by her sides, her eyes with that dreadful blankness fixed on us, and her voice went on and on obsessedly, while Christopher gazed at me in despair, and the gun never wavered in my hand which was unable to press the trigger and release us, with violence, from the spell.

I remember she said a lot of rambling words about 'Zaina'. "She plots against me—she's wicked——" (strange accusation from Elizabeth), and then I understood she was speaking of Harif: "He's a Communist, you knew that, didn't you? But he's only using *them*, as well. He's worse than that, much worse." She cast a look of indescribable cunning over her shoulder, and whispered: "He does everyone dirt, in the end. But you mustn't say I told you——" She put up a hand as if to wipe her cheek, and scrubbed and scrubbed at it obsessively as though she were

202

trying to eradicate a bloodstain; I was grotesquely reminded of Lady Macbeth.

"You're all alike." I started, but she was speaking to Christopher, not me. "All of you. Harif and Zaina, and you and Jenny. You just make use of me. While it suits you, and then. . . ." The accusation on her lips was both absurd and sinister—the curse coming home to roost with a vengeance. "But I'm not going to be made use of any longer——" Her eyes swivelled round to me, filled suddenly with hatred. It was as if a dead electric bulb had blazed into life, and I was correspondingly startled. "I hate you, Jenny; but I hate Harif more—he thinks I'll help him, but I won't."

I looked helplessly at Christopher. It seemed as if nothing could check the soft, mad monologue—except the gun in my hand. I saw him turn slowly back to the bed, lowering Ilona towards it. I still don't know what he intended to do. Elizabeth's rambling speech had stopped. Her silence drew my eyes back to her. Perhaps, too, I had subconsciously been aware of a barely noticeable sound such as an arrow's flight makes through the air. I saw my sister's already staring eyes widen, saw a lock of shock mould itself suddenly on to her features like a deathmask. She gave a little gasp, her hands jerked up to chest level, and she fell forward on to her knees, down on to the floor at my feet. For a paralysing moment I thought: 'But I've done it. I've killed her. . . .'

I must instinctively have pulled the trigger of the silenced gun. Yet at the same time I knew, in a confused way, that I *hadn't* . . . my hand had been perfectly still. I looked down aghast at Elizabeth's body lying almost across my feet; and then up again—straight into Harif's face. He was standing just outside the door, ignoring me with the same indifference Elizabeth had shown—had he even *noticed* the gun in my hand?—and on his face was an expression of cold anticipation which I'd already seen twice before. His right hand was raised, the gun he held in it now covered Christopher.

22

Let them be hunted soundly: at this hour
Lie at my mercy all mine enemies.
                                    THE TEMPEST

All this takes time to write, but in reality it was only a matter of
a second or two. I had barely time to think: 'We've had it, we
can't get out of *this*,' and at almost the same instant to realize that
now I was going to shoot without compunction, when Christopher acted. He must have possessed a sixth sense I didn't—or
the proverbial eyes in the back of his head. For before Harif
could fire again—or did he intend to, perhaps he wanted
prisoners?—Christopher had suddenly whirled about and,
Ilona still in his arms, made a lightning sideways kick at the oil-
lamp. He didn't succeed in putting it out, but it rolled over on
to the bed, scattering sparks and splashing out oil on to the
coverlet, which promptly caught fire.

For a bewildering second the light shot up—unsteady light,
not like the former dim glow, but leaping fire with leaping
shadows too. It confused Harif more than it confused me. My
gun was steady on its target. His held fire, wavering from Ilona
to Christopher, and back again to Ilona as Christopher swung
round. This time I found determination to act, and my courage.
I shot Harif as cold-bloodedly as he'd shot Elizabeth a moment
since. As I watched the repetition of that awful sagging at the
knees, the slow final slide to the floor, I simply couldn't believe
in it. I remember saying confusedly over and over again: "I've
done it, I've done it; Christopher—I've done it," on and
on like a stuck record. And I put up a trembling hand to my
forehead and wiped the sweat from my eyes. I couldn't look
downwards again. I heard Harif make a small sobbing sound
once, and then there was nothing else except my own harsh
breathing, and the crackle and smell of fire as the flames caught
hungrily at the long curtains beside the bed.

And I still barely remember how we got out of that place.
I know Christopher's hand pushed me ahead of him out of the
door, and I stumbled and almost fell over Harif's body. Outside

in the corridor Christopher whispered: "Hold her a moment, Jenny," and thrust Ilona into my arms. Her head was inert against my shoulder. I held her awkwardly, the gun still dangling from my hand, while he brutally seized the corpse by its shoulders, and dragged it backwards into the room. I saw it like a vision in a nightmare, silhouetted against leaping flames. Christopher's muscles strained under the weight, and beyond was the hunched form of Elizabeth, her blonde hair mercifully hiding her dead face. And over all was the sibilant crackle of fire. *Götterdämmerung*, I thought insanely; and wanted, with hideous inappropriateness, to laugh.

Now Christopher was taking Ilona from me, and urging me in whispers to get back along the passage. As we went, stumbling in the dark, I looked over my shoulder once, but there was nothing to see except the crack of light under the door, now orange instead of yellow, flames instead of light. The house still seemed unnaturally silent. There was no longer any sound from below. We negotiated the up-and-down stairs safely, before suddenly a door opened somewhere beneath us on the ground floor, and a voice cried out, a high agitated note of questioning.

Christopher's hand in the small of my back propelled me violently up the opposite corridor outside my former room . . . I was stumbling and gasping with terror. This was true nightmare. In one moment, I knew, my feet would refuse to move. We reached the passage end just as feet began to stumble on the stairs. I had time to see the little window ahead of us, still open, before Christopher reached the oil lamp and turned it out. Behind us, in the sudden darkness, there must have been confusion on the staircase. I heard a babble of voices, and a cry . . . probably someone calling for light. Luckily our remaining enemies' wits weren't too quick—perhaps they thought the lamp had just blown out. At least they didn't appear to realize yet that something was seriously amiss . . . but they would soon. The smell of fire was strong.

"Get out on the sill, Jenny," Christopher was whispering to me, "there's a sloping roof two or three feet below—swing down, I'll give you Ilona."

Amazingly, in my state of physical weakness, I still managed to do that apparently simple thing—terror can temporarily paralyse, or it can strengthen. Trembling with fear and reaction I obeyed like a puppet, taking Ilona's weight obediently into my arms, and then waiting for Christopher to join us. I felt he'd never come, although it was only a second until he climbed out on to the sill—just as a light sprang up behind him, revealing him clearly as a dark and appallingly obvious target. I shut my eyes. This was the end. I heard a shot, the slap of a bullet against the window frame, and a high whine, like an enraged wasp, as it ricocheted past my ear.

I opened my eyes again in time to see Christopher fling himself down beside us on the roof. Then he was half-pulling, half-carrying us down the slope towards the welcome cover of the palms. Friendly, they seemed now, with their promise of protection. We were on the ground, well-hidden beneath their feathery tangled fronds, before the first pursuer appeared, climbing cautiously out on to the sill after us, a gun wavering wildly in his hand. I can see him now, if I shut my eyes. He came sideways, like a giant crab scuttling towards us.

"Keep *down*, Jenny—round on your left—quick—there's a door." Sobbing, I felt with my hands along the rough surface of the high wall. I didn't dare look back again, knowing that man was climbing so tenaciously after us. . . . Here at last was where Christopher had got in: my hand encountered wood, my fingers scrabbled at the door's edge . . . I couldn't open it. And then I felt it being pushed inwards towards me, and I screamed. Now I come to think of it, it was the first real scream I ever uttered, and it was a good one. I heard it echo about us, high wide and handsome. The pressure of the door had forced me backwards against Ilona and Christopher. What looked to me a battalion of armed men was pouring through it. (Long afterward I learned there were only three or four of them.)

Christopher's voice was jubilant in my ear. "*Saved*—d'you hear? You're *safe*, Jenny," and then, ridiculously, "This is what the doctor ordered. . . ."

They went past us, and I stood there beside him gaping like a lunatic. I saw moonlight glitter on belts and bayonets as they went. I heard shouts and shots and confusion. There were the

206

palm fronds swinging and swaying over us, and behind us everything seemed to be run suddenly in reverse, like the wrong way of a film, with our pursuer going back through the window as hastily as he'd come out of it.

I saw the amazement mixed with amusement on Christopher's face. I remember Ilona's chestnut head against his shoulder. I remember saying, "How *bloody* funny, what the doctor ordered," and then starting to laugh, and hearing Christopher say, startled: "Why, *Jenny*. . . ." And then, except for the moon going round and round above us in the sky, like a comet, like a mad hornet, like a soup plate with Elizabeth's dead face appallingly etched across it, I remember nothing more at all. . . .

Nor do I remember a great deal about the next three weeks. Ilona and I were taken to a nursing home, run by an order of nuns. (Very different, this, to that dreadful hospital.) And there Ilona, with a child's recuperative powers, quickly recovered, except for a certain look of strain about the eyes which no child should have, and a temporary reversion to babyishness, which was admirably coped with by the nuns. Luckily there were other children for her to play with, when she wasn't sitting quietly in my room reading, or absorbed in some old French games that the Mother Superior found for her.

I wasn't frighteningly ill to a child—only to myself. I smiled and spoke and slept like someone normally alive, but inside I felt dead. Finished. For a week or two Christopher came every day at three o'clock to visit me. He would sit and read the papers, while I lay and stared at the ceiling, or wondered what the headlines meant—even the English headlines. I never asked questions, and he offered no answers. I might have demanded explanations, but I didn't. At that time I mightn't have understood them, anyway. They hardly seemed to matter any more.

Elizabeth was dead; but I was intent on watching a fly walk across the ceiling. A trap had been laid for me, and I had walked into it, and been freed—but I was only interested in counting the notes of a particular bird in the garden: up the scale, except for one note, and down again. I did a lot of painful concentration on that bird: it filled a vacuum, which might otherwise have attracted something else.

After a fortnight Christopher ceased coming, and I listened passively while the doctor told he had gone back to England; flown. He was wanted on a job. There was a letter for me, but I didn't bother to read it for another week. Sometimes I picked it up to look at the envelope, which was addressed to 'Mrs. Jenny Emerson' almost as though I had a whole person's personality; and then it was all too much effort, and I put it away again.

Still, however much one wants to escape, one can't do it for ever; and since I couldn't or wouldn't make efforts for myself, other people began to exert pressure from outside. I could have screamed at them to go away and leave me in peace, but lacked the strength of mind, so I allowed myself to be gradually manipulated back towards taking responsibility, but with inner resentment. Why should they expect me to deal with my own life? I'd already dealt with enough. Yet it was during those spells of brooding resentment that my thoughts began to make sense again. Even a negative chain of reactions was better than nothing, it seemed, for bringing me back to life.

So I was soon playing games with Ilona, and sitting up for most of the day; and I read Christopher's letter, with dread which turned to relief. For it only said: 'Au revoir, and get better soon, Jenny, because then they can fly you home; and you and Ilona can stay up in Cumberland till you're completely well. Mrs. Shaw' (his housekeeper) 'is a marvel, as you know, and she'll love to look after you both. I shall be unable to get away at first from the *Subscriber's* clutches, so you'll have perfect peace with the hills and the lakes and the lambs. Love, Christopher.' It was a rather dry ending, but at least it didn't sound as though he wanted to force explanations on me.

All I had to do, it seemed, was sit back and someone would look after me for ever and ever, amen. No need to think of anything unpleasant, because what I didn't ask no one would tell me. Even the quiet authority that Christopher had assumed wasn't annoying, although at one time it would have nettled me. The Mother Superior was welcome to look at me as though she thought I lacked backbone. The world, I felt obstinately, owed me forgetting. So when we left Alexandria Ilona would come with me to Cumberland, and amongst the sheepbells and harebells we would holiday and holiday. . . . Even thoughts of Christopher didn't make me uneasy, because John would quite likely send him abroad again.

This glossy complacency lasted me all through convent farewells, and back to England; right up to the moment, in fact, when I casually picked up a morning paper, and read that Clayton had committed suicide in his cell, after being remanded in custody on an unspecified charge.

It was only a jolt, however; one which barely affected the surface of my mind, and then let it settle again into peace. We travelled on up to Cumberland, Ilona and I, and were made very welcome by Christopher's housekeeper; and in the old grey stone house, with its hall smelling of beeswax and roses and old wood, it was almost possible to believe that modern life didn't exist, that nothing rough nor ugly could ever have happened to the idle, indulged pair that were Ilona and me. Only one thing ruined the spirit of this unrestricted holiday—our constant longing and need for George.

And there was just one day which wasn't pleasant, for other reasons: when Morell and two quiet-voiced men—colleagues of Christopher's?—journeyed all the way up by car to see and question me; but I still evaded asking questions and, probably primed by Christopher, they forced no information on me. Their manner was sympathetic, and discreet. Matter-of-factly, as if we were doing a joint jigsaw puzzle, I filled in missing pieces for them. These were things which hardly scratched the surface of my indifference. George's death wasn't mentioned, nor Ilona's kidnapping; there could be no trial for either, no need of my help in this respect, since all three of the people chiefly concerned—Elizabeth, Clayton, Harif—were dead. Yet, from a journalist's memory, I could dig up facts. Facts about the engaging of Clayton, about my friends and enemies, about Mademoiselle Khahn.

Morell was very friendly, very kind, but I couldn't warm to

him. Eventually he snapped shut his black notebook, glanced out of the window at Ilona playing in the garden, and gave me a brief nod. "Thank you very much, Mrs. Emerson. We'll try not to bother you again, unless we have to——"

He waited. Was there a faint look of interrogation about him? He was giving me the chance to ask questions. When I merely rose to my feet and held out my hand to him, he looked mildly astonished. "All this must have been a bit of a shock to you, Mrs. Emerson . . . I daresay you feel that you don't understand it yet."

"A bit of a . . . yes, I should think we *might* almost say it had."

"Well. . . ." He gave me a doubtful sideways look; retreated into what he evidently thought of as humour: "We shan't be prosecuting *you*, anyway, you'll be glad to hear!"

"Prosecuting—me?"

"For theft and, er—threatened forgery. Mrs. Hellevan's passport and cheques."

"Oh, *that*. Oh but," I said idiotically, "Marjorie wouldn't mind."

"Perhaps not." He smiled gently beneath his moustache. "Ordinarily speaking, Mrs. Emerson, *we* should."

I had a flash of temper.

"If you'd prevented the kidnapping of a child in cold blood, instead of using her to further your ends—whatever those were," I said coldly. And stopped. I prayed he wouldn't tell me what they were.

He didn't. My antagonism had put a stopper on revelations. Morell and I, with the two smooth men whom I inwardly termed Christopher's accomplices, walked to the gate, and made polite meaningless conversation as we went. When I turned back again up the path, between the clipped hedges and sweet-smelling grass and budding flowers, I felt like the factory worker who makes the jigsaw pieces and never sees the finished picture. Like the factory worker, I didn't give a damn.

A letter from Marjorie was lying on the hall table; a typical Marjorie letter, full of warmth, and concern for Ilona. There was one too from Lucy Starr, which I didn't understand: it read like an agonized and guilty cry of self-reproach. I let the untidily-written pages slip through my fingers, and picked up the next letter instead. Christopher's. . . .

He wrote to forewarn me that he was coming home, as if the house were mine. My heart warmed to him for his sensitivity; and then I felt chilled again as if a shadow had fallen across me in the hall. He would be here soon, and when he came . . . I found myself unwillingly thinking of Clayton's shifty face, of Elizabeth's body sprawled face downwards in the House of Palms . . . hastily I picked up my other letters: from John and Miranda, from the Reverend Mother of the Kensington convent. This last brought me a feeling of comfort, although even here were reminders of Elizabeth. The nuns were praying for her, they had said a requiem.

I put down the letter more thoughtfully than I had picked it up. George had seen through Elizabeth; so had Bill and Marjorie; now, in this letter from the old, kind nun, although there was nothing to pin a certainty on, no lack of charity, there was a reticence about my sister which made me wonder. Had she really *ever* been so loved and trusted by everyone as I imagined? Was it I alone who had been completely taken in by the smooth surface of the *sainte nitouche*, as Father's language would have termed her? I hastily stifled my ungenerous thoughts. She was dead. I mustn't add lack of charity to the other troubles that had been between us, terrible though they were. The nuns in their choir stalls were praying for her, as I, too, if I went to Mass tomorrow. . . .

The interruption was Ilona, flying in through the garden door which always stood open in this weather to the windy, sunshiny day outside. She was carrying a vast bunch of wild flowers tangled with the earliest roses filched from the walled garden behind the house. She tripped over the cat, said something she hoped I hadn't heard, saved herself by a remarkable feat of balance, and flung herself on me, flowers and all, with some of her old gaiety. "For you, Mum—wasn't I clever to find them, and aren't they gorgeous, and—*oh*, when's Christopher coming?"

"Soon, darling." My voice must have sounded odd, for she gave me a queer look and muttered: "But don't you *want* to see him? I do——"

I put the flowers down carefully on top of that unwelcome letter.

"It would be marvellous, honey," I said evenly, trying hard not to disappoint her, "but of course he *may* not be able to get away just yet." In spite of every effort, I could hear the hope in my voice. "He can't always choose his times, you know." But of course—being Christopher—he both could, and did.

23

Your tale, sir, would cure deafness.
THE TEMPEST

The sky was very high and clear and light. There seemed a great deal of it—more than would be seen in the south. There was nothing soft about the air, it was like a chilly stream, running gently against my face as I lifted it to heaven. Right up in that enormous sky a hawk hovered, a tiny pitiless speck seeking food. The prettiest thing about this county was the sound of sheep bells. It was all around me, a continual small sharp ting-ting-ting as the black-faced ewes moved on the rocky slopes to crop the already close-bitten turf. Lavender and blue and grey-green were the shadow colours on the lower slopes of the hills— those great round-headed near-mountains which reared up towards that dazzlingly empty sky. Empty except for my hawk, which suddenly plummeted downwards and disappeared. My eyes searched everywhere for him, conning first the slopes, then the trees in the hollow, then the spread of blue water beyond the house.

Nothing moved except the ewes and—far below me—Ilona's small jersey-clad figure putting a pony through its paces in the paddock behind the house. Jonathan Shaw, the housekeeper's son, was with her. She would come to no harm. I smiled tenderly to myself. She was recovering fast from her later ordeals. The wound of George's death went deep, and would take long to heal—if it ever did. I was glad when comedy entered the scene, in the shape of Clemmie bobbing at the pony's heels like a fat white ball. They were having the whale of a time. Jonathan could be trusted to see it kept within bounds.

My hawk had totally vanished. In the sky above, two larks had risen and were giving out their sweet long trill. How many larks is an exaltation? I wondered as I watched them. I hoped the substitution of them for my hawk was a good omen.

I was so busy watching them that I never noticed Christopher until he had reached the bottom of the slope where I had perched myself on the biggest boulder I could find. He was climbing rapidly, with the deceptively easy stride of the natural athlete. His head was bent, and he never once looked up as he climbed towards me. There was about him an air of purpose, and a faint stiffening went over me. The larks singing so high and clear, Ilona happy on her pony, these were all I wished to contemplate at present. I felt something inside me go hard and resistant. Christopher was the only person now who could disturb me, and I steeled myself against him. He had arrived the day before, and so far I had managed to fob him off, by Ilona's presence, and then by early bed.

"You're very interested in those larks."

There was a hint of amusement in his voice. Perhaps my strained attention had been too contrived. I laughed back at him, but warily, with no intention of letting down my guard.

"You aren't bored up here, Jenny?"

"I think it's perfect heaven. So does Ilona."

"You both like it, do you?"

I nodded; and he went on, "You mustn't do that, you know."

"Mustn't like it?"

"Mustn't couple yourself constantly with Ilona. You're always doing it now. Like a sort of shield. There's a separate Jenny, you see."

I almost reminded him that he once said there wasn't, but his manner no longer held its former aggressive quality, only a great kindness. So I agreed, and said it was a habit I should probably get out of as soon as Ilona went back to school.

"It's easy enough to fall into—*too* easy, when we've been only in each other's company for several weeks."

He nodded, but abstractedly. I could feel his thoughts entirely on one track, like a powerful locomotive pulling straight on its iron road. I had an uneasy feeling that this particular one was going to run me down, and I should never feel quite the same again. I might not want to, of course; it all depended, so much, on what unwelcome things he had to say.

The larks had ceased their song, and plummeted, first one, then the other, to the earth.

"That's an excellent seat for one, but hardly big enough for two. If you've the energy to climb over the brow with me, Jenny, there's a much bigger rock slab which could cope with both of us. It has a magnificent view."

"A place in the sun." I got up.

"It's what you ought to have." He put his hand under my elbow and helped me up the hill. I was still shamefully weak from the long rest in bed, and was glad of his arm. We settled ourselves comfortably on the grey ledge of rock, and Christopher took some chocolate from his pocket and handed it to me.

"Keep up your strength."

"You were right about the view. It's quite gorgeous."

"It is, isn't it?" He was not really looking at it, just staring into space, his mind obviously set on a single purpose.

"It's the light," I said hurriedly, "the light on those hills, but mountains they are, really, aren't they, and I think it's a bit——"

"Jenny," he interrupted, "do you, or do you not, want to know the real truth about why George died?"

Here it was.

"I don't want to," I said honestly, "not any more. Not since they're both dead. I suppose I ought to hear, but I just can't bear it. I feel—I feel it won't do any particular good, and I just want to keep it all out."

"And you think that would be altogether satisfactory—for ever?"

"No—no—it's just I don't want to hear about it *now*." I couldn't try to explain. I looked across at the view and repeated wretchedly: "Not now."

"There might easily come a time," he said, almost to himself, "when I no longer felt I could tell you."

There was the high arched sky, and the beautiful view, and beside me the insistent sense of something dark and urgent, which Christopher knew and I didn't, about to overwhelm me. I still tried to hold Christopher's determination back, by pitting my will silently against his, but in the end the quality of his silence broke me down, and I heard my own voice say wearily, "Tell me, then."

My giving in didn't seem to make it easier for him. A frown appeared to have fixed itself permanently on his face. He sat and stared at the close-bitten turf. I looked at the view, so haunt-

215

ingly beautiful. When he didn't speak I said lightly, sorry fo him now, "You see, it's so peaceful, isn't it? There's nothing wrong with the world when you get right away, up here."

"That's what you think, Jenny." He raised his head at last, and smiled, though sombrely. "Yet even the insect life under your feet is busy eating each other up in a way that would make your moralists die of horror. It's just the whole thing, taken all in all, that looks grand, and peaceful too."

"Then I'd sooner be taken in," I said absently, trying not to think of George, "if it's nicer."

He didn't laugh at that, the sombreness had definitely won.

"It's what you always wanted, at one time, and lived very successfully with it till it crumbled. Do you really want to go on living like that, in ignorance?"

"I suppose," my voice was small, "it depends on what you're going to say was underneath." For an awful moment I thought he meant there was something I didn't know about George. To my relief he spoke of something else.

"It may look peaceful, Jenny, but it's not: that's the crux of it. We all live on more than one level now, and the danger is that we forget it. But we can't afford to forget: to ignore the depths of power and hatred, and cruelty and—yes, *meanness*, in other people and ourselves. How often, when you were living your gay happy life in London, Jenny, did you think of that?"

"As little as I could. It always seems somehow to make it real."

" 'Seems', Madam! Nay, it is; I know not 'seems'."

"All right, you needn't quote at me. Point taken."

"There's another thing," Christopher continued glumly, "which we all forget. When you read the daily papers you get convinced that things happen because they're made to, by a few determined people. Or that they were inevitable, right from the start. You forget that it's not just when great men have migraines, or five minutes' vanity, that things go wrong. It's that we're all acting like that, all the time—and God knows when we're going to rub it off, our tiny misery or vanity, on something that will bring down the whole house of cards on top of us."

I felt scared, and grew flippant: "*Darling* Christopher, you didn't warn me I was in for a lecture on historic cause and effect. Or a sermon."

"All I'm feebly pointing out, Jenny, is the old, old truth: great oaks from little acorns grow. And acorns scattered at random, too, as they usually are. Or, as the Chinese put it rather more exactly, a mandarin in Peking is killed by an unconscious gesture made in Paris. We're more terrifyingly bound up with each other, all of us, than we care to believe."

"You're saying, I think, that—that George was the mandarin." Christopher nodded.

"Yes. Except that the original gesture wasn't unconscious, but was certainly not directed at George. He was killed, as people all too easily are, by the recoil from a gun."

"You got me confused once by bringing in Mrs. Maclean, when you were cross with me in Paris. And what seemed to be a private greedy murder turned out to have been done by a sort of gang—and an international one, at that. It's still hard to understand how Elizabeth became a pawn in that sort of game."

"Elizabeth was hard to understand, anyway. No one could better dissemble than she. The diary was proof of that."

"The diary!" I gaped at him. "How did *you* know——"

"I saw it. Oh——" he grinned at my dumbfounded face—"not later on, when you did. (Marjorie, by the way, told Morell about it; Ian Maddox too, when he recovered—more of that, later.) No. *I* saw it when we were children. When she wrote it. A few days before she left. It was an eye-opener, I can tell you."

I was remembering the diary. "She wrote in it that she told you nothing. . . ."

"She didn't." He gave me a rueful, sideways look. "She left it open on the table one day, when I was round at your house, and, horrid little boy that I was, I read a page. It happened to be a particularly juicy bit. So I'm afraid all inhibitions went, and I just read on."

"You knew," was all I could say. "And you never said anything! Not even when she went——"

"I was a sensible child, and I knew at once we were all better off without her. I didn't read as far as the drugs, or I might have

217

given her away. But I must admit it made me determined to keep a very close eye on her when she returned to England, particularly as I was briefed to do so."

"*Briefed?*"

"Yes. You see, she was your sister. And you were already a bit suspect."

"*I* was!" I was stunned. "*Suspect?*" I was also stung. "*Christopher*—of what? Or rather—by whom? And why suspect by *you*, anyway?"

He was digging at the turf with his fingers, taking a great interest in some clover. "Hey look, Jenny, is this a four-leaved one——"

"No, it's not," I said indignantly. "As if it would be, anyway, with you drivelling on like a madman. Come on—out with it—air your paranoia."

"Don't laugh at me."

"I'm not. I never felt less like laughing in my life. I feel—I feel as if I've got muddled up with James Bond."

"So you have, in a way." He was grinning now, but I didn't smile back. "Poor Jenny, and poor innocent Geneviève. You never guessed, did you, that in my capacity as roving journalist, I naturally had my uses elsewhere."

"Bond in person, then. Congratulations."

"Nothing so grand. Just someone who was paid to keep his eyes and ears open. Who was a natural for keeping his fingers in other people's pies." There was a note of mocking self-dislike in his voice now; of bitterness. "I'm what's known as good with people, you see. I had a knack of unlocking other people's tongues, over a glass of wine, of course. And then passing back what I heard."

"To Intelligence, I take it."

"Sometimes, yes. But there are other rackets than the political ones. And sometimes they get intertwined."

"I don't follow you."

"Oh come, Jenny. There are rackets which deal in people's weaknesses. And people with weaknesses are good political prey. So the two things often run hand in hand. And if you get someone entirely devoted to his own interests, as Harif was, he can often play one thing off against the other, to his own profit. Your sweet brother-in-law——"

"So he *was* that," I said slowly. "But I guessed, of course. Elizabeth had worn rings on both hands, when she came to us first. George noticed the marks. I know, of course, Moslem women don't wear wedding rings—but there's no bar, is there, against them wearing rings on either hand, as ornament? In fact, haven't I heard that it's the Moslem custom to weigh them down that way?"

"Clever Jenny. Yes—Elizabeth was no more than seventeen when she became a Moslem—and Harif's wife."

"*Seventeen!*" At that age I had achieved my goal of the first lacrosse team. While Elizabeth had been preening herself in silk and scent, sunning on tropical beaches, ski-ing at Gstaad ... I felt a strong, illogical feminine indignation.

"Goodness, all that, at that age! I feel cheated."

Christopher roared. "Oh Jenny, you are marvellous. But I really can't see you, my dear, shacked up with Harif."

"That sod," I said, with feeling.

"Exactly."

"And Father was 'Barfleur'—I suppose he already had his bolthole fixed, when he snatched Elizabeth."

"It seems so. Now that we've been able to pry back into his past, it appears that he'd known the Khahn family for some time —had met them in Paris, and joined in the son's debauches with alacrity. A shady business, for which he'd always used a different name. It must have come in useful, when he took Elizabeth. He was a shrewd man, your father, probably he had a definite rôle for her to play. She had striking promise as a beauty—and was just as astute as he was. It was her job to get money for them both. He must have counted on Elizabeth's ambition and vanity aiding his, but she surpassed his hopes. She made a try for, and got, Harif himself."

"They took risks, didn't they? Suppose she'd been recognized, on a trip abroad?"

"There wasn't much risk. I've seen photographs of her at that time; with make-up, and *couture* clothes, she looked more like a woman of twenty-five than a girl of seventeen. They toned her down considerably for her return to England!"

"Good heavens!" I sat up very straight. "I must have seen her, in Paris."

"Did you—when?"

"The year before she reappeared. At a dinner, before a masked ball. The Khahns were pointed out to me. There was a blonde woman, in a fantastic jewelled mask. It must have been Elizabeth. And Harif was there, too. To think that I saw him then, and never recognized him when I walked into the Hilton."

"He was there, was he?"

"Yes," I said grimly. "He watched us meet. And Elizabeth, I think she nearly fainted. She looked most peculiar at one moment."

"No doubt it was a strain—acting under Harif's eye."

"Yes," I said, in a small voice. This time it was I who dug with my fingers at the turf. Its spongy surface smelt sweet, with the pungent smells of cropped grass, clover, trefoil. There were rabbit messes in the grass. Small, furred independent life had been that way; it was good to think of it, indifferent to human twists and horrors.

"Christopher, you haven't told me *why* she was acting. *Why* she was sent—or came. *Why* I was 'suspect'." I swallowed. "You've not told me a thing yet—you're stalling."

"Oh heck. Why did I ever start on this?" He looked disconsolately at me, and ran his fingers irritably through his hair. I noticed it was turning grey. Greyer, surely, than it had been last year. It was odd to think that I was probably the cause.

"You just have to put two things together: Harif was a man with fingers in many pies—and I couldn't keep mine out of other people's."

"You did it for a good motive, anyway," I said warmly.

"No one ever really knows their own motives."

"True. But Christopher, the Khahns were fabulously rich!"

"Façade. The solid gold background was all gone. Nasser put paid to that. They were a type he looked on as utterly useless, and he milked them accordingly. So Harif took to dabbling here and dabbling there. He had links with Communism, which is one side of the story. But you have to understand that the position of Communists in Egypt is totally anomalous—on one hand help from Russia eagerly accepted, on the other many Communists in prison. So Harif didn't allow himself to be too much entwined. He would have been like a man walking one tightrope above another."

"I'm glad he fell off," I said feelingly. And then I shuddered. I still couldn't quite get accustomed to the fact that it was my hand which pushed him.

"Bloodthirsty girl. No—sorry, Jenny, my dear, you're right, of course. One can't be too thankful there were no nets underneath. He was the lowest form of animal life, with extensive profits from the dope trade."

"*Dope.*" I looked at him, my eyes wide with horror. "Why, that would explain—Christopher, did Elizabeth——"

"Yes—she drugged, all right. Remember how her moods puzzled you?"

"Ye-es. And you said she looked dead—and then other times she'd get all lit up and gay, for no apparent cause. You said—you said dope ran all through this case."

"So it did." Christopher sighed heavily. His hand closed over mine, firmly. "You see, in my probings and peerings, I'd run across Harif's dope-running organization. I was beginning to get thoroughly in his hair."

"But I can't see what that had to do with us—me, and Ilona; and——" my voice faltered on the last word: "George."

"No. But let me tell you the story first." His grip on my hand was almost painful, but I ignored it; just nodded, staring at the view. Clouds towered in the distance. The great hills, the further ones, that is, were threateningly dark, almost malign. I felt as though the shadows they cast were creeping nearer to me. "Once upon a time——" I said flippantly, trying to be light about it.

"Around eighteen months ago, to be exact. The police in quite a few European countries began to be worried about an increase of drug-taking. Particularly amongst teenagers. They knew a lot of it was seeping in from the East, but though they pulled in some small fry here and there, no one seemed to know anything, or if they did, they wouldn't talk. I was in Paris and Brussels for John about that time, Switzerland too, and—like a good many other people—I was asked to keep my ears open. As

221

a matter of fact I wasn't too willing. I hadn't found the police very co-operative before, they aren't fond of lone wolves, as you can guess; in fact, with my sometimes unlucky tongue, I'd got properly across that stick, Morell; and he got across me. So when I did, by pure gambler's chance, actually get a line on these people, I decided to follow it up a bit on my own. Wherein," he added grimly, "I was unwise."

I remembered Harif's face, and shuddered. "Unwise is a mild term, I'd think."

"I'd managed to get John interested in financing me—on consideration, of course, that he got the story if anything blew. So I was able to go in for corrupting the already corrupt; my contact, for a nice heavy sum, was to introduce me as someone ready and willing to pass the stuff, and in an admirable position to do so. Of course I was using a false name, and was only an up-and-coming reporter. I'll spare you the details, but the long and short of it was that on a certain night teeming with rain I was taken out to a small café in a Paris suburb to receive my—er, initiation into the ways of my charming fellow-travellers.

"It was all very dull, on the surface, and tatty, and mediocre. Squalid is the word, really. My contact was a little underfed man, with bad breath and bunions. We sat at a table just inside a porch, with the rain spitting in on us, and all the time he did nothing but complain about his stomach and his feet. If he made, as he claimed, a packet out of his antisocial activities, it hadn't done him much good. There were a few other people sitting around, habitués, I supposed, and behind us at a table were a couple who might have been Arabs. The conversation about bunions went on and on, and I began to get pretty restive, and so in fact did the little man.

"In the end he blurted out that he didn't think the chap we'd come to meet could be coming, and we'd better go. He got up and went inside the café, and when he came out I thought he looked thoroughly scared. He insisted we'd better go. At once. It had all fallen through. He'd fix it another time. I didn't believe him, of course; I knew I'd never see him again, something had put the wind up him properly. I was mulling it over, with him tugging at my arm, when I became conscious of a muttered conversation behind me. It was in Arabic, which I know a bit. I didn't get much. Just a few words about the boss himself being here. Anyway, it decided me; I made a pretence of leaving with my friend, hung around for a bit, and then I went back.

"It was quite dark by then, and the café seemed to have closed down for the night. Not a sign of life, I felt I was wasting my time. But there was a telephone kiosk on the corner, and I took shelter there for a few minutes. I even made a call, to a—er —friend."

"A blonde friend, I take it."

"Red-haired, actually. I'd just left the box, still with a watchful eye cocked on the café, when a man came out of it by a side door and down the road towards me. I was too late to get out of the way and anyway I wanted a look at him, but I didn't really think I'd get it because it was now so dark. He had his hat pulled down low, and his coat collar up, and the rain was probably getting in his eyes, because I don't think he saw me coming till I was right on top of him. As luck would have it, we were bang opposite a side turning, and a car was coming down it with its headlights on; I got a good look at him, and was conscious of a pretty nasty stare in return. I couldn't recognize him at the time, and it wasn't for months later, just before Elizabeth's return, that I saw him again, lording it at a Paris first night. Of course it was friend Harif."

I said nothing. Christopher withdrew his hand from mine, fumbled in his pocket for cigarettes. When he had lit one he sat back, hands linked together between his knees, and sighed heavily.

' It gave me a jar; it gave him the hell of a worse one. We ran into each other in the foyer, came face to face just as we had in that road. It was quite unavoidable . . . After that, he must have made a few simple inquiries. Elizabeth wasn't with him, or I'd have got even more of a surprise."

"*I'm* surprised he didn't get you bumped off at once."

Christopher shook his head. "He may not have been quite sure, for a bit. After all, there's no reason why I *shouldn't* have been walking down that road . . . Only perhaps later, when he

223

found out I was a . . ." he gave me his self-amused smile, "well-paid journalist, and when perhaps he *had* come to hear about my shabby friend with the bunions and the too-eager young reporter . . . One can't be sure."

"So why didn't the police act straight away?"

Christopher, for the first time in my long acquaintance with him, looked bashful.

"Because I didn't tell them."

"Christopher, you *clot*."

"Granted. But Jenny dear, don't you know your Ogden Nash? 'Vanity, vanity all is vanity, That's any fun at all for humanity'? I'd had some pretty scathing moments with the police before. I just thought I'd start another spot of investigating on my own, before laying any ideas before them."

"Well," I said heartily, "I never really believed in *everyone* having a good strong death wish before. . . ."

Christopher winced.

"Don't, Jenny, please. You can't imagine what I feel about it now."

But I could. The day was bright, and yet suddenly I felt as though surrounded by invisible darkness. I was remembering George. . . . And my terrified Ilona; now happily at play in the fields below us, but with who knew what hidden scars on her mind? The wind, which had been fresh and down-scented, blew with an icier edge to it. I couldn't look at Christopher any more. I said, on a whisper: "You still haven't said—how did *we* come into it?"

24

. . . What's gone, and what's past help,
Should be past grief. . .

THE WINTER'S TALE

We sat in silence for some minutes. The light now had that
slow golden deepening of afternoon, just before the sun drops
behind a light mist, and the air strikes with sharper, more
treacherous chill. All the colours grew intense, the silence
more profound. Clemmie's bark, Ilona's laughter, rose with
extra clarity to us where we sat. I gave a little shiver, hunched
myself deeper into my thick Shetland sweater. Christopher put
his hand over mine. "Cold, Jenny?"

I shook my head. He hadn't really been smoking, only pulling
at his cigarette, jerkily. Now he ground it out savagely into the
turf, scarring it with black. Not till then did he answer my
question.

"Jenny, it was the most appalling and damnable piece of bad
luck. Harif had a crooked mind which automatically worked
sideways. You heard Elizabeth say that he did everyone dirt.
By the same token his left hand never knew what his right was
doing. So when he ran into trouble on the right, what better
than that the left should deal with it? Leaving the one dark
side he wanted untouched by hint of suspicion unclouded and in
the clear. And at the same time Fate handed him a lovely little
bonus, all for free. Lucy Starr."

"*Lucy?*"

"Jenny, stop jumping. You look like the dog with eyes
like windmills. Yes, Lucy was desperate for money, as you
probably know. Things were getting worse, with her mother. So
she started, in all innocence—*almost* all innocence—supplying
one of those agencies who make up the foundations of gossip
columns, with snippets she gleaned during her job. She chose a
Swiss agency, because it was far afield. After all, she was
herself the person who read up the foreign papers, so she felt
pretty safe. It was Lucy who gave them the full column on
you."

225

I gaped at him. "*Lucy?* It doesn't make sense—why, *she* showed it to me."

"I know. She was fond of you—and she'd got thoroughly scared by the happenings after Elizabeth's return. She felt responsible, *and* she felt she must open your eyes. So she cooked up that story. . . ."

I was speechless. Was nothing or nobody as I'd thought them? All outlines blurred? I could have sworn to Lucy's probity. And then, remembering the sick mother, I reproached myself. Who was I to dictate her priority of loyalties? It was plain enough where they would lie.

"As bad luck would have it. Elizabeth and Harif were in Europe at that time. Elizabeth must have seen the article. Perhaps she prattled to Harif. Perhaps—who knows?—she even mentioned me. Anyway, the coincidence must have struck him enough for him to mull it over. Here were all sorts of interesting things tied up together and which might, with any luck, pay off a dividend. He was heartily sick of Elizabeth, anyway. She'd failed to have children, and after the Moslem fashion he'd lately taken a second young wife of whom she was morbidly jealous. And now here was Elizabeth's sister, rich and talented, and working for the very same newspaper which was employing me. Surely, with a little ingenuity, he might rid himself of at least two of his problems at the same time? And with enough red herrings strewn around to bewilder the keenest-nosed of hounds. Perhaps it immensely tickled his perverse sense of humour, when Elizabeth, always with a nose for money, suggested getting in touch with you again. It seems in character."

"How do you know all this?"

"A few inquiries have been going on while you and Ilona have been convalescing . . . Zaina, the younger wife, knew a little. So did—" Christopher smiled grimly, "Mademoiselle Khahn. She had a most interesting time with the *gendarmerie*."

"That awful woman," I said feelingly. "I'll never be able to bear Paris again. And then you turned up raving like a madman about Mrs. Maclean, and implying that I was some sort of fellow-traveller. I certainly thought you'd gone mad. And so had I. You were so hostile—you didn't *believe* it? Why, that would have implicated me in killing George. Why, it would have meant I connived at Ilona's kidnapping!" I floundered helplessly, and stopped. "Christopher, you *couldn't* have believed it!"

"*You* seemed to believe I'd murdered George and abducted Ilona."

"Yes, well," I admitted, "I'd found the telegram you sent Elizabeth crumpled up in her waste-paper basket. I thought you were in league with her."

"Was *that* it?—I thought *your* accusations were all part of your act. No—I was Commie-hunting, thanks to Harif stirring up the muddy pool with his little stick. He was a brilliant improviser—so long as he could make you and Elizabeth look pretty peculiar, and involve me in the whirlpool, he didn't mind what strings he pulled—or where. I told you he had dealings with Communism—he had a pretty general system of lobsterpots out, old Harif! He just let fall that the financial reward could be great, to Party funds, if a little phoney information could be dropped about you just where it would cause most interest. D'you *now* remember Jim and Dorothea Arkroyd?"

Slowly I searched my memory—there was a tenuous thread somewhere which would lead me to the clue; and then all at once I got it: that euphoric birthday morning, which now seemed so long ago. My feeling of condescending pity for the shabby couple who had just been jailed for ineffectual spying—the woman with the crumpled cream bun face, and the man with slitty eyes.

"Yes, I remember."

"Well, it was dead easy. They were dismal failures—they'd already been jettisoned to the wolves. A little false information about you was simply planted amongst their papers. A photograph of you; a mention of vague 'activities' on your trips abroad, of 'meetings' with one or two thoroughly suspicious characters; and finally the statement that Elizabeth, under her maiden name of Lemprière, was coming to England. Of course it sounded too odd to be genuine, but it was puzzling enough for me to be asked to keep an eye on you . . . And when Elizabeth actually turned up, and the most sinister things started to happen—well, *I* thought I was going mad, as well."

I put my hand up to my mouth. The horrible ease with which

227

I'd been sucked into the whirlpool! And George—When I thought of him, I would gladly have shot Harif all over again. In the stomach, at that. "But Elizabeth—why did she play along with him?"

"All Harif wanted was for me to give him the chance to wipe me out while embroiled in a different dirty business to his cherished sideline. It didn't matter how or where, so long as it looked as though I'd met my end following up a totally different line to the one he was actually interested in . . . All Elizabeth wanted was money and power. She hoped to regain hers over Harif if she provided him with the former. Unfortunately, she was also an improviser. When George got uneasy about her, and started to make a few discreet inquiries on his own, he had to be killed."

"I never *knew* he made inquiries," I said miserably. "And then, when he was killed, that brought in Morell."

"Yes—and you. Harif must have been dancing with joy, in the wings."

I thought back, painfully. "But Christopher—look, it doesn't make sense. They tried to kill *me*, as well."

"Oh no."

"*What*! You mean that I was imagining things—there was *nothing* in my drink that night?"

"I said, *they* didn't. That was where human nature ran out again, like a racehorse which won't keep to the straight. Elizabeth decided to throw over Harif, and play the hand to suit herself. She wanted you out of the way, and she suborned Clayton. With Clayton, money talked louder than anything else. You always disliked him, didn't you?"

"He gave me the absolute creeps."

"Well, like many horrible characters, he was oversensitive to being disliked. He had an almost pathological hatred of you."

"I know. I always felt it."

"And 'way back in his life Clayton had a bit of a record. Attempted blackmail. Of a petty kind."

"He would—now I come to think of it, he had a blackmailer's personality. Disgusting, somehow."

"Yes—well, he had a habit of storing away information about

people, like a squirrel with nuts. And somewhere his large ears picked up the rumour that we'd once been engaged. That was probably something else that Elizabeth reported back to Harif along with the information that Clayton had found me kissing you, and thought I was still mad about you. Good news, again, for Harif. He could, perhaps, count on me following you up for more than one reason, if you disappeared. He must have been absolutely furious if he ever came to learn that Elizabeth had tried to do you in. It would have made her doubly expendable, in his eyes.'

"Why did she want *me* out of the way, though? Jealousy—hate?" I looked sideways at him, knowing there could have been a reason. "Anyway, it seems a bit extreme."

He hesitated. "I'll come to that, it ties up with me, really."

I grinned. "Christopher, you destroyer. As bad as Bond in every way."

"Don't say that. And, as far as 'extreme' goes, don't forget that she drugged."

"Marjorie and Bill found her quite terrifying. I suppose the drugs had affected her personality, deep down."

"Yes. They would. And talking of your chum Marjorie, Jenny, you owe her a lot. Bill eventually made her go to the police, who sensibly dragged Morell back from Paris, where he was wasting time on a dead end already covered by me. Marjorie's statement on her missing papers, on the diary, plus all you ever told her—poor Jenny, what a night you spent!—was illuminating. We knew then that you might turn up anywhere as Mrs. Hellevan. But by that time you'd skipped out as Marian Said. We lost you from your hotel, and Interpol clumsily let you slip at the airport. Eventually I flew to Egypt after we found out that 'Marjorie' had acquired a visa by dubious means—my dear, your nerve! If we hadn't discovered *that*, someone would eventually have dropped me a clue, of course, to take me to Alexandria. It had just crossed my mind already that it might be your destination, when I found the copy of *Justine* left behind in your bag.

"It was in Egypt that I got a report from back home—after Marjorie's revelations, a second careful check-up of the Arkroyd papers, *and* an interview with Dorothea Arkroyd, had led to the belief that someone had deliberately planted that ridiculous stuff about you. I'd no reason of course to connect Elizabeth with Harif at that stage, or I'd have known at once who was responsible. As it was everything was getting murkier and murkier, and I'd lost you to boot, since you were registered at your hotel not as Hellevan but Said. I was getting pretty desperate about you when dirty friend Ibrahim turned up from his dirtier House of Palms. Harif's tatty chums were as many as plums in a pie, so he'd tracked me down without much trouble. Of course the whole thing smelt strongly of fish—but I was feeling pretty Bond at the time, and by then, knowing how wrong I'd been, almost out of my mind about you as well."

I made a small sound, quickly choked back.

"You see, Elizabeth and Clayton were right about me." Christopher brushed his hand wearily across his eyes. "You *were* the reason I hadn't married. We just got off to a bad start, that's all. It was when we were engaged that I first got the chance to do a bit of Bonding. More by luck than anything else I got hold of a certain bit of information where others had failed. I—I think you saw a change in me, Jenny. It was a strain keeping the whole thing from you. In the rather unpleasant way of young men I began o blame you for not understanding something you couldn't possibly understand, and for not having the self-confidence to keep your end up. I was overexcited . . . and self-important . . . and unkind."

"You weren't exactly unkind—only withdrawn."

"Thank you, sweet Jenny. If it's any comfort to you now, though I suppose nothing is, it was a tremendous shock when you threw me over for George."

I gasped. "But—but I *didn't*! You didn't want me! You didn't make the smallest effort to stop me, when I broke it off."

"No," Christopher admitted with a wry smile, "I was beginning to think that a wife and two jobs were too much to undertake, altogether. But my male vanity had a nice picture of you waiting sad and dangling for five or six years, while I roistered over Europe and then condescended at last to come home and pick you up and settle down. When instead I picked up the paper and found you were engaged to George—it was a black moment. You see, in my selfish way I loved you. It never occurred to me that you could love anyone else."

I heard him with stunned amazement and a sense of indignation, which boiled down together to something like . . . passing regret for the girl whose youth had been spoilt? I don't know; I was conscious anyway of the warmth of Christopher's hand in mine. He put up his other hand and touched my hair.

"Jenny, I'm a bit of a bastard and I—I hated you. I didn't dare think of you any other way. My hatred for you was a very nice spur to—to all sorts of things. I took pleasure in telling myself that a woman who switched immediately from one man to another wasn't worth having."

"It wasn't immediately. It was *months* afterwards, I married George. And you never raised a finger to get me back. And anyway no one could help loving George, he——" My voice quavered into silence.

"Jenny darling, I know. He was a perfect charmer, and far nicer than me, and no one could help it, as you say; and you had a perfect right to love anyone you pleased, after the way I behaved."

"I never had the smallest idea you felt like that!"

"Why should you? And it was all the worse because every now and then I had to see you and George together, and realize what I missed."

I couldn't say anything. I could only remember the regiment of hot or icy-looking blondes, and Christopher speaking always with that edge to his voice, and occasionally looking as if he longed to strangle me.

"I'd just reached the point of not hating you any more, and knowing regretfully you were the one person for me and I'd mucked it, when I had a telephone call one day, and—and the Arkroyd papers had revealed the specially-planted beans. It was almost a relief to be able to . . . despise you, though paradoxically it didn't make you any less attractive. It seemed the irony of ironies that I should be asked—naturally enough, as we both worked for John—to keep a check on you and try to find out what you were up to."

It suddenly occurred to me that Christopher was getting more and more uneasy, and had taken refuge in uncharacteristic wordiness. Now I had caught the unease. He was skirting a subject which he knew would give me pain. His face was thoroughly unhappy, his hold on my hand so hard that it was painful.

"You'd better tell me," I said.

"Tell you what?" Caught off-guard, he avoided my eye.

"Whatever it is you're so carefully keeping from me. About George."

I heard him swallow. His voice was harsher. "The hell of it is, Jenny, that you aren't ever going to forgive me, if I do."

I couldn't say anything for a minute, and when I did the words fell with the awful finality of an executioner's knife.

"*Yours* was the 'unconscious gesture', then, that actually killed him."

He nodded, and withdrew his hand from mine as though he felt I might violently repudiate his touch.

"Go on." My voice was flat and dull. I stared at the landscape in front of me. Colour had seeped away from it, and it was cold, cold as the air of the approaching dusk.

Christopher spoke low and quickly, as if he half-hoped I wouldn't hear what he said. "I was asked to find out what, if anything, George knew. As far as the Arkroyd papers showed, you were simply running around in dangerous company: a bit more than running around. Naturally enough, I decided there was a man in it somewhere. There was nothing to pin down, but it was probably what we were meant to think. You travelled a lot—there might have been someone you'd met abroad. If you deceived George you could have deceived anyone. Two or three meetings can decide these things, after all. I was still more certain when you left, taking Ilona with you."

"I *didn't* take Ilona."

"It was carefully made to look as if you connived at it, let it happen, and then . . . followed. When Elizabeth failed to get you, she herself had somehow slipped back into Harif's net; perhaps the drugs had begun to undermine her. She lacked the ability to carry the thing through on her own. Curiously enough— ironically—I don't think Harif can have cottoned on to the fact that she was using them; or he'd have realized what an uncertain quantity it made her. The whole thing anyway was game within game within game, d'you see, like Chinese ivory boxes. Skilful, and muddling. It gave me considerable headache working it out even afterwards, when I knew it was a desperate chase after a really-abducted Ilona, instead of you in with it all and pretending you weren't. Of course, we'd been thoroughly muddled by the Arkroyd papers."

"And having them, you went ahead and let it all happen!"

"My dear, we weren't interested in stopping you. We were out to catch whatever bigger boy you seemed to be mixed up with."

"At Ilona's expense. What a wicked thing to do."

"Ah no—that was a terrible mistake. Naturally you weren't expected to be long parted from her. Now that Clayton and Harif are both dead, it seems unlikely we shall ever know whether it was Clayton himself, or one of Harif's dingy accomplices, who pushed Morell's man under a train; anyway, Elizabeth got away with Ilona while all other eyes were on *you*. We decided you'd realized you were watched, and had put on an accomplished, if painful, act. It hardened me considerably towards you. After that you were our only link with them. Just in case you really gave us the slip that tatty hotel near the Luxembourg had been tactfully mentioned in the Arkroyd papers, so that I should know where to look for you."

I took a deep breath. "Christopher, you're still hedging. What about—George? You said you had to find out what he knew. You didn't ask him—you didn't tell him——" My voice died away in my throat, leaving an empty ache. I knew the answer. I hated Christopher.

"Jenny, please. . . ." There was a pleading note in his voice. "I *had* to know."

"You pumped him—and he guessed. You came round and did an act after he died. I thought you were *sympathetic*."

"But I was, I——"

My voice had been almost strident with horror. Now I could only whisper: "*After he had killed himself.* . . ."

"Jenny, my dear, no. Is that what you think? He didn't— Jenny, please listen."

I had risen. Tears were streaming down my face.

"I won't listen—I don't want to hear any more—there was nothing unconscious about what you did—it was deliberate, deliberate—because you were jealous——"

Christopher had stood up too, he held my arm. I couldn't tear myself free. We stared at each other like open enemies, only I was warm with fury, and Christopher looked as though someone had carved him out of ice.

"Ah, go on, hate me, Jenny. There's nothing I can do about it except say that it wasn't deliberate, though I grant you the jealousy. I will tell you the truth now, though, if it kills me. I suppose you'd say that I owe God a death."

I was silent.

"I've said George wasn't satisfied about Elizabeth, he was making his own inquiries. When I started pumping him too, he was certain. But somehow Elizabeth had guessed George was getting on to her. She knew he had an important appointment that day. She thought it was to do with her. In fact he was seeing someone from Intelligence, and when George didn't turn up he would have gone round to your house, only it might have been unwise; and George's secretary said he had a bad cold and hadn't been in all day, which sounded reasonable. Elizabeth had seen the red light—she killed him, working it up to look as if you'd done it—and, irony of ironies, she muddled Morell by trying to pin the cause for your action on me." He sighed heavily. "Hares starting in all directions."

"That cinema business——"

"Yes. She and Clayton worked it out together. He bought her ticket. She hung around and waited till you left the house. Later she slipped away to the cinema—there's an emergency exit door by the front stalls. Clayton was able to get out as if going to the Gents, give her the ticket, and she slipped in that way when no one was looking. Fairly foolproof."

"Yes. And—what—did—she—say—to—George?"

My arm was almost numb from his grip, but I hardly felt it. Christopher was staring bitterly away. He looked like someone who has lost.

"I don't know."

"I thought you knew everything. Just a bloody puppet-master with your hand on the strings."

"Jenny—don't. I suppose she pretended she'd come back to try and charm him out or buy him out, or something. Till she got her chance."

"To slip him the amytal. The *coup de grâce* after she—and you—had poisoned his mind against me. He died—thinking the things you hinted. . . . Perhaps he even thought, when he got dizzy——" I stopped. I could not go on. Ilona's small yellow figure swam across my blurred vision—a dot of gold in deepening shadow which threatened to obliterate her.

"I don't think he ever believed them. He was bewildered, puzzled . . . he thought someone was tricking me."

"You don't think—don't *think*, but you don't *know* . . . Oh but he died, and now I'll never know. . . ." I had my hand to my mouth and was biting my knuckles till blood streamed over them, unaware of what I did. Christopher's voice was insistent in my ears: "Jenny, listen. You *must* listen. *You* knew George—was there any difference in his attitude to you that day?"

I thought back agonizedly, as I had done so many times before. There was nothing. Blank. Only the memory of George saying: 'I must see him . . . it's something we'll have to discuss, Jenny, you and I.' Now that sentence held such terrible meaning for me, I could no longer remember the tone in which he said it. . . . Surely he was the same to me as usual . . . surely? But it was before Elizabeth, at that final interview, added her lies to whatever Christopher had already implied.

Christopher's voice roused me from silent despair.

"And the ultimate irony was that she'd decided to strike out on her own, jettison Harif, murder you, get her hands on the money—and on me. How she thought to get away with it all I can't begin to imagine."

"I wish she had, except for Ilona," I said dully. "I wish I was dead. And I wish she'd got you, if that's what she wanted. You deserved each other."

But even then I knew that I was being unfair. The first shock was wearing off, although it was quite as bad as I had thought it would be. Now I should never know what George had been thinking of me when he died . . . yet while I blamed Christopher aloud, I knew it wasn't really his fault. I was taking out my grief on him. What else could he have done . . . in reason? The trouble was that I didn't want to reason, or be fair; I only wanted to hurt him as he'd hurt me and George.

I was like Elizabeth, after all: I wanted to kill.

All this time I had been staring at Ilona, and now became truly conscious of her again. She was alive, at least. Alive because Christopher had saved her; and so was I. 'Eunostos', the safe return. I found myself wishing I could take back my words. In my heart of hearts I didn't believe that George had died mistrusting me . . . it was just so unbearable not to *know*.

"You'll get cold, now the sun's gone in. Time to go back to the house." Christopher sounded like a polite stranger.

"I'm all right," I muttered, but I began to walk slowly down the hill towards the rapidly darkening valley, stumbling over the tussocky grass as I went.

"Here—you'd better take my arm, Jenny, you're tired, and it's steeper than it looks."

I shook my head and walked stubbornly on, tears still blinding my eyes and threatening to overspill. After about ten yards I simply ceased to see where I was going, and when I came to a particularly large tussock I fell over it, coming down hard on my knees with a jolt which finished the last of my self-control. After that I just lay on the grass and cried, like a child, like Ilona.

For anyone so tough Christopher was as efficient as a nanny. He let me cry for some time until I was too cold and miserable to have any more fight left in me, and then he simply yanked me up and into his arms, and comforted me as if we had never quarrelled and George's death didn't lie between us to make everything impossible.

I began to say it was impossible, but he cut me short with:

"Ah, Jenny, don't start developing attitudes, for God's sake—you *know* inside yourself it wasn't intentional; and I didn't have to tell you, only I couldn't have seen you again if I hadn't, and given you the chance to forgive me—which, thank God, you have."

236

Then I began to say weakly that I didn't mean to do that at all and he'd said himself I couldn't; but he only continued to stroke my hair, and to say, "Anyway, George couldn't have borne you and Ilona to be out in the cold, he'd have liked to know someone was looking after you."

"It's too soon to think about anyone but George, and——"

"Of course it is. All the same, I'm here, for when it doesn't seem too soon. Come on down to the house now, and have some tea."

I went with him, not feeling anything very much, except exhaustion. Light was streaming across a daffodil sky, on the verge of sunset. The great hills looked wild and ferocious, like beasts closing in on a camp-fire. Down in the paddock I could still pick out Ilona in her yellow jersey from the shadows which already engulfed the house. I shivered. In spite of everything it was oddly comforting to be with Christopher. We went down the hill hand in hand.